"Wha[...]

She d[...]ng in her
hand. He [...] to get them, and she lifted
her face to his. Langston froze, then slowly backed up an
inch or two to look into her eyes. She thought he was
going to kiss her. Amazingly, she didn't turn her cheek
to him, or raise her hands to stop him, or even lower her
eyes. Instead, she raised her lips to meet his. Pleasure
shot through him like a bullet to the heart.

Langston looked down at the keys. Reggie followed his
gaze. He bent and picked up the key ring and held it
out to her. She looked at the keys in his hand and caught
her bottom lip with her teeth. She was mortified. He
could see that. But he held out the keys anyway, and she
reached out and took them. Then she looked up at him
and reached out to hook one hand behind his neck and
pull his head down so she could kiss him, long and hard.

He should have felt victorious, but instead he felt humbled, awed by the intensity of their shared contact. Her
lips were blood-hot under his. Her hips were soft under
his hands, not bony protrusions like those of his last girlfriend. He slid his hand up to her waist and around to
her back. He gloried in the feeling of her flesh through
the silk blouse that flowed over her and covered her voluptuous figure to her knees. She felt great. He wanted
to touch every inch of her, to kiss the chestnut-colored
skin that was hidden from him. He slid his hands down,
and she ended it.

"I think I should take you home," she said.

"I don't," he protested, but without force. Reggie had
surprised him with that kiss. She had given him more
than he'd expected. He didn't want to push it, or push
her. So he slowly backed away, letting her go.

**BOOK YOUR PLACE ON OUR WEBSITE
AND MAKE THE ARABESQUE
ROMANCE CONNECTION!**

We've created a customized website just for our very special Arabesque readers, where you can get the inside scoop on everything that's going on with Arabesque romance novels.

When you come online, you'll have the exciting opportunity to:

- View covers of upcoming books

- Learn about our future publishing schedule (listed by publication month and author)

- Find out when your favorite authors will be visiting a city near you

- Search for and order backlist books

- Check out author bios and background information

- Send e-mail to your favorite authors

- Join us in weekly chats with authors, readers and other guests

- Get writing guidelines

- AND MUCH MORE!

Visit our website at
http://www.arabesquebooks.com

MAD ABOUT YOU

Roberta Gayle

ARABESQUE
BET
BOOKS

BET Publications, LLC
www.msbet.com
www.arabesquebooks.com

ARABESQUE BOOKS are published by

BET Publications, LLC
c/o BET BOOKS
One BET Plaza
1900 W Place NE
Washington, D.C. 20018-1211

First Printing: June, 2000
10 9 8 7 6 5 4 3 2 1

Printed in the United States of America

One

He was the hottest thing to hit the big screen since Denzel Washington, and he was hers. Regina Primm could barely contain her excitement as she walked through the lobby of the Westin Hotel. She held herself in check as she made her way to the door, because if she actually started skipping across the marble floor she'd completely blow the image she'd spent the last hour creating of a smooth, self-contained professional who could successfully shepherd Langston Downs through the maze of previews, interviews and public appearances during his promotional tour here in Seattle.

He was the biggest client Regina Primm had ever represented, and he had the potential to be her biggest success ever. The raw material was there in abundance. And more. Not only was he the most gorgeous man she'd ever seen, but he also had talent and drive and, well, everything she could have wished for. The qualities that had made him the driving force behind the championship football team he'd played on in high school, and having been recruited by many colleges, as well as having been a high draft pick by each and every team in the NFL seemed to have served him well in his first foray into the film world. As a supporting player in *Heart of Soul,* he'd amazed audiences and nearly won an Academy Award. Reggie was convinced his second film, *Under His Skin,* would be even more successful than the first.

She sang along with the Four Tops on the radio all the way to the bar where she had promised to meet her best friend that evening. Reggie felt triumphant and excited, and a little bit scared at the thought of actually having gotten Langston Downs as a client. True, it was the film company that hired her, but she'd still be working with the best-looking man in the movies, maybe the most scrumptious black man ever to draw breath. And who was she? Just another overweight, overworked, ordinary woman struggling to make her new business a success.

This is it! she thought, forcing any lingering doubt to the back of her mind. *This is the dream.* She parked the car and strode into The Plum Bar with renewed determination. She would pull this off. She was good at what she did, and she'd proven that already today by selling the services of her small public relations firm to the film's producers. How much easier it would be to sell the sexiest man in America to an eager female audience. "I'm going to enjoy this," she said with exhilaration. She squared her shoulders and walked toward Bebe and her husband, Neal, who had staked out the pool table in the back of the room. As usual, Bebe was shooting, Neal was watching.

"How'd it go?" Bebe asked as soon as Reggie was within shouting distance. The bar was crowded and loud, and the only reason she could hear her friend was because the pool table provided a buffer to the noise the bar's other patrons were making.

"Great!" Reggie shouted back. "I did it!"

"Wow, Langston Downs!' Bebe said, sounding slightly envious. Her wide, sincere smile let Reggie know her best friend was happy for her anyway. Bebe Klein and she had been inseparable since the third grade, when they'd found out they were both getting braces on the same day. They had sworn to stick together all the next day and defend each other to the death if necessary.

A lot more than the wire on their teeth had kept them together through the years. Bebe was the only Jewish black girl at prestigious St. Mary's in the years she and Reggie attended the snooty pseudo-prep school. She was so fair she could easily have passed for white if she had wanted to, which didn't endear her to the six other black students in their class. Her mother was Jewish, her father African-American. The gene mix hadn't been kind to her; she'd inherited her mother's nose, and her father's overly large teeth.

They survived the adolescent horror of junior high school together. Bebe earned the nickname Tits on a Stick after a growth spurt in the seventh grade turned her from a skinny, leggy girl to a skinny teenager with a large chest. Reggie earned her own sobriquet, Porky Pie, because she was overweight, wore braces and glasses, and was as dark as Bebe was fair, putting her at the bottom of the list of untouchables for both the black and the white students. In a school in which wearing patent leather out of season earned scorn and public derision, Reggie didn't fit well into designer jeans, nor could she keep her thick, frizzy hair under control. She and Bebe had supported each other through it all. It was a friendship Reggie cherished.

When Bebe was thirty-three, a nose job and a tanning salon had given her the profile and complexion she'd wished she'd been born with, and caps on her teeth made her wonderful, sincere smile a beauty to behold. Recently, she'd been photographed for a *Cosmo* article on sexy lawyers, and she'd been voted by that magazine the sexiest one, black or white, male or female. She was also one of the brightest and most dedicated people Reggie ever knew.

"How about you? How's the case going?" Reggie asked. Bebe's current crusade involved going after the owner of a low-income housing project which had been hideously mismanaged. The responsible party was a scion of one of Seattle's oldest and wealthiest families, and had the added misfortune of having been a member of their class at St. Mary's.

Usually Reggie discouraged her best friend's vengeful preoccupation, but in this case Reggie had been totally appalled to find out how blatantly he'd misappropriated funds and risked lives, and she was squarely in Bebe's corner.

"We're going to skin 'em alive," Bebe said with relish. "Look at us, Reggie. I'm beating the stuffing out of the most popular guy in class, and you're working with a superstar quarterback. I bet those guys on the football team will wish they'd been nicer to you now." Bebe loved taking on their old classmates, and generally getting in their faces whenever possible.

Reggie didn't share her friend's thirst for vengeance. She was just glad the football team, the basketball team, and all the other

teams were in the past. "You would have hated him in high
school. He'd have been the Prom King, King Jock, and King of
the World if the girls at St. Mary's had been voting," she said
as Bebe re-racked the pool balls.

"Who cares?" Bebe said, taking the break and sinking the
three ball. "You've got him now."

"Yeah, I've got him." A shiver of anticipation ran down her
spine. Bebe scratched and Reggie lined up her shot and sank
the nine ball as she explained. "Of course it's just a glorified
baby-sitting job, but hey, I'm going to be paid really well. And
who knows what could come out of this. It's Hollywood we're
talking about here."

"Do you get to see the film?" Bebe asked. "Now? Before it's
released?"

"I'm sure I will. Although I don't think it's quite there yet.
They were talking about reshooting a scene or something."

"It's not done? It's supposed to be released in a month," Bebe
asked, surprised.

"It's done, I think," Reggie answered. "They tested it. Or
anyway, they said it 'tested well' on women my age." She exchanged a wry look with her friend. "So I guess it and I were
made for each other."

"Oh really," Bebe said. "Does that mean every woman our
age will enjoy it?"

"I guess so." Reggie threw her a glance pregnant with laughter. "They gave me a whole batch of demographic information
to help me focus my publicity campaign."

"How kind of them," Bebe said sarcastically.

"They can be as patronizing as they want. I think they just
hired me to keep Elaine happy. But my ego can take it, as long
as they don't get in my way. I'll enjoy promoting this film to
my peers. I helped the author get established, promoted the book
the film is based on, and set up the sale of the book to the film
company. And without any demographic research at all, I might
add," she said facetiously. More seriously, Reggie continued, "I
love this project. And between that and the fabulous salary I'm
getting paid, I'd be willing to dance naked in the street to sell

tickets to this flick." Reggie hadn't felt so invigorated since she'd
first gotten her business license.

Bebe thought of the one thing that could dampen her enthusiasm. "Unless they've completely ruined it," she said sadly.

"Elaine would have told me, I think. She's seen it." Reggie
answered. "My first assignment is to get Mr. Downs to a shoot
or session of some kind in two days. So I'll ask if I can see the
movie before then, just to be sure."

"Ask if you can bring a friend. I want to see it, too. Especially
if I get to sit in the dark with Langston Downs while I watch."

Neal just listened quietly up to this point in the conversation,
but his wife's lustful expression finally moved him to comment.
"It's not a date, dear," he pointed out.

"Not for me," Bebe quickly agreed. "I gave up dating a couple
of weeks after I got married," she joked.

Neal was a musician who taught at a prestigious music school
on Bainbridge Island, and composed his own music rather successfully besides. He was the leader of a wildly popular local
jazz group, and managed also to fit in time to compose background music for films, a profitable sideline that few people
knew about. He had unlimited creative energy when it came to
his art, and like so many talented artists, he could barely be
moved from behind his keyboard. Reggie could never have fath-
omed Bebe's attraction to the tall, thin, slightly myopic music
professor if it hadn't been for her friend's predilection for men
with long-fingered, graceful hands.

Bebe kissed her husband on the cheek. "Not for me, dear,"
she repeated. "But Reggie's available, aren't you, Reg. And she's
always had a thing for Downs."

"I do not," Reggie protested.

Bebe pursed her lips in a silent whistle. "I hate to have to say
this, but you lie, girl."

"I loved the character he played in *Heart of Soul,*" Reggie
clarified. "But Langston Downs is a jock, and a world-class
skirt chaser according to the newspapers. He's probably a big
jerk. I doubt we'll have a word to say to each other, except for
business, of course."

"Of course," Bebe echoed.

"Anyway, even if I were interested in him, which I'm not, I doubt a celebrity like Langston Downs would be interested in me."

"Why not?"

"Well, for one thing, he dates movie stars and models. For another thing, he's an athlete who's probably only interested in women who have abs of steel, not to mention buns of whatever."

"Speaking of buns—"

"Which we are *not*," Reggie said emphatically. "Even if he was the slightest bit interested in me, which I'm sure he won't be, I've never been any good at talking to men."

"You talk just fine to me," Neal interposed.

"I talk fine?" She raised her eyebrow. "Don't you mean I speak well?"

"Whatever," he agreed. "Don't go getting all professory on me. I'm just trying to say in my ungrammatical way, I've always enjoyed talking to you."

"You don't count. You're not a man, you're a husband," she said flippantly.

"Ouch," he said, wincing.

Bebe gave her a shove. "Hey!"

"No offense," Reggie apologized. "Good-looking guys like that are not attracted to frumpy women like me."

"You don't look frumpy to me," Neal said. Reggie walked past him to take her next shot, and he grabbed her and bent her back over his arm and buried his face in her neck. "In fact, if I wasn't so afraid of my wife, I would be all over you."

"Hey!" Bebe yelled. He let Reggie up again as Bebe raised her pool cue and pretended to threaten him with it from across the table.

Reggie straightened her skirt and continued on around the table to the most advantageous position from which to take her final shot. "No problem, Bebe. Your man is safe around me." She lined up to sight the eight ball. "He's a great guy, but he doesn't compare to Langston Downs." The game was over.

"Now I'm hurt," Neal said.

"I win," Reggie retorted callously. "You know I've always

secretly loved you," she whispered loudly to him across the table as Bebe racked the balls up again.

"I heard that," Bebe said.

"I can't stand it when you two girls fight over me," Neal said, tongue in cheek. "I'm going to go talk to Alfie." He went to the bar. The bartender was an old friend of his.

"I didn't mean to hurt your feelings, but he's my dream client, not my dream date," Reggie said firmly to her best friend. She loved kidding around with these two, but she didn't need to feel any more insecure about her femininity than she already did— not with the big meeting coming up in the morning. As she always told her clients, confidence was nine-tenths of the game. "I'm already putting together the campaign to promote him within the African-American community," she offered, as a new topic for conversation. "I called a bookstore and a radio station from the car on the way here, and we have appearance dates at both."

"Let me guess, both were run by women?" Bebe said cynically.

"Actually, the radio show is with a man—that sports guy on Cool Jazz. I'm sure I can get Downs on National Public Radio, too."

"Do any of his fans listen to NPR?" she asked teasingly.

Reggie bristled. "I do," she replied.

"You're not his usual fan. I think he's more popular among fourteen-year-olds. Boys and girls."

"I'm going to change all that, remember?" Reggie said. "Besides, it's not like he's completely unappealing to our . . . demographic. You like him—"

"I'm a lech," Bebe interrupted.

"I like him, and so does my mother."

"I just meant that no sensible woman would seriously want Langston Downs. He's too slick and smooth and good-looking. I don't think anyone over sixteen would fall for that guy."

"I don't know. His name has been linked with a number of women who are all grown up. Didn't he date Vanessa Williams for a while?"

"Venus or Serena Williams, you mean?"

"No. Vanessa, the actress. Not a teenager."

"If you can believe the tabloids, he's dated everyone."

"All I'm saying is that just because teenage girls think he's all that, doesn't mean he's into teenage girls."

"I was just joking, jeez, Reggie. When did you become this guy's press secretary."

Reggie brought her watch up into her friend's face. "About four fifteen today?" she said wryly.

"Oh yeah," Bebe remembered. She laughed. "Well just don't let those too-good looks make you do something you'll regret."

"Such as?" Reggie inquired.

"Such as lose your head," her friend advised.

"You just said no mature woman could fall for him," Reggie reminded her. "Besides, he's a client. I would never . . ."

"Never is a long time, as my father likes to say. And I'm just saying you should watch out for him. As you said, he doesn't seem to lack female company of any age. He could be one of those men who can't stand to be near anything in a skirt without making a play for her."

"I don't think I need to worry about that. But, if it will make you happy, I'll keep my pepper spray handy."

"Good idea."

"I was just kidding," Reggie exclaimed. "I can't believe this conversation. Two minutes ago you were talking about how irresistible he is. Now you're suggesting he could be . . . what? A rapist?"

"They're not unrelated subjects," Bebe said. "If you think about it. Irresistible people sometimes can't handle being turned down."

"If he's irresistible, how can I turn him down? It's a contradiction in terms," Reggie said, teasing her.

"Don't start playing these word games with me," Bebe said. "You always win. All *I'm* saying is that it's a big myth that gorgeous, successful men don't rape women. It's when they're used to getting their own way, be they bullies or businessmen or sex symbols, they can get upset when they don't get their own way."

"Okay, okay, I was just messing with you, girlfriend. I will not make any assumptions, okay?" Reggie paused to let her promise sink in. "And you stop making assumptions, too. Just because he's a rich, famous movie star doesn't mean he always gets his own way."

Bebe grinned, and Reggie had to smile back at her. "In a just world, he'd have to pay for all his advantages by having some terrible deformity or something," she said.

"He might have," Bebe suggested. "Maybe he's plagued by recurring nightmares, or a terrible rash."

"Or . . . or . . . warts!" Reggie added.

"Impotence!" Bebe shouted.

"Now that would be a shame," Reggie said, shaking her head.

"And warts wouldn't?" Bebe asked.

"No, I mean there's a difference between something that he has to suffer in silence and something that deprives the entire female population of sex with a man who embodies carnal pleasure," Reggie explained.

"True," Bebe said, nodding. "Very true."

Two

Langston "Mo' Down" Downs couldn't believe his luck. No matter which way he turned, women stared, smiled at him, followed him. There was no way to get out of the hotel without one of them getting to him. They were growing bolder with each passing minute of his stay in Seattle. He could feel them circling, moving in. He was going to suffer, one way or the other. Either he was going to have to run through them with his head down and his backside protected, like a fullback on the one-yard line on fourth down, or he was going to have to pretend to pick up one of these meat eaters and dump her when he had made his getaway. Either way, his dignity was going to suffer.

Langston walked briskly down the hallway from his suite to the elevator, looking neither right nor left. It had been forever since he'd had a night alone like this, and he planned to enjoy it. He had always traveled with his team, practiced with teammates . . . virtually lived with them. When he'd started in the pros he'd been one of the youngest players, and some of the older guys had instantly adopted him, taking him under their wings. It had been kind of them—but it had left him without any experience in this kind of thing, and sometimes he wished he'd spent some small portion of his adult life living on his own, so he'd know how to handle it now.

He reached the elevator without incident and forced himself to stand still and patient while he waited for the elevator to come. When the doors finally opened, the car was blessedly empty, so at least he wouldn't be trapped in the box with anyone. He hopped in and pressed the button for the lobby, praying that no one else would end up sharing the small enclosed space with him for the short ride.

It had taken him all of the last year to get used to the concept of spending time by himself. After growing up in his mother's house with his three sisters, all of their friends, and, of course, his friends, who ran in and out of his mother's kitchen as much as he had himself, he had gone on to live with his team, and they became another family. He had taken on the newer, younger men and tried to guide them and keep them out of trouble, just as others had done for him.

In the year since he'd retired from professional football, his life had undergone so many changes. It wasn't just the career—even though just thinking about that made him nervous as hell—nor was it the new house he'd bought in Malibu. It was evenings like this one, when he was in a strange town without the team, where he wasn't expected anywhere, and could do anything that he wanted. The feeling of freedom was still new.

His agent, Tommy Ray, who was also a friend, thought it was hysterical that Langston was so excited by something that most adults considered commonplace. He also couldn't resist teasing Langston about wanting to be alone. "Hiding out, huh?" he asked when they spoke earlier that evening. "Or do you have some sweet little tidbit you're trying to keep a secret?"

It was no use trying to get Tommy to keep his smart mouth shut—Langston had tried. "Cut it out, man," he said anyway. "You know I'm not." He didn't mean to sound pathetic.

"It's completely up to you, guy," his friend said straight out.

"That's right. And I enjoy my solitude."

"You are one strange cat. Any other guy would love to have great-looking babes show up at his door naked."

"Try it sometime. I think you'll find it's not all it's cracked up to be."

"Just give me a week," Tommy said with heartfelt sincerity. "One week. I promise I will take advantage."

"I thought you were really into what's her name," Langston said.

"I am. But I can fantasize, can't I? I'm dating her. I didn't put a ring on her finger." He was incorrigible. Langston couldn't help laughing. If he'd been at home in L.A., Tommy would already have been at the house, forcing him to go out to some club or something.

He'd only relocated to the West Coast a month ago, but it was the home of a number of people he'd known for years, including his sports agent, his business manager, and other friends. And of course his new best friends were constantly calling: his new talent agent, director, producer, and even some of his fans when they managed to get his number. Tonight, he was truly without any obligations. No one even knew his telephone number, let alone his room number, and he could go to a movie, or just take in the sights, or do whatever normal people did. If he just wasn't recognized.

Langston had been named MVP two years in a row, but even that had not prepared him for the kind of attention that he had garnered by playing a supporting character in one film. When he played football, women had been some of his biggest fans, but when he played a football player in the movie *Heart of Soul,* they went crazy. They staked out his apartment building, they sent him photos—and proposals of marriage—through the mail, they approached him everywhere he went.

The elevator doors slid open. Langston kept his head down as he crossed the lobby. He had called down to the bellman to get him a taxi, so all he had to do was get outside and he'd be all right. He had already gotten in trouble once on this trip. A group of young women had surrounded him at the hotel pool the previous day and he was pretty sure someone had videotaped him as he'd tried to extricate himself from the situation. It had been embarrassing, but it had given him a reason to change hotels, and only his agent and his mother knew where he was staying now. Which was the only reason, Langston knew, that the producers of his latest film hadn't called and arranged for him to spend the evening with one of their baby-sitters. They didn't trust him to behave himself.

They didn't understand that he wasn't interested in young girls, or groupies of any age for that matter. He didn't want the notoriety, it just happened. He thought he heard someone say,

"Isn't that him?" And he quickened his pace. A moment later he was out of the tall glass doors. A bellman ushered him into a waiting taxi.

"Pike Place Market," he requested, and the driver pulled away from the hotel.

After a moment, the cabby asked, "You know there's not much down at the market at night. A couple of restaurants and bars still open on the pier, but the market's closed, and the boat rides and other tourist stuff."

"That's okay," Langston said. "I'll just take a quick look around."

"It's not too safe these days, with all the homeless and all," the man said.

Langston had not worried about his physical safety since he'd topped six feet right before his fourteenth birthday. People, even the truly desperate, tended to steer clear of big black guys whose biceps measured eighteen inches in circumference. *The guy's just trying to be nice,* he thought.

"Really, how about Pioneer Square then?" he suggested.

"Better," said the cabby, without enthusiasm. "There isn't much there either, though. The stores are all closed already."

"I know, I just thought I'd look around. I was there last year with some friends, and I didn't really get to see it. I thought it looked nice though," he explained.

"It does look pretty. I don't know how safe it is, though," his driver mused. "Cops keep the homeless out of there."

"Thanks, I'll watch my step."

"I can wait for you," the older man offered.

"I appreciate it, but afterwards I'm going to walk over to the New Orleans Bar."

"Enjoy yourself then, Mr. Downs," the old man said. Langston smiled, shaking his head in amazement. He read an article in the newspaper about how most Americans couldn't recognize the members of the President's cabinet. He was just an ex-football player, but he was recognized everywhere.

Langston was lost in thought as he walked toward the main attraction of the square, the fountain, lit up and glowing golden in the darkness just like it had been when he'd been here before.

That had been another life. He was starting to think he might prefer the new one. He stood for a moment admiring the Old-World charm of the sight. Someone giggled. Langston's blood froze. They couldn't have followed him *here*. Could they? He turned slowly to face the sound, hoping against hope that that high-pitched girlish giggle came from a parrot, or an alley cat, or anything other than a girl.

He wished in vain, he saw as he peered through the darkness at two very young, very star-struck girls. They were tiny. "You can't be over twelve," he blurted out.

Two smiles faded and were replaced with defiant scowls. "I am," one girl said.

"I'm almost fourteen," the other one piped in.

"What are you doing here?" Langston asked, incredulous.

"We followed you from the hotel," they said simultaneously, which set off the giggles again.

Langston thought he had seen everything when the girl showed up at his hotel room wearing a completely transparent outfit last year, but this was a new one. He couldn't believe pint-size teenage girls were stalking him now. The two of them stacked atop each other would barely have reached his chin.

"You shouldn't be out here," he said stupidly. "It's not safe."

They weren't just tiny, young, white girls. He could guess from their clothing, hair and mannerisms that they were over-privileged and overprotected as well. A few years ago, a man of color would have been lynched for just talking to girls like these. He had to get them back to the hotel immediately. He didn't know who needed protection more—them or himself—but he had a sinking feeling that he knew who was going to get into trouble on account of their escapade.

He walked them to the first restaurant he could find, sat them at a table, and bought them Cokes. They drank their sodas while he called the taxi service. "Fifteen minutes," the dispatcher promised. It was too long for Langston, but short of leaving them there to fend for themselves, he was forced to wait with them. His mother would have killed him if he left these defense-less waifs alone on the city streets.

"We were in the lobby when you left," said the thirteen-year-old.

"Our brother wouldn't let us play Commando," said the younger one, whose name, she had volunteered on the walk, was Sam. "If we got your autograph we knew that would make Ben sorry," she said, clearly relishing the prospect.

"Ben's your brother?" Langston asked. "He was supposed to be watching you?" He sought further clarification—and a scapegoat in case the press and the kid's parents were awaiting his return to the hotel.

"We're old enough to take care of ourselves. We don't need anyone to watch us," Sam protested.

"Apparently you do," Langston chided her. "You were supposed to stay in the game room, weren't you?" She set her chin mulishly. He aimed his stern gaze at the younger girl. "I'm sure you weren't supposed to leave the hotel, and you knew it. You look smart enough to know better than to wander around a strange city at night."

"But we thought you were going someplace cool," Molly whined. "Not some boring old fountain."

"Molly!" Sam's harsh voice made her little sister jump.

She recovered quickly. "Well, we did."

"Okay, okay!" Langston did not want them to start bickering. That was all he needed. He'd witnessed enough arguments between his older sister's teenagers to know that that kind of melodrama could get ugly.

He got them back to the hotel without incident and even gave them the numerous autographs they requested for themselves, their friends, two boyfriends, and even their father. "How about your brother?" he heard himself say before he thought about it. That was one of Langston's biggest problems. He hated to disappoint even the brother of his two pint-sized stalkers.

"No way!" Samantha said.

Molly shook her head in emphatic agreement. "He has to be punished," she explained in a patronizing tone.

"Oh sure," Langston agreed helplessly and made his escape as quickly as he could.

Back up in his hotel room, he ordered room service and a

movie on Spectra Vision. It wasn't the same as going out, but at least he didn't have to worry about anyone intruding on his privacy.

There was a message from his agent, Tommy Ray, waiting for him when he got back. "A woman named Regina Primm will be contacting you. Be nice," was all it said.

He crumpled the short note and threw it in the trash. He had never heard of her, but with a name like Primm he didn't think he'd forget. If his agent said to be nice, he would, of course, be nice. However, when the phone rang halfway through the movie, he ignored it. He called the operator for the message an hour later.

Ms. Primm's voice on his voice mail matched her name, "Mr. Downs, I hope we can meet tomorrow morning as we don't have much time to get acquainted. I'll be at your hotel at nine, unless you care to suggest an alternate time or place. Leave a message on my machine to confirm the appointment after you get this message, if you please? Thank you."

She sounded professional, competent, and controlled. She did not sound like a groupie. Langston tried to figure out who she could be as he prepared for bed. Her voice mail message, when he called to confirm the meeting, was also professional, but didn't give the name of a company, only "Regina Primm," like her message, and his agent's. Perhaps it was a name he was supposed to know.

She knew where he was staying, and only Tommy could have given her that information. His agent wouldn't give his address to just anyone. She had to be connected with the film company or the movie he was in town to promote. She could be some local film distributor's wife who had been promised a meeting.

He shook off the slight feeling of unease he felt. If Tommy gave her his number, she was safe anyway. His agent knew better than to give his number to any of the brand of women he'd dubbed meat eaters years ago. Langston had only been nineteen when he first realized there were plenty of women who went beyond simply categorizing men as slabs of meat—they actually wanted to take a bite.

His mother taught him not to treat women as objects, ever,

and she'd been equally strict on the subject of behaving like a gentleman. Langston had never shared his father's or his grandfather's illusions about women being the gentler sex. His mother was the one who raised him after his father's death when Langston was five, and she never implied she or any of his sisters were in any way weaker than he. Tricia Downs had been a member of the illustrious Tuskegee track team and had just missed qualifying for the Olympics herself. Langston had inherited her athleticism. More importantly, when her first husband died, and then his stepfather was crippled in an accident and left it up to Tricia to raise Langston and his three sisters alone, he saw how strong his mama was.

It was she whom he emulated when he worked so hard at school in academics and in every sport he could participate in. He chose to pursue his career rather than go on to college because he wanted to take some of the financial burden off of her. Mama hadn't liked it, but she supported his decision when she realized she could not talk him out of it. Then she began a campaign that continued to that day to talk him into going back to get his degree. Langston liked school. He would have liked to continue his formal education. But the one time he did take a couple of college courses, he found it impossible to be a normal freshman in the sea of admirers who had eagerly followed his career in the NFL. It wasn't worth it. He might have kept trying, but two girls in the school, whom he had thought of as friends, both filed paternity suits against him and that had been the end of college for him. He was exonerated—he hadn't even slept with the first one—but the stigma still clung to his name. It didn't help that he voluntarily gave both girls the money they had needed so desperately that they'd taken him to court. The press had branded him a ladies' man long before those incidents, and Langston couldn't bring himself to be cold enough to his female fans to escape the barrage of insinuations and accusations the media threw at him.

He loved women. His mother, his sisters, and the wives of his coaches and teammates, all were precious to him. Beyond that, he liked flirting with intelligent women, enjoyed the feel and taste of female flesh, and had no desire to live as a monk.

Langston threw off the covers, warm at the thought of how long it had been since he'd had any kind of relationship. He still hoped to meet his perfect match. Once or twice he thought he had, but it never worked out. Unfortunately, it seemed the good ones were all taken, and he was left with man-eaters and teenage groupies. The few women he met who came closest to his ideal—independent, unattached women with both looks and brains—only seemed to be interested in brief affairs with him. He could understand that they didn't want marriage to a dumb jock who didn't even have a bachelor's degree.

He put all thought of the mysterious Ms. Primm out of his mind. He refused to lose sleep over a woman he hadn't even met. He'd know soon enough.

Three

Reggie arrived early, as usual, at the hotel. She called Langston Downs from a house phone.

"Hello?" His raspy baritone had enchanted fans of his first film, Reggie among them.

"Hello, Mr. Downs, this is Regina Primm. I'm in the lobby. May I buy you a cup of coffee or some breakfast?" Reggie didn't want to be alone with the star, yet. She preferred meeting him outside of his hotel room, on more neutral ground. She didn't trust herself not to reveal what a huge fan she was, and it was important to behave like a consummate professional.

"Sure," he answered, and they arranged to meet in one of the hotel's quieter restaurants.

She went into the restaurant and asked for one of the tables toward the back of the room. Reggie ordered a pot of tea for herself and organized her files and her notepad on the table in front of her. Langston Downs surprised her by appearing only a few minutes later, just as she finished pouring and adding sugar to her tea.

She rose. "Good morning," she said, signaling to the waiter who had escorted him to the table that he should remain for a moment. "How about some coffee?" He nodded. Reggie looked at the waiter, who said, "Of course," and left. Then she sat down at the same time Langston did. So far, so good. She didn't think he could detect her rapid heartbeat. She'd imagined herself meeting this man, as thousands of other women probably had, but she'd never dreamed it would really come true. And her fantasies hadn't included her having to behave completely professionally.

Reggie finally took her first real close look at him. He was closely shaved and his hair, which appeared to be wet, was pulled back in a short black ponytail. She assumed it had been straightened for the movie he'd just appeared in, and it gave him the roguish look of a pirate. His eyes were hidden by sunglasses, but she'd have recognized that strong square jaw and that famous mouth anywhere.

His clothing was casual but elegant: a golden yellow designer shirt and loosely cut nut-brown trousers cinched in at his waist with a thin belt. He didn't wear a tie or jacket. She was dressed in her best black linen power suit, in slacks rather than a skirt, her Hermes scarf draped loosely over the white silk blouse, her long jacket open and flowing over her hips. She'd had her hair braided and coiled up into a crown on her head, a style which would last for the entire two weeks of the assignment, and one that added an inch or two to her height so he wouldn't tower over her five foot three inch frame quite so much.

Reggie cleared her throat, realizing that while she'd been giving him the quick once-over, he'd been doing the same. "Shall we get right down to business?" she asked.

"What business would that be?" he responded with a slight smile.

"Didn't they tell you?" The waiter arrived with his coffee, and Regina waited until the young man had left again before she continued. "I own a small public relations company here in Seattle, and I've been hired to escort you to your interviews with the Morning Show and KXGA, which were set up by the studio. Also, I'm going to promote you locally and accompany you to the spots I hope to set up for you." She quickly gave him a summary of her plans for him, stumbling at first over the details, then slowly finding her rhythm.

"Ah, so you're my new nanny," Langston said, removing his sunglasses and reaching for the creamer.

"You don't need a nanny," she said, although at that moment she wasn't sure. "You're a grown man. I've been hired to raise your profile among a certain demographic in this area. That is, you are already popular with sports fans, young and old, and young men and women who enjoyed your last movie, but this is a different kind of project. This is a period piece, and the producers feel it will appeal to the intellectual elite . . . and women ages eighteen to thirty-five in general."

He took a sip of his coffee and set it down. "So you were hired to—what did you call it?—raise my . . . profile. Is that all you're supposed to raise?"

Reggie wished she could wipe that smug expression off his face, but she knew that humoring him would make her work easier. She kept her cool as she answered, "Do I look like the kind of woman whom they would hire to . . . um . . . raise anything else?"

"You look smart," he answered immediately. "You sound like a professional. In New York, the production company hooked me up with a woman who . . . How do I put this politely?" He took another sip of coffee while he thought. "I'll just say her bra size was bigger than her IQ. I wouldn't have minded their condescension, except that they seemed so surprised that I managed to ditch her . . . every time. At least this time they assigned someone with a brain."

"Mr. Downs," Reggie started to clear up his assumption that she was being paid to do anything more than promote his new film.

"Langston, please," he interrupted. "If we're going to be spending a lot of time together, you might as well call me by my first name."

Reggie didn't want to start trading insults with this man. He was a client. There was something about the way he watched her, though, that got under her skin. He examined her like he might examine a microbe under a microscope. "Fine. Langston." She spoke slowly and clearly so he couldn't misunderstand her. "I was hired for my expertise as a manager. Not for . . . anything else. The time we spend together will, I assure you, be spent promoting you and this film. I managed Elaine Fuller's publicity when her book was first published. That's why they hired me."

Under His Skin? My movie?" he questioned.

"The book on which the film was based, yes," Reggie confirmed. "So can we get back to business now?"

"All right," he agreed slowly. "Sorry if I offended you."

She bowed her head regally in his direction, acknowledging, and tacitly accepting, his apology. But she didn't believe it for a moment. Regina knew his type. They'd plagued her for most of her life. Men like him used their good looks, charm, and sizzling sensuality to get whatever they wanted. They counted on their attributes to get their way with women like her who were unattached (and therefore starved for affection) and older (and therefore desperate) and less than beautiful (and therefore frustrated). She could have told him she felt not one iota of desperation.

While it was true that when she was growing up her dark complexion and kinky hair were not considered assets, her parents and teachers praised her intelligence, which gave her a different yardstick to measure her worth by. It served her well.

She didn't have to be intelligent to realize as a teenager that she would never appear on the cover of *Vogue*. Her weight aside, until recently only black women with light skin, thin noses, and "good" hair could aspire to fit the ideal of beauty touted by Madison Avenue and Hollywood. When she traveled abroad after college, she found places in which her exotic appearance was regarded as inherently beautiful. Cosmetic companies and the mainstream media in her own country were even beginning to recognize the existence of a population that praised "phat backs" and naturally curly locks.

It was possible that she would never get over her insecurities about her appearance, but Langston Downs would be blind to the kind of beauty she valued most: Neal's love for her best friend, and her youngest little niece who was newly walking and was a wonder to behold as she dared to explore the world. She didn't need, or want, his admiration.

Reggie managed to keep her voice calm and steady despite her desire to puncture the huge ego sitting across the table from her with a sharp word or two. "Here is the itinerary I've created so far. I've only had one day, so I'm waiting for a number of calls before I'll know the final schedule, but we do have some definite dates. Those are printed in black. Possibles are in blue. The two red items are the most important. Do you have any questions?"

"One or two," he said coolly.

"Oh lord," she groaned inwardly. But she smiled and asked, "Yes?"

"Do you like your work?"

She examined his face closely, but could see no sign that he was less than serious. "Um-hmm," Reggie cleared her throat. "Yes, I do."

She was about to suggest they meet at eight the following morning so she could drive him to his interview at Seattle's KXGA radio station when he took off his sunglasses and focused his big brown eyes intently on her face. It knocked the thought out of her head. "And . . . ?" he asked.

Reggie suppressed the urge to whip out her pocket mirror and check her face for smeared lipstick or dirt stains. "And?" she echoed.

"Why do you like it?" he questioned.

"My work?" she repeated, then felt her cheeks grow warm with embarrassment as he nodded. "I enjoy helping writers to promote their books, which is what I specialize in. Whether it's an author or a musician or a visual artist, I like seeing talent recognized and knowing that I was a part of creating that recognition." He listened to her with an intensity she recognized as a trait of the character Jed, whom he played in his first film. She had fallen in love with Jed. Those magnificent, warm, brown eyes were even more beautiful in real life than on the screen, and as she stared into them, the people in the room around them receded. It was easy to forget Langston Downs' less appealing personality when she sat face to face with this magnificent man whom women dreamed of meeting and talking to—like this.

As he nodded and said, "I see," Reggie thought perhaps he wasn't such a jerk after all. He seemed to be truly interested. "You must know all the best clubs and party spots, too," he said, jolting her abruptly out of the fantasy.

"What?" She became aware of the bustling waiters, the busboys who hovered not far from the tables, and the other patrons eating, talking and laughing at their tables not far from hers.

"You people always throw the coolest parties at the coolest places," he clarified.

Shaking her head, Reggie bid farewell to any thought of finding a kindred spirit in her new client. "Yeah, sure," she confirmed.

"So is there going to be a party for me?" Langston asked.

After his unenthusiastic welcome earlier, she was surprised he so quickly accepted her role in his life. "Do you want a party?" she asked in return.

"Why not?" he responded casually.

"Why indeed?" she mused softly. "I'll see what I can do," she said to him. Then before he could ask anything more, or make any other comments that could annoy her, she quickly ended the meeting. "So, I'll be in touch concerning your schedule, and we'll meet here tomorrow morning at eight to go to your interview at the radio station."

"Fine. I'll see you then." He stood as she did and shook her hand when she offered it to him.

Reggie wondered what he would do with the rest of his day, now that he had the day free. "I hope he doesn't do anything . . . scandalous," she told her mother when she met her for lunch.

"Scandalous?" Her mother repeated the word, smiling.

"You know what I mean, Mom. He's got a reputation for . . . fooling around, with young girls. You saw that newspaper article in the paper this morning." Her mother ushered her into her sunny kitchen where the table was already laid out for lunch.

Jenny still looked remarkable at the age of seventy-five. Her golden brown skin was only faintly lined at the corners of her mouth and eyes. Her big brown eyes and high cheekbones gave her a timeless beauty, and her reddish-brown hair caught the sunlight and formed a halo of curls around her head.

She bustled about, bringing lunch to the table while Reggie sat down. "I saw his face in the photos, too, and I'd say that man was being hounded by those girls, not the other way around." Her mom always called things the way she saw them.

"That doesn't mean he didn't earn the rep," Reggie said peevishly.

"It doesn't mean he did, either. You're just annoyed with him because he didn't know who you were," her mother said in acerbic tones as she served them both lunch.

"I'm annoyed with him because he insulted me," Reggie corrected her. "Not just because he didn't know who I was."

"All right, so he made a mistake. He didn't have all the facts. You said he was okay after you explained the situation, right? So be grateful for small favors. He didn't turn out to be the pig you thought he might. He could even be a pretty nice guy."

"I sure hope so," Reggie said. "We'll be working pretty closely together."

"Mmmm, now for that I would go back to work," she sighed loudly.

"Mom!" Reggie exclaimed, pretending shock.

"That is one pretty man."

"He knows it, too," Reggie said. "But he didn't seem too conceited." Not that she was acquainted with any men as attractive as he was. They were few and far between in the real world. "He was very sure of himself, and a little arrogant, but he was relatively down to earth."

"That's all you can ask," her luncheon partner commented.

"I can ask for a lot more than that . . . but I won't," Reggie replied. Her mom finished her minuscule lunch and began clearing away the dishes. Reggie would have helped but she knew her mother would not thank her for it. Jennifer Primm fought hard to preserve her independence. She said she liked waiting on her family now that she didn't have to anymore, but Reggie believed she didn't want to be a burden on her children.

"I just hope he doesn't say anything embarrassing on the radio tomorrow."

"Why? What would he say?"

"I don't know." Reggie had to think for a moment about why she'd said that. "He didn't seem too bright, I guess. Not that he said anything unintelligent, but I just didn't get the impression that he was one of the intellectual elite either. I suppose I expected him to sound more like the character he played in his movie, and he sounded more like a football player. Which makes perfect sense, when you think about it."

"What does a football player sound like, honey?" Her mother gently prodded.

"Don't start with me," Reggie warned. "I promise not to judge Langston Downs without getting to know him." She held her hand up as if she were swearing in a courtroom, but her mother gave her a swat anyway.

"Don't be fresh," she admonished.

Reggie didn't think Langston Downs cared one iota what she thought of him, but her mother was obsessed with avoiding labels. She felt they demeaned everyone, both the labelers and the labeled. "Yes, ma'am," Reggie appeased her. Even though it was a pain at times, Reggie was secretly proud of her adherence to her principles. If everyone listened to Jenny Primm, the world would be a much nicer, more tolerant place. So she tried. But in this one instance, Reggie refused to worry about it . . . much.

She felt enough anxiety about working with a former star football player and current film idol. Reggie refused to add to her burden by trying to collect more information before she judged her new client. She would brief him in the morning before the interview. If he appeared to understand her instructions and spoke sensibly, she would let him field the questions by himself. She hoped, for the sake of their work together, that he was not an idiot. But if he asked her any more questions about partying, she would tell him to keep his mouth shut until he was prompted, and then stick to succinct answers. She planned that evening to compose a short script containing only a few safe, stock answers to frequently asked questions, just in case Langston Downs really was a dud in the brains department.

Four

Ms. Primm and Proper was going to drive him insane. Reggie briefed him in the hotel when they met, and again in the car on the way to the radio station. He wondered how stupid she thought he was as she stood blocking his way into the studio to ask him, *"Titanic* was the most recent period piece to become a blockbuster, so you may be asked whether *Under His Skin* will appeal to audiences who enjoyed that movie."

"Uh-huh," he mumbled. He looked around to see if anyone was watching. Fortunately for him, they were alone in the narrow hallway.

"What will you say?" Reggie pressed.

He consulted the list in his hand. It was a learned response. The lady nearly blew a gasket when he'd responded without glancing at her cheat sheet first. "I think this film will have wide appeal to audiences of all ages who enjoy a good romantic action adventure."

She nodded, apparently satisfied.

"I feel like a trained monkey," he said under his breath.

She heard him. "I'm sorry. This interview will kick off the round of public appearances in the region, and I want it to go well."

"You said that before," he told her.

Reggie had the good grace to look embarrassed by his reminder. "This shouldn't take long, and then we'll know where we stand."

Langston resisted the urge to pick her up and move her out

of his way. He resorted to sarcasm. "Well, I'm standing here, and you're standing there, blocking my entrance into the interview."

"Oops," she said, moving aside. "Good luck, Mist——" For a moment her chagrin was visible, but she quickly rearranged her features into a smooth smile. "Break a leg, Langston."

Reggie looked so nervous, he couldn't resist teasing her a little. "So, what's the name of this flick again?"

"Oh my lord," she groaned. She looked like she was about to pass out, so he relented. "Just kidding." He chuckled.

She gave him a weak smile in return. "I knew that," she insisted, but she couldn't look him in the eye.

He took her chin in his hand and lifted her face so she couldn't avoid looking at him any longer. "Really, it was a joke. You've got to loosen up, Reggie."

"I'll try," she muttered. It didn't sound as though the prospect appealed to her. Langston wasn't a bit surprised. She was so tightly wound up, he was tempted to flub the interview just to see her blow. But of course, he couldn't do that. He wanted to be taken seriously as an actor. He was good at football, he used his brain, and to those who knew the sport that made him a great player. But no one took football players seriously off the grid iron. As an actor he had come to be seen as a whole person, complete with brains, heart, soul, and the rest of it. He wasn't about to give that up just to rattle his publicist, no matter how much he would have enjoyed it. He wasn't educated like Ms. Regina Primm and her friends, but he approached his acting career with the same dogged determination he had called upon to tough out fifteen years in the pros. He didn't feel inspired by the script, the other artists he worked with, or the camera. He just slogged along, hoping he was fooling everyone. So far, it had worked. He pretended to be someone else, and they bought it.

Some day he might learn more about this craft than to do what he was told by the director and the cameraman and the dialogue coach and the lighting guy. For now, he didn't understand a word of language that dominated his fellow actors' conversation about their work. Such foreign phrases as method acting or Strasberg or Stanislavsky were indecipherable. He tried reading about them, but the explanations were as confusing as the lingo itself. He understood why actors seemed to perpetually "study" and to vie to work with certain "masters" of the art. Acting, even more than football, was not something one could learn alone in a room with a book. And he was too embarrassed to try to get into any classes. It was too late. He couldn't go into Meryl Streep's classroom at Yale and ask her how it was done. He couldn't ask anyone to teach him the basics after making a successful film. He would look ridiculous. So he dutifully answered the stock questions put to him by the radio talkshow host, just as he'd been instructed.

Reggie beamed at him when he came out of the booth. "You were great," she raved. "I'm sorry if it seemed like I . . . uh, implied—" she floundered.

"That I am an idiot?" he supplied.

"No, no. I never thought anything like that," she deferred.

She was adorable, all flustered and discomposed. He liked her better this way than when she was composed and self-assured.

Reggie had anticipated every question in the interview, and Langston was glad to have a professional on his side, but he wondered if she could be fun, too. How thick was that veneer of self-assurance she wore like a cloak? If she had a healthy sense of humor, that would make the next two weeks easier to bear. It was definitely an idea worth exploring.

She was saying, "I thought you did a wonderful job."

"For a moron?" His voice was harsher than he intended, but it seemed like a good time to find out if Regina Primm could take a joke, albeit a pretty lame one. "I don't know if I can work with someone who has so little faith in my ability to handle a simple interview."

"I'm sorry if I gave you that impression," Reggie said sincerely.

He didn't change his tone. "It's a little late for that now, don't you think?" He watched as she tried, unsuccessfully, not to let her frustration show.

She straightened up and looked him straight in the eye. "Of course, I can assure you that I won't make that mistake again."

He pretended to consider her words, then turned away. "Not good enough. You're fired." Maybe he was pushing it, but Langston wanted to get a rise out of her, see what she would do when pushed past her limit.

And that got her. "You can't fire me. You didn't hire me," she spluttered angrily.

He turned to face her. "I'm sure my producers can find another publicist." Something in his expression must have given him away. Reggie, who had been staring up at him in disbelief, started to protest, when suddenly she narrowed her eyes and refocused on his face. His lip twitched involuntarily and Langston knew she saw it when her eyes narrowed even further.

"Is this your idea of a joke?" Reggie asked.

"Yeah," he admitted. "Funny, huh?"

"Ha, ha," she said sarcastically. Then she smiled ruefully and he knew there was a woman he could enjoy behind that stiff, stuffy facade.

"You got me." He smiled back. "Truce?" She offered him her hand to shake.

He took it. "Let's start again. Okay?"

"Okay." This time her smile was warm and genuine. Langston fell into step beside her as she started toward the elevator, pleased with the result of his little experiment. He'd broken through the wall of reserve she'd erected at their first meeting. He had to take some of the blame for her behavior, since he'd caused part of it, at least with his insensitive remarks at their first meeting. Now that he'd repaired the damage he'd done, though, Langston thought he was going to like this woman. He liked females with spirit. And there was something about her that made him want to shock her out of her equanimity. At the same time, Reggie was such a tiny little thing, and he felt protective.

"Great. Now how about some lunch?" he asked.

"It's only ten o'clock," Reggie answered.

"Late breakfast, then," he suggested. He wanted to spend just a little more time with her—off the clock.

"I had breakfast. How about some coffee?" she offered.

"Done."

"The hotel restaurant again?"

"No, I've been living in that place. How about some place the tourists don't know about?"

"Well, there are lots of ordinary little coffee shops, but . . ." Her voice trailed off as she considered the alternatives.

"But—" he prompted.

"They're not glamorous or anything," she finally concluded.

"Perfect. I love ordinary. Really," he added when she looked at him doubtfully.

"Okay." She led him to the car, then drove him to a hole in the wall which could have been located in any city in America. There was no menu, but rather paper plates pinned to the wall with breakfast specials misprinted in felt-tipped marker.

"I don't suppose they have any cappuccino here, huh?" he teased.

She came right back at him with, "You wanted ordinary, you got it." At that moment, he was sure Reggie Primm could be a fun girl if she loosened up a little.

"No, seriously, it's great." After the waitress took their order, he confided in a near whisper. "It's amazing. I can spend two hundred bucks a night for an elite hotel, and still I can't avoid being asked for my autograph everywhere I turn, but everyone here averts their eyes as soon as they recognize me."

"It's only polite to let a man eat in peace," Reggie answered. "Even if he does order the pig-out special."

"Hey, it sounded good. Anyway, I'm just replacing the pounds I sweated off during that interview."

"Sweat? You? Try pulling the other one," Reggie said unsympathetically.

"Hey, those things are hard work. Put me up against a two-hundred-fifty-pound linebacker any day."

"You looked like you were enjoying yourself thoroughly."

"You know the old saying. Never let 'em see you sweat."

"So why are you telling me?" she inquired.

"I don't know," he answered honestly. "Something about you inspires confidences."

"When I'm not calling you a dumb jock," she joked.

"Hey!" Their food arrived before he could protest further.

She waited until the waitress left them alone again, then said, "I'll tell you a secret." She crooked her index finger, and he leaned across the table toward her. "That's my job," she whispered loudly. "I'm in public relations, remember?"

"That must be it," Langston said nodding.

"Don't worry," she soothed as he sat back again and attacked his second breakfast. "You'll get used to it."

"To what?" he asked.

"Telling me your deepest, darkest secrets. Everyone does. I have that kind of face," Reggie said, shrugging.

"What kind of face is that?" he asked.

"You know. Everybody's favorite sister. Maiden aunt. Nun. Friendly, open, trustworthy. All that good stuff."

"Um hm," Langston pretended to consider her words carefully, then shook his head. "You don't look much like a nun to me. In fact . . ." He let his voice trail off, as his eyes travelled down from her face, following the neckline of her blouse past the top two open buttons to the shadowy hollow between the swell of her breasts.

"Hey!" It was Reggie's turn to protest.

"No offense intended."

"None taken," Reggie said letting him off the hook. He waited for her to respond equally suggestively or flirtatiously. Most women seemed to. Instead she looked a little hurt, when he looked back up at her face. "Does that mean you *don't* trust me?"

"I told you about the sweating, didn't I?" he said reassuringly. She smiled smugly secure in the illusion that he agreed with her assessment of herself. "But it wasn't because of the way you look," he continued and her smile faded.

"All right, Mr. Downs. Why then?" she challenged.

"I don't know," he said, studying her carefully.

"So what do I look like to you?"

"Definitely not anyone's maiden aunt. They're like seventy years old. With glasses."

Reggie looked stunned for a moment, but she quickly recovered. She leaned across the table again, and he leaned toward her like before. She looked to the left. Then the right, then leaned even closer. "Contacts," she muttered, as if it were a state secret.

"I would never have known," he whispered back conspiratorially.

She nodded. Then sat back. Langston took another bite of his eggs, bacon and homefries, chewed, and swallowed. "So, is that why you got into your current line of work? Your ability to give people confidence?"

"Actually, it just sort of evolved naturally. I was teaching creative writing, and then other writing courses. After some of my students got published I started to help them promote their work. When the university laid me off, I started my company."

"A professor? Really? I'm impressed."

"Adjunct professor getting my degree with the help of a grant. When the money disappeared, so did the job."

"That's too bad. Do you miss it?"

"What?"

"Teaching."

"No," she said forcefully. "I liked it, but it's really time-consuming. I taught English 101 and Composition, and most of my students were freshmen. They weren't very interested in writing. Or thinking for that matter. They just wanted to pass the course."

"And I bet you were a hard grader," Langston commented.

"I take exception to that remark. I was very fair."

"A hard grader, just like I said," he said smugly.

"Well, the students seemed to think so, anyway," she agreed with a rueful smile. "How'd you know?"

"I didn't get the impression, before, you know . . . that you . . . um . . . suffered fools gladly."

"I thought you agreed to forget that," she complained.

Damn, Langston thought. He honestly didn't intend to bring up their earlier disagreement. He guessed her implication that he was a dumb jock still rankled, especially now that he knew it came from a college professor.

"Forgive, yes. Forget, not quite yet," he said. "It's only been a couple of hours." He excused himself.

"But I apologized."

"Only because I forced you to," he stated dispassionately.

"Tricked me, you mean," she said, apparently still not reconciled to his little joke about firing her. He wasn't the only one who hadn't forgotten the earlier conflict.

"A guy does what he has to to get respect," he joked.

She took him seriously. "That can't be a problem for you."

"Why not?" he asked flippantly, finishing off his breakfast.

"Let's see, I suppose I figure a guy can't get much more successful than you are. You were a famous football player, earned millions of dollars, became a movie star, nominated for an Academy Award no less, and have thousands of fans all over the world. I don't know. That sounds pretty respectable to me." The sarcasm was evident, but there was no rancor in her tone.

He didn't feel he'd earned his Oscar nomination, but he deserved the awards he won as a football player. "It isn't like being a brain surgeon or a college professor. People do respect the money you can make when you can throw a football farther than most people, but they don't exactly give you credit for having intelligence. In fact, most people think the two are mutually exclusive."

"After they see you in *Under His Skin,* that perception will change I'm sure," Reggie said simply.

Langston hoped she was right. "Thanks," he said. "I appreciate the vote of confidence. But you haven't even seen it yet."

"I know the story. And Elaine told me you did a wonderful job. No one will believe a—you'll pardon the expression—a dumb jock could play that role."

"I don't know. I haven't seen it."

No one expected the character he played in his first film to be as popular as the leading man, or to be nominated for any awards, or for the role to lead to a career as an actor—least of all Langston Downs.

His second film was more upscale than his first. The historical settings, period costumes, and accents had all served to make him feel like a more serious actor as well. But Langston didn't know if he'd pulled it off. He was not at all certain that he could keep fooling people.

As a young man, he'd seen Courtney Vance—younger, still—perform opposite James Earl Jones in *Fences* on Broadway. He'd watched Larry Fishburne and Cuba Gooding, Jr. slowly work their way up the Hollywood ladder and succeed because of their amazing talent. By comparison, he lucked into the roles he played. His first film was affectionately known as "Jerry Maguire Two" because the film's white star—his character's best friend—struggled with reinventing himself after retiring from football. Langston played Jed, a football player coming to terms with the end of his own career after a bad injury. Thus far, critics gave him credit for performing well, but they did point out that his first film role was tailor-made for him, and perhaps he wasn't acting but instead was just playing himself.

It was true that the hardest part of the job had been the interminable waiting and then replaying the same scenes over and over again, but Langston was proud of the acting he'd done in the love scenes. It had been much more difficult than he would have thought to have the crew watching while he and his professional, and absolutely breathtaking, co-star fell in love on camera. That was work. Jed said and did and felt things Langston had never experienced, but he made it real. He was so convincing, his own mother had warned him against trying to break up his film lover's real-life marriage. Langston was even compared favorably to Cuba Gooding, Jr., and while he wasn't sure he deserved that, he felt good about it. It proved that not all his success was pure luck.

Still he wished there had been a college degree in the bio Regina Primm had undoubtedly been given.

"Will you be at the screening tonight, then?" Reggie asked him.

"I don't think so," Langston replied. "It's embarrassing to have all those people watch you watching yourself."

"I thought the audience was going to be a small group of people connected to the film," she said, puzzled.

"I guess it is. I still don't think I can do it. Unless you go with me."

"Me?" she asked surprised.

"Yeah, I told you before, you give me confidence."

"But, but . . ." she spluttered. "Isn't there someone else? I thought you were dating a Spice Girl or a supermodel or something."

"Reggie, Reggie," he remonstrated gently, shaking his head. "You should know better than to believe everything you read in the gossip columns."

"Well, I do, but . . . you said yourself during some interview or other that you were seeing someone special. I remember that."

"I always say that," he said, smiling.

"So you're not dating Ginger Spice or Tyra Banks?" she pressed. "I've seen photos of you with both of them."

"No. We're just friends. That's all."

"That's all, huh?" she said suspiciously. "Then why say otherwise?"

"To keep the media off my back." Langston could see she was offended by his dating habits. He tried to explain, "I don't need a beautiful woman on my arm to give me confidence. You make me feel great."

"That's good," she said wryly.

He realized his mistake almost immediately. "Not that you're not beautiful, too."

"Better quit while you're ahead," Reggie warned.

"I mean, I want you to come, not as a beautiful woman, which you are, but as my date, because I could really use your support." She rolled her eyes. "So will you come with me? Please?" It didn't seem like such a farfetched idea to him. She said she was planning to go anyway, hadn't she? So why not go to the screening together so he wouldn't have to suffer alone?

"Wouldn't you rather bring someone you know?" she asked.

"I know you," Langston pointed out.

"Better than me," Reggie said. "I mean, not superior to me, but someone you know better than me. Like an old friend?"

"I like making new friends," he answered. "Don't you?"

"Sure, why not?" Reggie agreed, but she looked confused by the conversation. He couldn't blame her. He felt a little befuddled himself. Langston didn't know what it was that made him so curious about her, so intrigued with her . . . so attracted to her. She was adorable, it was true, but she was also an uptight, brainy, straitlaced snob, even if she had apologized for presuming to coach him before the morning's interview. He knew what she thought of him. She thought he was a fraud, which was probably why she didn't want to accompany him to the screening. That had to be why she was so reluctant to get to know him better.

Suddenly it occurred to him that he might have overlooked the obvious. "Or did you already ask a date?" he inquired.

"I asked an old friend," she admitted.

"A good friend?"

"Very," Reggie said.

Langston had assumed that since there was no ring on her third finger, Reggie wasn't married. But, these days, that didn't mean anything. "Just a friend? Or something more?"

She looked confused again. "More than what? Oh, you mean a boyfriend? Not that it's any of your business, but no. Bebe has been my best friend since grade school."

He felt an immense relief. "Oh just friends, then," he said sheepishly.

"Yes," Reggie stated firmly.

Langston was alarmed at how happy her answer had made him. This woman was not for him. He knew that. They had no future. They didn't even have a present. The only reason they were together at all was because Reggie was hired by the film company. She clearly had no interest in him, and she wouldn't even accompany him to the screening. She said no. Or not exactly no, but . . .

"How about we all go together?" he heard himself ask.

Five

As they made their way to the cash register, Reggie realized she hadn't been pressed so assiduously for a date since she made the mistake of flirting with the cashier at her favorite grocery store. It had started with a little laughter at the much older Japanese man's harmless jokes. She'd accepted his little gifts, packs of gum and candy bars for her nieces and nephews for six months, mistakenly thinking he saw her in the same avuncular light in which she perceived him. Despite her refusal of his proposition, then and since, Reggie couldn't convince him that her interest was purely platonic.

It wasn't the first time that a male friend had misinterpreted innocuous banter for an invitation, but, as usual, it came as a complete surprise to her after their little chats about Sujiko's family. She supposed she could understand it, sort of. He saw her shopping alone, week after week. Maybe he thought she was desperate enough to date a man who was twice her age and who had a wife and both children and grandchildren. She might even have given him that impression by being nice to him in the first place.

While she waited for the waitress to come to the cash register and take her money, Reggie looked at Langston, thinking that at least Mr. Tomiko fit the profile. Men who asked her out were generally sweet, suitable, unavailable, and completely unattractive. Langston Downs, on the other hand, barely fulfilled one of the criteria. He *wasn't* sweet, he *was* available, and he was *very* attractive. He was also almost as unsuitable a match for Reggie

Primm as Mr. Tomiko was. Unfortunately, she couldn't think of any sensible reason to turn down his invitation.

After she paid the check, they walked to the door, where Langston stopped with one hand on the door handle, and she realized that he was poised to open it for her while he waited for an answer. "Okay," Reggie said. "It's a date." He ushered her out the door, smiling.

At least Bebe would be happy at this turn of events. She would get her wish to sit next to the movie star in the small darkened theater. It was an opportunity that Reggie didn't think many women would pass up. So why was she so uncomfortable about it? Reggie asked herself. It wasn't like it meant anything.

The ride back to the hotel was relatively quiet. She pointed out Mt. Rainier to her passenger. The mountain's peak was still covered in snow, as it was for most of the year.

"It was hidden by the clouds before," Langston said, properly impressed.

"It is one of the highest peaks in North America," Reggie informed him.

"It's beautiful," he said. "Do people climb up there?"

"Yes. Mountaineering Inc. takes experienced climbers all the way up, and they teach beginners, too."

"What else is there to see here?" he asked.

"We've got lots of good tourist spots in Seattle. Near your hotel are the pier, the market, boat rides and the Aquarium. I love the museums of art and natural science, and the University of Washington campus. You should probably visit Westlake Center, where the Space Needle is located, or have you been there already?"

"I went, but it was so cloudy, I couldn't see anything. You get a lot of rain, huh?"

"Only thirty eight inches annually. It's not the amount of rain that makes the weather here so unappealing, it's the fact that most of it is in the form of drizzle and mist, so it rains often and it's usually cloudy even when it isn't raining."

"You sound like a professional tour guide," Langston teased.

"It's an occupational hazard," she quipped. He looked puzzled, so she explained. "I had a client who wrote a book about

Seattle and its history. Whenever I hope to promote a project I end up reading it, and hearing even more about it. By the end of the job, I sound like the book's author. I can't help it. My friends say I've become a walking billboard."

"For Seattle?"

"For most of my client's projects."

"Which projects were your favorites?" he asked.

"Heart of Soul," she answered promptly. It wasn't because he'd been nominated for an Academy Award for playing a character from that book. It was the truth.

Langston smiled and nodded. "Of course, but what else?"

"We're here," she said instead as they drove up to his hotel.

"Tell me more," he urged.

"Another time," she promised. "I've got to get back to the office."

"All right, then." He undid his seatbelt. "I'll see you tonight?"

"Right. Shall I meet you here?"

"Yes. Great." He opened his door, then turned back to her. "I'll be waiting." He jumped out of the car and strode away without looking back.

Reggie put the car in gear and drove to the office, growing slowly more and more nervous about their "date." There was nothing she could do about it, though, so for the rest of the afternoon she immersed herself in work and tried to forget about the evening. Unfortunately, she had to call Bebe and tell her about the change in plans, and her friend wouldn't let it go.

First, Bebe speculated that Langston probably never went to a movie without a date in his whole adult life.

"This isn't a date," Reggie explained patiently, again. But Bebe called back again to ask if perhaps she should bring Neal to make it a double date.

"It's not a date." Reggie's patience was wearing thin.

Bebe called a third time to ask, "What are you wearing?"

"Tonight?" Reggie asked, her mind on the letter she'd been composing on her computer as she tried not to lose track of what she'd been about to write.

"Of course tonight," Bebe said, exasperated.

"Don't take that tone with me, sister. Not after what you put me through today," Reggie warned. But she couldn't remember what she'd been about to write in the letter, so she sat back from the computer screen and concentrated on the question, "I'm wearing my taupe suit. I wasn't planning to change," she answered.

"He saw you in that this morning," Bebe protested.

"I really don't think he noticed what I was wearing," Reggie sighed.

"Still . . ." Bebe drawled. "You want to make a good impression. I think I'll wear the black cocktail dress I bought last week. Why don't you wear your cream silk?"

"If I change, I'll probably just change into another suit," Reggie said. "This is a business thing."

"So it's business? So what? When a client takes me to dinner at a fancy restaurant, I dress for the place, not the meeting. Who knows who might see you there?" Bebe argued.

"Well, we're not going anywhere fancy. It's a private screening, not the world premiere."

"If you want to wear slacks, you can wear that blue silk set you bought at Lane Bryant. You look great in that," Bebe replied, never one to concede.

"I'll think about it," Reggie agreed reluctantly.

"And wear some lipstick," Bebe ordered.

"It gets all over everything," Reggie complained.

"You want me to come over there and do your makeup for you, homegirl?" Reggie knew Bebe wasn't making an offer, but a threat.

"This isn't our prom, Bebe," Reggie said dryly. But Bebe wouldn't let her hang up the phone until she promised to make herself beautiful.

"Ha!" Reggie said aloud as she surveyed herself in her bedroom later that evening. "Yeah, right." It would take more than a little silk and lipstick to make her beautiful. It would take a medical miracle to bring her up to par with the least attractive of Langston Downs' women.

Ginger Spice is probably a brainless bore, she said spitefully to herself. *Well,* she thought, grabbing her purse, *I'm not competing with anyone.*

"You look great," Bebe said when Reggie picked her friend up on the way to the hotel.

"Sure I do," Reggie said with a grimace.

"I hate it when you do that," Bebe said. "You're a beautiful woman, and everyone can see that except you."

"Hey! I see those heavy women walking down the street stuffed into their spandex and falling out of their tops, thinking they look great. You want me to be like them?"

"No, I just . . . You could use a little of their vanity . . . uh, I mean confidence," Bebe retorted.

"They could use a little bit of my common sense. Big girls should not be wearing anything skin-tight."

"You are not wearing anything like that. So how come you're still putting yourself down?" Bebe asked, sounding exactly like her Jewish grandmother. "Did you take a look at yourself in the mirror this evening. You are sizzling girl." She continued, sounding like herself again.

"I think I look . . . okay."

"You look better than okay. Your hair, your nails, your face . . . you look lovely."

"Oh and you're not biased at all. Face it, Bebe, I'm not exactly a supermodel."

"So who is?" Bebe asked, once again reverting to the Yiddish inflection of the old country.

"Langston Downs' usual companions for an evening," she promptly retorted. "So just take that little matchmaking mind out of overdrive and look at the facts."

"Which are . . . ?"

"Pretty face or not, I'd have to lose a hundred pounds before that man would have the slightest interest in me."

"Hey! He isn't married to any supermodels, is he?"

"I got the definite impression he's just playing the field," Reggie informed her.

"So you're not out of the game," Bebe said triumphantly.

"Can we drop the sports analogies, please?" Reggie begged.

"You started it," Bebe said childishly.

"And I'm finishing it. We're here," she said as the hotel came into view. "Now. Just be good," she admonished.

Langston was waiting for them as they pulled up to the entrance.

Bebe jumped out of the car, forestalling him as he started to open the back door. "You sit up front. My legs are shorter," she argued, rushing around to climb into the passenger seat behind Reggie. Langston quickly complied. Reggie shot Bebe a look in the mirror which she pretended not to see. "I'm Bebe Klein, Mr. Downs," she introduced herself.

"A pleasure," Langston said, turning in his seat so that he could see her in the back. "Call me Langston, please."

"Call me Bebe," she instructed in turn. "Reggie told me you had a great interview this morning." Reggie had actually given her a blow-by-blow account of the entire embarrassing incident.

"It felt pretty good," he said modestly. Reggie would have told Bebe not to bring it up, but she assumed her friend would have the good sense to know better without being told. She should have remembered Bebe's complete lack of tact. In her professional capacity, Bebe Klein was a master of subtlety, but when it came to her personal life, discretion and diplomacy were neglected in favor of a direct, almost painfully honest approach to every situation. It was as if she used up her quota of finesse in her work.

"You must have given a lot of interviews in your former profession."

Langston winced. It wasn't obvious, but Reggie caught the slight movement and felt bad for him.

"Bebe just can't help interrogating everyone she meets," Reggie said apologetically. "Get some sense, girl," she said to Bebe. "Langston isn't on the witness stand."

"Just trying to make conversation," Bebe replied, unruffled. "So, Langston, what would you like to talk about?"

"Reggie," he responded instantly. "Your friend is very close-mouthed."

"You have a very different view of her than I have," Bebe said. "Closemouthed." She made a sound halfway between a giggle and a snort. "Right." He just looked at her inquisitively. "What do you want to know?" she asked.

"What else did she say about me?" he inquired.

"Hmm," Bebe murmured, considering his request.

"I mean, she knows all about my exploits, but I hardly know anything about her."

"That doesn't seem fair. Let me see. What can I tell you about my Reg that doesn't violate the friend-friend privilege?"

"You're a lawyer?" he asked.

"Oh yeah," Reggie said emphatically, "And be careful what you say, Bebe. As a lawyer you know the penalties for slander."

"I don't need to lie about you, honey. I know all your deepest, darkest secrets."

"Just remember who got you into this screening in the first place," she warned. "And by the way, here we are," Reggie announced, hoping to cut Bebe off before she could make any revelations that could embarrass or humiliate her.

"Safe and sound," Langston teased.

"With my dignity intact," Reggie said, relieved. But he had already jumped out of the car and was on his way around the car to her side. Reggie resisted the urge to open the door herself before he did it for her.

"Who said chivalry is dead?" Bebe taunted.

"Stop trying to make trouble," Reggie chided her. Then she added for her ears alone, "Remember, I'm on duty here. This is part of my job." He opened Bebe's door first, then hers.

She stepped out of the car, and Langston closed the door behind her. "You look nice tonight," he said.

"Nice work if you can get it," Bebe murmured as he turned away. Reggie led the way into the building and held the door open for Langston. She ushered him inside but grabbed Bebe's arm and held her back. The hallway was too narrow for the three of them to walk abreast, so Langston strode ahead.

"Cool it!" she ordered. Bebe did not look intimidated.

The screening room was relatively small. Wood-paneled walls gave it a cozy feel, and the ten or twelve rows of plush, upholstered chairs looked very comfortable. They watched Langston meet and greet his director and various men in suits, with a handshake and a smile for each one. For the women, he had a kiss on the cheek and a squeeze of the hand, which, judging by their reactions, they loved.

He made a quick circuit around the small room, then came back to Reggie and Bebe.

"Are you originally from Hollywood, or did you just pick that up?" Bebe asked, an admiring tone in her voice.

"It's not that different from my business . . . I mean, football. Money's the name of the game, and the stars have to press the flesh just like agents do. Sometimes better. If an agent loses a contract point, he negotiates one for another client. For us, it's . . . personal. Most of the players either love it or hate it, but we all do it."

"What about you?" Bebe asked. "Did you love it or hate it?"

He flashed that devilish grin and shrugged as he said, "I loved it, of course. After a while, it becomes second nature."

"Especially if you're good at it, I imagine," Reggie said. She envied the ease with which he claimed the attention of those he met. And even more the ease with which he charmed them all. It was something she had to do in her line of work as well, but for him it seemed effortless. She always felt like she was putting on a show.

As if he'd heard her thoughts, Langston echoed them. "It's not real, but it becomes your automatic response to everyone, or anything, new."

"So have you been schmoozing with us this whole time?" Bebe asked, pouting.

"Not at all," he said quickly. "I'm enjoying your company." He bent closer to them and whispered. "I feel like I can be myself with you."

It was almost certainly a line. But if it was what he really felt, Reggie wished she could have felt the same way. She couldn't be herself around Langston, though. At least not for long. There were moments between them, but . . .

She liked him because he didn't seem phony or disingenuous, but she wasn't sure she trusted him. There was a gleam in his eye at times that made her feel as if he had some unknowable motive for acting so friendly toward her. She'd noticed it again when he questioned Bebe about her in the car. She felt he was fishing for some information to use against her, somehow.

Reggie shook off her paranoid delusions as she, Bebe, Langston, and everyone else took their seats in front of the blank white screen that covered one wall of the room they were in. After the lights were dim, while they waited for the film to start, Reggie indulged in one last flight of fantasy. Langston's knee was against hers, his elbow rubbing hers on the armrest, and she let herself wonder, *What if he had meant to ask her out on an actual date tonight?* It was an outlandish idea, Reggie Primm, the publicist, and the playboy Langston Downs, together. Would he take her hand? Entwine his long sensuous fingers in hers? Put his mouth next to her ear to whisper of his desire to touch her?

That was as far as Reggie could get in her imaginings since she found it extremely hard to believe he would find her attractive after he'd been with models and actresses. He was too beautiful to be a match for her. Reggie felt an awareness of the width of his shoulders, the white flash of his smile, and the musculature of his long legs.

She felt as though they were cocooned by the soft velvety sweetness, and she would probably have made a complete fool of herself if Langston had spoken to her or touched her at that moment. Luckily, though, he was speaking quietly but intensely with the man who was sitting on his other side.

Bebe spoke into her ear, snapping her reverie. "I like him."

"I was sure you would," Reggie replied. "He's a charmer."

"You say that like it's a bad thing," Bebe said. "Aren't you glad that he turned out to be a good guy. He could have been a conceited jerk. Most guys in his position would be."

"I thought he was when I first met him. All right, before I met him," Reggie admitted. "I had preconceptions. I made assumptions. He's a rich, handsome jock, so I thought he'd be big and dumb and full of himself. So did you. Remember?"

"And you were dreading it," Bebe reminded her. "So be happy. Langston Downs is a doll. This is going to be a great week."

"Two weeks," Reggie corrected her, trying to match her friend's enthusiastic smile. "Great!" she said aloud. But even to her own ears, her voice sounded less than convincing. Even though she had met the enemy and found out he wasn't the enemy, she still dreaded spending two weeks with the man. She had no idea what he was capable of. He had a reckless streak which was, Reggie was sure, part of the reason the film company had hired her. She'd read enough of the press coverage on Langston to know there was no telling what he might do next.

It was her responsibility to make sure he didn't set foot over that thin line between good publicity and bad publicity. As thrilled as Reggie was to have Langston Downs as a client, she wasn't sure how she was going to keep him in line if she couldn't keep a professional distance. She didn't want to be attracted to him. And she was. But she couldn't tell Bebe that. She could barely admit it to herself.

Luckily, the credits began to roll up on the screen and she didn't have to tell her friend anything at that moment. Reggie lost herself in the film for the next two hours and change. By the end of the viewing, she knew she was going to have to be even more careful than she had thought because Langston Downs could make a woman forget herself with that little-boy grin of his without even trying. All he needed to do was turn that smile on her and she would melt. For the last couple of hours he'd done just that, and he hadn't even known it.

The select audience was too sophisticated to applaud when the film ended, but their excitement was tangible. And, in Reggie's opinion, the film deserved it. She didn't know the business well enough to be certain, but she felt pretty sure that *Under His Skin* was going to be so successful it would make Hollywood rethink the conclusions that had been drawn when *Beloved* had a mediocre reaction at the box office. Period pieces featuring black characters could be blockbusters after all. Reggie was a huge fan of Toni Morrison's and had enjoyed the adaptation of her Pulitzer-Prize-winning novel to the big screen, but *Under His Skin* was so easy to like, and the characters so appealing, that the actors couldn't help but be nominated for the Oscars. The story was so heartwarming it had men and women alike laughing through their tears.

"I predict a big hit," she said to Langston before the crowd could descend on him with their congratulations.

"Definitely," Bebe agreed.

"It looked good to me, but I'm biased," Langston added, pretending modesty, but it was obvious that he was pleased with the outcome.

"Everyone here is probably a little biased," Reggie said judiciously. "But that doesn't mean you're wrong. It's good. Really good."

"You'll have to help me celebrate. Okay?"

Reggie hesitated. She suspected Langston's idea of a celebration would be a loud, possibly drunken, out-of-control affair. She pictured the 49ers pouring a cooler full of liquid over Joe Montana's head. But she could try to steer him away from the worst of it, and perhaps even get him back to his hotel without the paparazzi catching him in some disreputable pose.

"Okay," she said. But only Bebe heard her. Langston was already in the center of a group of admiring fans.

"He's working the room again," Bebe observed cynically.

"Where do you think we should go?" Reggie asked.

"I have to head home. I've got to appear in court in the morning," Bebe answered.

"That never stopped you before."

"I've got some paperwork to do tonight. I already put it off to come here."

"Okay, so, any suggestions?" Reggie asked, hoping she didn't look as disappointed as she felt.

"How about the Blue Room? Neal played there last week and it was cool, mon," Bebe said in a rather awful impression of a rastafarian.

"Sounds good. Thanks."

She introduced Bebe to the producers and was introduced to the film's director, and then the women waited patiently for Langston to work his way back to them. He didn't take long, and then he swept them inexorably along before him as they exited the room. His joy was infectious, and the three of them joked and laughed on the way to Bebe's house, where Reggie dropped her friend off.

The car was quiet for a moment after the good-byes had been said, and then Langston turned to her. "Where to now, teach?"

"I thought we'd go to the Blue Room. A jazz bar," Reggie offered for his approval. "I don't know who's playing tonight, but Bebe said it's a nice place. Neal had a gig there last week."

"Her husband is a jazz musician?" Langston said, surprised.

"Yeah. Why? What's wrong with that?" Reggie asked.

"Nothing. Of course, nothing. I just would have thought he was a lawyer because of the way she talks about him."

"How's that?"

"You know. Like he's the same as her."

"Why shouldn't she?"

"She's a lawyer," he said.

Reggie looked at him, annoyed. "He's a musician, not a murderer."

"My bad," he confessed.

"They are a great couple," she said, obviously offended.

"I'm sorry," Langston said sincerely. "Forget it, okay?"

She relented. "Okay."

They arrived at the bar just after nine thirty. After the beautiful clear day, the evening was balmy, the stars bright overhead. The night air felt satiny against Reggie's skin.

"Shall we?" Langston offered her his arm and when she stuck her hand in the crook of his elbow he covered it with his own and folded it, and her, close to his side. "This is going to be a great night," he said, guiding her toward the door.

Six

The Blue Room was a big dark cave of a place, the deep blue of the evening sea. The effect, Langston felt, was that they were underwater.

"Come on up here, Mo," the bandleader urged suddenly after a couple of numbers. He shook his head. The man turned to the audience undeterred. "Come on, folks. Help me out! Get him up here!" The crowd started clapping and cheering for Langston. They weren't going to leave him alone.

"Vinnie saw you sing it in St. Louis." Langston vaguely remembered. "You can do it," the man shouted nodding toward the drummer who smiled and waved.

Apparently, the drummer had heard him sing somewhere before, and felt he had been good enough to merit an encore on stage tonight. "No, no. You go on," he shouted to the bandleader.

"Get him up here!" the saxophonist yelled, and the applause grew louder, the crowd even more insistent, until they were clapping, stomping and shouting in unison, "Mo, Mo, Mo!"

"Go on!" Someone yelled from the table next to where Langston and Reggie were sitting. Reggie slid down in her chair away from the spotlight that was trained on him. The band didn't realize it, but their behavior was not helping him out. His fans were determined. All this attention was clearly making Reggie uncomfortable. She was trying to fade into the background. Langston almost wished that Bebe hadn't left them alone together. Almost.

He really did want to be alone with her and have her smile

at him like she had once earlier that evening. That smile gave him chills; it was so sexy, so inviting. At that moment he thought he'd finally won her over. But the glare of the lights and the enthusiasm of the crowd had had a startling effect on Regina Primm. She smiled, she even laughed, and she looked quite gratified. For him. But she retreated back into the professional persona in which she treated him as a client rather than as a friend. He could almost see the walls go up around her as she became his publicist again. All the progress he had made in getting to know her and letting her know him was lost. Her smile was genuine, encouraging, and totally impersonal.

Langston finished one beer and picked up another of the pints that had been delivered to the table, compliments of various fans scattered throughout the audience. The rhythmic chanting, "Mo, Mo, Mo," grew louder as he stood. The audience sensed that they had won. Cheers and shrill whistles of approval followed him to the stage.

The microphone held down at his side, Langston conferred with the band's leader, the pianist. Luckily, his favorite song, "God Bless the Child," was a part of their repertoire.

"This is my mother's favorite song. I wish you all could hear *her* sing it," he said to the audience, and to Reggie, whom he couldn't see beyond the bright lights that shone on him at the center of the stage. He sang for her, and he thought he sounded alright. His initial embarrassment faded and he enjoyed performing for the lively audience. Perhaps it was just the adrenaline coursing through him, but he felt alive and freer than he had in a while.

When the music died, the crowd went wild. He gave one quick bow, jumped off the stage before anyone could stop him, and made a beeline for the table. He didn't sit down. He urged Reggie up and they scooted out of there before the cries of "More, Mo, more," had faded. Once safely outside, he let out his breath in one long rush of air. It whistled through his teeth, and Reggie laughed breathlessly.

"So you weren't as cool as you looked up there, after all?"

"I'm cool," he said. "I just . . ."

"Just what?" She cocked her head and twinkled up at him.

She seemed pleased with the revelation that he could be as insecure as anyone else.

"I'm not a singer. I know it, and you know it," he said.

"You sounded good to me."

"Really?"

"Now you're fishing for compliments."

"No, I'm not, I'm . . . curious. You're not . . . handling me, by any chance?"

She held her hands up in front of her, palms open. "I'm being completely honest with you."

"Completely?" His voice took on that rough, rasping quality that gave him away whenever he was near a woman he liked. His sisters told him it turned women into jelly, but he didn't do it on purpose. It just happened. "Because it means a lot to me, coming from you." Her smile faded as she looked up into his eyes, and for a moment he saw something in her face, behind her guarded expression. Deep in her big brown eyes, Langston thought he glimpsed an echo of his own desire. Reggie turned away and started walking toward the car and he fell into step beside her.

He was probably projecting his own feelings onto her, he told himself. It had happened before. Women like Reggie weren't interested in men like him. They saw right through the looks and the charm to the man beneath. That man wasn't a warrior, or any of the worthy things people liked to attribute to professional athletes. He wasn't particularly brave, and he certainly wasn't noble. He worked his butt off to succeed in the one arena where his talents were worth something. But a perceptive woman like Reggie would not be attracted to a man who couldn't sustain a meaningful relationship beyond a few weeks.

He didn't want her to find out that he was indeed the dumb jock he'd been labeled so many years ago. He liked her. And he respected and admired her. She seemed to like him. It would be nice to have a woman like this for a friend. If he were smart, he wouldn't start anything.

Still, she was lovely in the moonlight.

When they reached the car she stopped. "So? Enough celebrating? Are you ready to go home now?"

"Your place or mine?" He kept his tone light.

"Oh, I don't know . . . how about you go to your place and I go to mine?" she replied.

"That's a new and novel idea," Langston said. Still keeping it light.

"I bet," she muttered under her breath.

"What do you think I am?" he couldn't help asking.

"Hey, I'm sure a lot of women find you absolutely irresistible," she said, appeasingly.

"But you're different, right?" His voice was that husky rasp again, but this time he wasn't flirting with her. Langston wanted to bug her, to put a dent in her self-possession, to make Reggie Primm admit that she wasn't completely immune to the chemistry between them either. "You don't find me irresistible at all?" he said, purposely baiting her. He had no intention of doing anything more than challenge her, but the fear in her eyes goaded him on. He took a step closer, backing her into the side of the car.

"This can't be the first time a woman hasn't been interested in your . . . line," she said, irritated.

"Most of the women I meet, do."

"Do what?" she asked nervously.

"They like lines, like 'Your place or mine'. They laugh. And sometimes they even say 'Yes.' But when they don't, they don't get all huffy. They take it as a joke."

"A joke?" Her voice cracked.

"Why are you so uptight, Reggie?" he asked. "What did I ever do to you?"

"I'm not," she retorted weakly.

He ignored her. "Why did you freeze up on me like I made some unforgivable remark?" he pressed.

"I don't know, I—"

Once again, he didn't wait for her to come up with some polite way to insult him. He cut her off. "What are you afraid of, Reggie?"

She dropped the car keys she had been holding in her hand. He started to lean down to get them, and she lifted her face to his. Langston froze, then slowly backed up an inch or two to look into her eyes. She thought he was going to kiss her. Amaz-

Roberta Gayle

ingly, she didn't turn her cheek to him, or raise her hands to stop
him, or even lower her eyes. Instead she raised her lips to meet
his. Pleasure shot through him like a bullet to the heart.

Langston looked down at the keys. Reggie followed his gaze.
He bent and picked up the key ring and held it out to her. She
looked at the keys in his hand and caught her bottom lip with
her teeth. She was mortified. He could see that. But he held out
the keys anyway, and she reached out and took them. Then she
looked up at him and reached out to hook one hand behind his
neck and pull his head down so she could kiss him, long and
hard.

He should have felt victorious, but instead he felt humbled,
awed by the intensity of their shared contact. Her lips were blood-
hot under his. Her hips were soft under his hands, not bony protrusions like those of his last girlfriend. He slid his hand up to
her waist and around to her back. He gloried in the feeling of
her flesh through the silk blouse that flowed over her and covered
her voluptuous figure to her knees. She felt great. He wanted
to touch every inch of her, to kiss the chestnut-colored skin
that was hidden from him. He slid his hands down, and she
ended it.

"I think I should take you home," she said.

"I don't," he protested, but without force. Reggie had surprised him with that kiss. She had given him more than he'd
expected. He didn't want to push it, or push her. So he slowly
backed away, letting her go.

The night air felt cool against his overheated skin. His breathing settled slowly back into a normal, even rhythm. He took the
keys from her and unlocked and opened her door, then stepped
back to let her climb into the car. She barely looked at him, but
slid quickly into the driver's seat, and unlocked his door with
the mechanism on her arm rest. He made the journey all the
way around to the other side of the car without thinking of a
single thing to say to her.

"So," Reggie said when he buckled his seatbelt. "We're off."
She started the car.

Langston sorted through various conversational gambits, dis-
carding immediately phrases such as "Wow that was great!" and

"I can't wait to do it again." Finally, he settled on, "Don't be embarrassed," but before he could say it, Reggie spoke.

"Are you shocked?" she said.

"I've been kissed before," he responded, hoping to put her at ease.

"Sure," she glanced over at him quickly. "We're both adults."

"Yes, we are." He tried to give her a reassuring smile but she had her eyes on the road ahead and didn't see it. "Definitely over twenty-one," he added inanely. He sensed that she relaxed a bit after that.

Langston felt the same way he had after he experienced his first earthquake: tense, unsettled and disoriented. The aftershocks kept jolting through him. He could still feel the imprint of her hand on the back of his neck. She was strong. And soft. And she intrigued him more than ever.

"Good," Reggie said finally. "I'm glad that happened. Now we can get back on track and put all this silliness behind us instead of having the miscommunications of the past two days between us."

Had it only been two days since he met her? It felt longer. But he didn't really know her at all. "Sounds good," he said aloud. "How about we forget all that stuff from before and start fresh. Knowing what I do now, I can't wait to get to know you better."

"Whoa, cowboy. You don't know anything about me," she protested.

Langston might have argued with that statement, but he chose a less confrontational path. "I'd like to know more, as I told you before. This is the perfect ope—" he caught himself before he finished saying "opening" and said instead, "opportunity," for fear that his wording might be misconstrued.

The last thing he wanted was to offend her.

"Langston, we are going to be working pretty closely together for the next few weeks and if today was any indication, it's going to get complicated if we don't set a few ground rules."

"Such as . . . ?" he asked, his spirits sinking. He didn't think kissing was going to be allowed.

"Well," she drawled. "I don't think I . . . I mean we, can't afford to get personally involved. We have to work together. And dating is stressful enough without the added pressure of having to be on top of each other all day."

"I'll take that chance," he joked. She didn't laugh. "Okay, no dating. We can still be friends, right?"

"Right," Reggie agreed hesitantly.

"Friends can do a lot of things together," Langston pointed out happily, thinking, *They can go to movies, or dinner, hold hands, kiss! Friends could even become more intimate on occasion.*

She looked at him suspiciously. "Good," was all she said, but he was sure her little mind was working overtime to figure out some way to expand on her ground rules. But she didn't say anything more about it, and soon she was pulling up to the front door of his hotel.

"Thanks, Reggie," he said.

"It was fun."

She seemed happy. Whether that was because he'd agreed to her edict or because she really did have a good time with him, he didn't know. Maybe she was just relieved because the evening was over.

"I hope you enjoyed yourself," he said. "I know I did."

"Definitely," Reggie said. "I never went to a screening before. It was a blast."

"A blast?" He chuckled. "That's an expression I haven't heard in a very long time."

"Sorry," she said flippantly. "I meant it was . . . way cool."

"Like groovy, huh?"

"Oh yeah," she said halfheartedly. She wasn't in the mood for this kind of chatter.

"Well I guess I'd better go in," he said reluctantly. "See you tomorrow."

"You have that interview with the reporter from *Essence*. My friend Tamara will call in the morning to tell us when and where exactly. Around ten probably. I called to confirm this afternoon. Then, in the afternoon, you have the lecture with Elaine at the university."

"Oh," he responded, less than enthusiastically. "Right!" He

could just picture the scene. All those students to speak with and ask him questions he wasn't sure he could answer. Then, afterwards, they would want autographs and crowd around him, preventing any kind of escape attempt until he either ran through them or bluntly told them to let him out. He hated both alternatives.

"Do I detect a note of reluctance?"

"Not really. I'm happy to do the class. But . . ."

"But what?" she asked.

"Maybe it's just me, but I'd rather play to a ten-thousand-seat stadium than speak at these intimate little affairs. They've 'got you,' you know. There's no one else for them to feed on, and nothing else for me to do but provide fodder for the animals."

"What else would you do? They want to know how your work is . . . what it's like. They want to *be* you."

"They just think that," he said. He smiled so she'd know he was joking as he said, "It ain't easy being me."

"Oh you poor thing," she shot back at him.

"They only want to know about the movie stars I've met and the fancy parties I've been to. They don't want to know how I got there."

"So tell them the truth about being a star," Reggie said bluntly.

He didn't answer. Langston knew all about telling the truth. It was not recommended. No one wanted to hear a guy who was famous complain about feeling persecuted by his fans. And even less did they want to hear a man who made millions of dollars a year complain about the work had to do to get to that point. His own brother-in-law joked about Sammy Sosa huffing away at a million-dollar pitch with a million-dollar swing. And this from a man who adored Sammy. Frank was a great guy and he and Langston could hang out, but he could not empathize with Langston's frustration with the stories the media made up about him. As far as his brother by marriage was concerned, it was a fair and even an appropriate price to pay for success at Langston's level. If Langston was maligned and slandered, he had two choices. In Frank's opinion, Langston had the money to sue the bastards. Or he could live up to, or rather down to, his rep.

For him to insist that reporters go out and find a real news story and just . . . leave him alone . . . was not realistic.

Langston didn't think it would fly with the university students either. "Hey," he said to Reggie. "I'll tell them the story that the movie is based on. I'll be a walking advertisement for the book in fact. That should make Elaine happy."

"Did you read it?" Reggie asked.

"No," he said, sarcasm dripping from his voice. "I'll just wing it."

"No offense intended," she excused herself. "Elaine said she didn't think anyone involved read the book. It wasn't a criticism."

"Well, Elaine was wrong. I read the book a couple of times."

She seemed at a loss for words. She took a moment to recover and then said, "Anyway, that's good. This almost sounds like a plan. So. You're all set for both events for tomorrow?"

Langston nodded.

"I'll call you in the morning," she confirmed.

"See you tomorrow." Langston hesitated briefly, then opened the door and stepped out of the car. Before he closed the door, he stuck his head back inside. "This could be the beginning of a beautiful friendship, sweetheart." It was his best Bogart impression.

Reggie smiled, uncertain, and then nodded. "Uh, sure," she agreed, but she didn't look at all convinced.

Seven

When Reggie arrived home, the little red light was blinking on her answering machine. If she'd thought about it, she'd have known Bebe would call.

"How was the rest of your evening?" her best friend wanted to know.

She couldn't call her back. Not yet. Reggie didn't know what, if anything, to tell her about that kiss. That stupid kiss. She couldn't believe she'd done that.

When Langston leaned down to get her keys she had been sure he was going to kiss her. And he knew it. She could tell when he looked at her that he knew what she'd been thinking. That would have been embarrassing enough, all by itself. But, then, to actually *kiss* him. She groaned, thinking about it. How could she do that? She would never be able to look him in the eye again.

She knew he enjoyed it. Maybe even as much as she did. He certainly seemed to get into it. And, luckily, he didn't push it. He'd been perfectly nice about it. He agreed just to be friends.

She had to listen to her mother's message three times before she got the gist of it, which was to call as soon as possible and tell her Mom how the evening went.

Reggie decided it would be best to call right away. Otherwise her mother, an extremely early riser, would be calling her at the break of dawn. It was eleven o'clock. Mom wouldn't be asleep yet, she reasoned as she dialed.

"Hi, Baby," Jennifer said when she picked up the phone. As

soon as she heard her mother's voice, Reggie realized she had
not called to avoid an early-morning interrogation, or to satisfy
her mother's curiosity. She called Jennifer Primm at eleven
o'clock at night because she needed to hear her mama's voice.
Thirty three years old or not, she still felt comforted just hearing
her mom's loving voice saying, "Baby."

"Hi, Mama, how are you? I didn't wake you up, did I?"

"No, no. I was just listening to a tape."

"Book or music?" Reggie asked.

"Book. Now that's enough about me. What happened with
Mr. Movie Star?" Reggie settled back comfortably onto her bed,
covered with pillows and throws and told her mother about the
"date," just like she had when she first started dating.

"We saw the movie. It was fantastic. Bebe loved it, too. And
Langston seemed happy with it. Everyone did. He was so up
from the thing, he asked if I'd go help him celebrate. Of course
I agreed."

"Of course," Jennifer said, without a hint of censure in her
voice.

"We dropped Bebe at home."

"She didn't go with you?"

"She couldn't. She had to work. Tonight and tomorrow early,"
Reggie explained succinctly.

"So where did you go?"

"The Blue Room. Some band we never heard of was playing
and we had just decided we liked them when they announced
to the room that they were happy to see Langston Downs in the
audience. It turns out they were big fans. *And* not only that. They
wanted him to sing with them."

"Sing?" Her voice held the same amazement that Reggie had
felt at the suggestion.

"Apparently, he got drunk one night in Nashville or someplace and he got on stage with a friend's band and sang with
them. And the drummer in the band tonight was there that night,
and he requested a repeat performance.

"He does have a lovely speaking voice, but . . ." her mother
said dubiously.

"The drummer liked it enough to remember it, and he got the whole place to get Langston on stage."

"That can't have been hard."

"It took a little while. That other time Langston sang in his friend's band, he was drunk! Tonight he hadn't had enough beer to lose his inhibitions completely, so it took some coaxing. But they did it."

"The band?"

"Everyone. They loved him. They loved him before he went on. By the time he sang his mother's favorite song, I thought they were literally going to bring the house down. I've never seen anything like it."

"It sounds like you had quite an evening."

"Yes. It was pretty amazing. By the way, you're never going to guess what his mother's favorite song is."

"What?" she asked, her curiosity piqued just as Reggie intended.

"You're going to love this," Reggie chortled. "It's 'God Bless the Child.' "

"But that's my favorite!" her mother exclaimed.

"I know. It's one of mine as well."

"And he really sang it?"

"Closed his eyes, threw back his head, and roared, Mama."

"Wow!" Jenny said, which was the perfect comment on the evening's events as far as Reggie was concerned.

"Yeah," she said, in complete agreement. She sighed, finished with the part of the story she planned to share with her mother. She couldn't tell anyone about what happened between Langston and herself.

With that sixth sense she seemed to possess, Jennifer Primm asked her the one question she didn't want to answer. "So you like him now, huh?"

"Mom, I never said I *didn't* like him," she prevaricated.

"I know. But I also know you were disappointed when you met him."

"I wasn't—" Reggie started.

"Who do you think you're talking to, baby." Reggie knew better than to argue when her mother used that tone of voice.

"Yes, Mama," she said.

"It's not surprising. You meet this . . . this bigger than life character, and you expect him to be—I don't know what. A prince, maybe. It's almost impossible for a real human being to live up to that kind of buildup."

"Yeah, I guess I was a little bit hard on him," Reggie grudgingly admitted. "But there was no harm done."

"Judge not, the Bible says."

"Yes, Mama," she said again.

"It's perfectly understandable," Jenny continued. "We have visions of people, of what they are, what we think they are. And he's a star, a real live movie star. But in real life he's still just a man. And you've got to remember that."

"I will, Mom."

But Jennifer Primm was not finished. "A good-looking man, Lord knows," she added.

"Mom!" Reggie said, laughing.

"I'm just stating the facts. It's easy to see how he might turn your head."

"He hasn't. I mean, of course he's . . . handsome, but that's not why I like him."

"I'm not accusing you of anything."

"I just want us to understand each other. I'm not interested in his looks," Reggie insisted.

"Umm hmmm," her mother murmured. Reggie could tell she didn't believe her.

"He's a client. I don't get involved with my clients," Reggie reminded her.

"This is not your ordinary, run-of-the-mill client. You have to admit he's something special."

"He's big. This is an important opportunity for me. Which is why I have to be especially professional on this job. This would not be a good time to forget that. I plan to work my butt off."

"Don't forget to enjoy it while it lasts," Jennifer admonished.

"I'll enjoy the memories. I have two weeks to show Hollywood what I can do, and that's all I'm interested in doing."

"So what's on the agenda for tomorrow," Mama asked.

"I got him the interview with Tamara for *Essence*, remember?"

Reggie was proud of her work for Langston. In only one day she booked her big star client into dates at every major regional event. This interview was the icing on the cake. She had pitched a story about black historical films to *Essence,* and they bought it—that was a coup no one could have expected of her.

If Reggie was going to play with the big boys, she was going to show them she was more than a mere baby-sitter for their talented, if temperamental, leading man. She could get them coverage. In *Essence.* And baby-sit. Of course, at the moment, she didn't feel like a very responsible baby-sitter, but at least he hadn't been photographed by any paparazzi since she'd had the care and keeping of him. So she'd been unprofessional for a few minutes that night in the parking lot. This article would make up for it.

"He's going to be interviewed in the morning."

"Did you give them a list of questions? They usually ask such stupid ones."

"You know Tamara, Mom. She doesn't ask stupid questions."

"I guess not. But I hope you get final approval of the piece."

"I trust my friend, Mom. Besides, I'll be there, too."

That's probably best," her mother said. Reggie agreed. There were not going to be any embarrassing revelations in this article. She was determined to keep it serious, high-minded, and focused solely on Langston's work in the new movie. No personal questions.

Reggie had an idea that would effectively prevent a repeat of the incident that night as well. "Tomorrow afternoon, Langston and Elaine are going to give a lecture at the university and there's going to be a small reception afterwards. Would you like to come?"

"Me?"

"Yes, you, Mom." It would be easy to keep her thoughts out of the gutter and her hands to herself with her mother in the room.

Tamara called the next morning at nine a.m. as promised, but she sounded half asleep. "It always takes me a while to get going in the morning," she explained. "I just need that first pot of coffee and I'll be off and running, sweetie."

"Okay," Reggie accepted her assurance. "When and where do you want to do this?"

"Ten thirty? At the hotel?"

"Sounds good," Reggie told her friend. "Call up to the room from the lobby."

After she hung up with Tamara, she called Langston's room. He didn't answer, so she left him a message. "I spoke with Tamara Jones from *Essence,* and she'll meet us at the hotel at ten thirty. Where do you want to give the interview? In your suite? Or at the restaurant? For the next half hour you can call me here, then I'll be leaving to come to you."

Langston called a couple of minutes later. "I was in the shower when you called." An image of him dressed only in a towel flashed before her eyes.

Reggie cleared her throat. "Umm, would you be comfortable speaking to Tamara in your rooms? It will be more private."

"Sure, if you think that's best," Langston answered.

"Okay. I'll meet you at about ten."

Reggie dressed more carefully than usual because they had the cocktail party that afternoon, and not, she told herself, because she would be attending with Langston Downs. The university staff was pretty conservative so she foreswore her usual pant suit for a dress—a flowing calf-length dress of ivory cream linen. Reggie preferred dark colors for their slimming effect, but since she was going to be wearing the outfit all day and into the night, she thought this would be more comfortable than any little black cocktail dress.

She examined her reflection with a critical eye. The woman in the mirror was at least eighty pounds overweight, and Reggie was, as usual, surprised to see her. She had a completely different image of herself. When she pictured herself, she imagined a normal woman who weighed the hundred and fifteen or hundred and twenty pounds a five foot three inch woman should. In her mind's eye, she was prettier; her eyes were bigger, her chin sharper, and her cheeks less round, and her body was perfect—not too thin and not too fat. The mirror was less kind, and so she saw herself as she really was. Reggie sighed. At least she didn't look too terrible. The bodice of the dress was loose, but tapered at the waist. The flowing lines of the skirt hid her large thighs and calves. Her strappy canvas sandals had no heels, but they showed off her ankles well enough. Men seemed to admire her rather large bust, but to her, only her ankles and small feet were truly feminine and attractive. To show them off, she sometimes wore high heels, but Reggie didn't want to feel sexy today. Not, she thought, that she was likely to feel anything but profound embarrassment around Langston Downs.

In the bright morning sunlight, he was bound to see her differently than he had in the moonlight. He would see the woman in the mirror—that unflattering image she found so unattractive. The flowing dress wasn't magic. It couldn't take off eighty pounds. There was nothing more she could do.

Reggie stood outside his hotel room and took a deep breath. It was time to face Langston, whether she wanted to or not. She squared her shoulders and knocked on the door. It was better this way. She was accustomed to platonic relationships with men. Now she could deal with Langston as a friend and client without any tension between them. He opened the door and smiled a greeting, which took her breath away. What had made her think she could have a friendly relationship with this man. He was just too beautiful.

He was wearing a navy polo shirt that showed off his powerful arms and a pair of worn blue jeans that molded to his long legs. As he led the way into the suite's sitting room, she admired his broad shoulders, his tapered waist, and his backside.

"Sit, please," he said. "This Tamara Jones, is she a friend of yours?"

"Yes. We went to school together. I asked her to keep away from your personal life." He looked at her quizzically. "Her questions. They should be about the film, your work on it, and what you think about the story," she elaborated.

"Sounds good," Langston said. "Do you want a cup of coffee or tea? I ordered a tray from room service with a pot of each. It got here just before you did. Everything should still be hot."

"I'll have a cup of tea. Thanks," she said. They were so civilized. He seemed to have forgotten about the night before. She should have been grateful.

She was, Reggie told herself.

"Milk? Lemon? Sugar?" he asked.

"Lemon and two sugars," she responded. When he brought her the cup, she chanced a quick look up into his eyes. He gazed down at her. There was affection in his expressive eyes. And something more. Appreciation. She felt her face grow warm and had to look away. Once she wasn't looking into those deep brown eyes, Reggie realized his appreciation might be for her work, not for her.

"We have the lecture at two," she reminded him. That had been her idea, too. Elaine had invited her weeks ago to a seminar she was teaching at the university. When she'd been hired to promote Langston Downs locally, one of Reggie's first calls had been to Elaine to ask if her new client could join the author at her podium. "You're not still nervous about that, are you?" she asked him.

"No, I think I'm ready. I wish I knew more about black American history, but I'll have Elaine up there to cover me. I called her last night and we talked for a long time. She says I know more than I think I know."

"Most people do," she acknowledged. "And I'm glad that you're comfortable with this because I got interest from *Entertainment Tonight, Inside Hollywood,* and some others concerning getting some footage, and a possible interview about promoting the film here in Washington state because the film is set here." *Under His Skin* was about a black settlement founded in the nineteenth century before the Civil War by an African-American named George Washington Bush. Reggie found that people were generally fascinated by the topic. Her promotion of Elaine's book fictionalizing the efforts of those early settlers to create a home in the untamed Pacific Northwest was her small company's first big success.

"You're going to tape the lecture?" Langston sounded less confident than he had a moment ago.

"Don't worry. You'll be great," she reassured him. "Believe me after playing this part, you know more about this subject than most anyone."

"Not more than you, though. Right, Teach?" he said.

"You've got a different perspective on George. You really did get under his skin," she joked. Langston groaned, but he smiled. "I'm sorry. I couldn't resist," Reggie apologized.

"Very punny," he replied. Reggie grimaced. "I know," he agreed. "I'm not as clever as you are." They were right back where they had started, but at least he looked more relaxed. Reggie thought he could handle the interview and the lecture with his usual grace, now. "Drink your coffee," she ordered.

It struck her as strange, all of a sudden, that she was privy to this side of him. If someone had told her a week before that Langston Downs, heartthrob, was insecure about his intellectual ability, or that he was embarrassed because he didn't have his college degree, she would have thought they were crazy. She never would have guessed this confident, even arrogant, man had any insecurities, let alone insecurities she could sympathize with.

It had taken only a short time for her to learn these things about him, and in those few days, she'd learned also to care for him—enough to want to alleviate his fears. It was bizarre that he had won her over so swiftly and effortlessly. Reggie wondered if it was always this easy for him. She supposed it was. That was why his was a household name. Making that name and that face even more recognizable was her only real concern, she reminded herself.

They sat in companionable silence in the sitting room of his suite. She looked around. It was a luxurious room, with a well-appointed bar, a large-screen television and a video cassette recorder. A walnut entertainment center against the wall stood facing a large, comfortable-looking couch and two armchairs placed kitty corner around a walnut table. The curtains had been opened to show off the view of Seattle. A wall of windows overlooked the rooftops and nearby Puget Sound.

Reggie marveled at how natural it felt to sit on a floral-patterned sofa across from the handsomest man in the country, sipping Earl Grey tea. The phone rang. It was Tamara, who was down in the lobby.

"Come on up," Langston said.

Tamara swept into the room like a whirlwind. Her avid eyes

took in every detail. Regina had never seen her friend at work before, and it was odd. She could almost see Tamara taking mental notes. The reporter cataloged Langston's clothes, his movements, and even the room he was staying in. But it didn't seem to Reggie that she saw Langston, even when she looked him up and down.

After the introductions were made, Tamara got right down to work. "What attracted you to this part?" she asked him.

"I loved the script and the character. I've never seen anything like this, and never heard of anyone like George," Langston replied. "I suspect this is a very realistic portrayal of the black frontiersman."

"I read the packet Reggie sent over, so I know the basic story of *Under His Skin,* but is there any particular theme or part of the movie that you thought especially interesting?" Tamara asked.

Langston thought for a moment. "I don't know how important it is, but I enjoyed the scenes where the others tried to get him to be the postmaster, then the sheriff, and finally the mayor. He kept turning them down. He just wanted to work his fields and orchards. They kept turning to him for advice on running the town. He was so out of his depth, it was ludicrous. In the face of their helplessness, he had to pitch in. No one else knew what they were doing either, so he made it up as he went along and as long as his solutions seemed to work . . ." Langston shrugged, on his face the same wry grin the character George wore during the scenes he was describing. Reggie smiled, looking at him and remembering moments in the movie. Suddenly she thought she understood why those scenes were so comical. It was because they were so real. And Langston gave Elaine's words that honesty and sincerity.

Tamara was smiling, too. "It sounds like fun," she said. "But it must have been difficult playing a black man in that repressive time period."

"Sometimes I got a little freaked out. We all did. The white actors, too. It felt wrong to me to be so submissive, so passive in the face of such blatant hatred. But once I got into it, I felt like his attitude was really courageous, even when he let white men walk all over him. George had a dream, and he'd sacrifice anything for it. In the end, it's easy to see how much strength it took, but while I was immersed in dealing with the day-to-day stuff, it was a struggle to keep my ego under control. Which was probably true for him, too."

Tamara's interview continued for another hour and her questions elicited various intriguing responses from her subject. Reggie's celebrity client had a viewpoint that she found both fascinating and amusing. She thought the article would be a really good one.

They both collapsed on the couch as soon as the door closed behind her. "Talk about waiting to exhale," Reggie quipped.

"She's a dynamo." Langston closed his eyes and leaned into the couch back. "I can't believe I have to go face a roomful of college students after that inquisition."

"Hey, it's going to be fine," Reggie soothed. "And you've got an hour or so to relax before we have to go."

"I'll need it."

She stood. "I'm going to make a few phone calls. Do you need anything?"

"Where are you going?" he asked.

"Down to the lobby, and then out to grab some lunch while I work on a few things," Reggie said, holding up her briefcase for him to see.

"How about lunch with me, instead? And no work."

Eight

Elaine Fuller mesmerized the audience with her sing-song voice as she told them amazing stories of the settling of the Northwest territories. Reggie was as enthralled by the lecture as the college students who filled the auditorium were—even though she had actually heard most of this speech before. Her old friend spoke for almost an hour, and by the end of her prepared comments, even the biggest Langston Downs fan had forgotten the movie star was up there on the stage with her.

Not for long, though. As energized and excited as the young audience had been during Elaine's presentation, a low murmur started when Langston stepped up to the dais—like an electrical current humming through steel wire.

He looked fantastic as always, and he handled himself just as well. Reggie's cameraman gave her an enthusiastic thumbs up when he finally put the camera down. "We've got some great sound bites," he said when she asked him if he thought they could get the tape on national television.

As she'd predicted, Langston was quite capable of holding his own as the students bombarded both him and Elaine with questions about the new film, the novel it was based upon, and the history that had inspired it. Everyone applauded wildly when the class moderator called a belated halt to the question-and-answer session, but it was clear that the seminar could have gone on for quite some time.

Reggie shepherded Langston and Elaine off the stage and into a small anteroom to wait until the room was cleared out. "You were—both of you—wonderful up there. They loved you," Reggie enthused.

"I thought it went pretty well," Langston said, looking at Elaine for confirmation.

"Very well," she agreed. "So why are we hiding in here?"

"We're supposed to meet the organizers of this little shindig, remember?" A cocktail party had been arranged by the university as a token of the history department's appreciation for the speakers' services. "If we didn't get you out of sight, we'd be hip deep in students with more questions."

"Oh, right," Elaine conceded gracefully.

"So we're just going to wait for the auditorium to empty out in this cozy little . . . um . . . coat closet. Okay?"

"No problem," Lansgton said reassuringly.

"It will only be for a few more minutes."

"It'll give me time to decompress. I don't know about you, but I was nervous," he said to Elaine.

This time she shook her head. "I've done this so many times now."

"You'd think I'd get used to it by now. But every time I speak in public, I worry that I'm going to say something stupid." His insecurity was endearing.

"You did great," Reggie assured him.

The party was in full swing when they arrived. Or at least as swinging as it could be with elderly, tenured professors, bureaucrats from the university's administration and officious student organizers as the attendees.

"They started without us, I see," Elaine said wryly. "Probably a good thing, too. Half of these stuffed shirts critiqued my novel when it first came out."

"I gather the reviews were not kind?" Langston surmised.

"They said I romanticized the era, the hardships, and the race," she said sotto voce.

"Not all of them," Reggie said reasonably.

"Only a couple had the guts to say what they all thought," Elaine shot back. Apparently, she still hadn't recovered from the experience.

"Water under the bridge," Reggie soothed. She saw her mom

and waved her over. "Elaine, you remember my mother, Jennifer Primm," she introduced her.

"Of course," Elaine said, extending her hand. When her mother failed to take the proffered hand, Reggie examined her more closely and made an astonishing discovery. Jennifer Primm's bright eyes were fading. Always dark as chestnuts, they were several shades lighter now, the color of maple syrup. Still beautiful, they had lost some of their shine. Reggie didn't say anything, just nudged her mother's arm forward with a hand behind her elbow. Jennifer looked down and saw the younger woman's hand. She took it. "Nice to see you again, Elaine."

Reggie introduced Langston next. "Mr. Downs, my mother, Mrs. Primm."

"A pleasure," he said. And actually bowed.

"The pleasure is all mine." She was purring. Reggie was amused, but at the same time she was a little dismayed. Jennifer Primm was nobody's pushover, but in seconds, Langston Downs had captivated her with his looks and charm.

Elaine wandered away to find a more receptive audience while Reggie's mom chatted animatedly with the movie idol. Her mother's dignified old face was alight with excitement. When Jenny told him she remembered him from the days when he had almost made the Olympic track team, Langston looked suitably gratified and, for the first time since she'd known him, quite humble. Watching them flirt, Reggie almost forgot about her earlier discovery. Almost. But in the back of her mind, she grappled with the unwelcome thought that her mother might be losing her eyesight.

At seventy-five, Jennifer Primm had a young soul, perhaps because of her boundless appreciation for life and all it had to offer, which Langston appeared to have discovered.

"Jenny, you're something else," he was saying, much to the older woman's delight. "I can't believe you remember that."

"I do." She nodded emphatically.

"Tell the truth, you wouldn't have noticed me at all if it weren't for my mother, would you?"

"It's true I did admire your mother and Wilma Rudolph and the other women on the Tennessee State team, but to be honest,

I would have noticed you anyway because you were so hand-some, even then."

"Mom," Reggie admonished.

She swatted at her like a pesky fly buzzing in her ear. "Go away, honey. I'm talking to Langston."

"Yes, go away, honey," Langston agreed. They angled their bodies away from her, not turning their backs completely, but effectively demonstrating that they didn't want her to intrude on their tête à tête. Reggie sighed, exasperated. Then she noticed Bebe heading directly toward them.

Thank goodness, she thought. Now she wouldn't feel like a third wheel on her mother's first date with Langston.

"Hey, Reggie. Sorry I'm late," her best friend greeted her. Bebe's eyes were glued on Langston from the moment she reached Reggie's side. "Good to see you," she said. Her gaze never wavered from his face. "What are he and your mom talking about?" she asked. "They're best friends already, I see," she continued without waiting for an answer. "Damn! That old lady works fast. She's got him eating out of the palm of her hand."

"And vice versa," Reggie replied.

Bebe shrugged as if it were the most natural thing in the world for a grandmother of five to be making eyes at a man who'd been dubbed the sexiest black man in America. "You should take notes, girl."

"Thanks," Reggie said wryly. "I'll do that."

"Do I detect a note of sarcasm?" Bebe asked facetiously.

"How would you feel if it were your mother?" Reggie responded.

"Jealous?"

"You would not," Reggie argued. "You'd be . . . you'd . . ." she spluttered.

"I'd what?" Bebe still hadn't even looked at her. Reggie was tempted to watch, too. She pretended to ignore the lively conversation going on directly behind her between her mother and her "new best friend," but she was straining to hear. It was rude to eavesdrop. If she managed not to gape, open-mouthed, at Langston when she met him, she could certainly resist the urge now, and keep her dignity intact. No matter how outrageously her mother was behaving, she planned to continue treating her superstar like any other client.

As if to test her resolve, the snippets of conversation coming from behind her grew more provocative by the moment, and Bebe's grin grew wider and wider.

"Oh, you are a big boy, aren't you?" Mom said. Reggie prayed she was talking about Langston's height and not his shoe size. Reggie saw Elaine nearby and considered dragging her over to break up the little parley.

"How did you like kissing that girl in that commercial. You remember that one . . ." Bebe laughed out loud, so Reggie couldn't hear the end of the sentence.

"Why don't you break those two up?" Reggie asked her. "You're obviously dying to get in there."

"I'm not messing with your mother. And besides, it's bugging you out, not me. You deal with it."

Resolutely, Reggie turned around. "I'm sorry to interrupt," she said insincerely. "But I think you've monopolized Langston for long enough, Mom. He should circulate a little."

"Okay, baby," Jenny Primm said tamely. Reggie was surprised at her compliance, until she turned to Langston to say, "Goodbye, Langston. I'll see you at the barbecue."

"Looking forward to it, Jenny." He winked. Reggie led him away. "She invited me to her place this weekend," he explained.

"I guessed," Reggie said briskly.

"The whole family will be there," he said.

"We usually are." They reached Elaine, who was speaking with a small group of men in suits. They were not wearing ties, so she guessed they were professors.

"Langston, I'd like to introduce you to Professor Blair and Mr. Andrew Chopinhauer."

Everyone exchanged greetings and Langston was soon the center of a discussion about the growing number of black historical figures in popular films, books, and even one stupid television program. The academicians agreed with him that the trend was a step in the right direction, but when Langston said it was time mainstream America finally found out that African-

Americans were instrumental to the history of the country, there
was a sudden lull in the conversation.

Elaine quickly stepped in. "Of course, even though information was available to those who were interested before, it wasn't
easily accessible to the general public, like major motion pictures are."

That started a lively debate which Langston listened to but in
which he didn't participate. Reggie knew he felt excluded from
the conversation about the merits of classical literature such as
the works of Turner, Douglas, Dubois, Hurston and even Wright
versus contemporary works such as *Beloved, Amistad, The Color
Purple* and *Rosewood.*

"Popular contemporary books are almost immediately
adapted to film, which makes the audience even larger," Professor Blair pontificated. "Millions see them." He was a tall,
thin scarecrow of a man, his face as spare and dire as the farmer
in *American Gothic,* albeit a mahogany version. His wire-
rimmed glasses made his long face look only slightly less
Gothic.

"But those books have not been read and studied and re-
printed for decades and until they are, we don't know how, or
even if, they'll be interpreted," Andrew Chopinhauer argued. He
was as stocky as his counterpart was spare, but he had twenty
years on the man. He, too, wore glasses, and his high forehead
was deeply furrowed.

"And what about the parallels that are drawn between successful literary works like *Beloved* and pure commercial fiction
like *Waiting to Exhale?*" Elaine chipped in.

Reggie drew Langston away muttering. "They'll be at this for
hours. You've done your duty. Do you want to go home?"

"I could use a beer," he said, putting down his untouched
champagne.

Reggie sympathized, but she couldn't think of any way to
tactfully bring up the subject she was certain was bothering him.
She brought him back to her mother, who was deep in conversation with Bebe. "We've come to say good-bye," she announced when they looked over.

"I was thinking of getting a drink, but Reggie can't drink and drive and I hate drinking alone in a hotel room. Would you kind ladies like to join me for a cocktail?"

"I've got to get home," Jenny said. "I promised to baby-sit for Rolanda tonight," she added in an aside to Reggie. "Thank you, though." She bustled off without a backwards glance at her latest conquest, but Langston stared after her, bemused.

"I'm game," Bebe said.

"You're driving, too," Reggie pointed out. If she was going to be nominated as the designated driver without so much as a by-your-leave, then no one else was drinking with impunity this evening.

Bebe had an answer for that. "Neal will come get me. We'll just go somewhere near my house, and he'll cab it over and drive me home in my car."

"I didn't mean to create problems," Langston said.

"You're not," Bebe retorted, with a pointed glance at Regina.

"Hey, I didn't start this drunk driving talk," Reggie said, glaring at Langston.

"You said the other night that you never drink when you're driving. At the Blue Room," Langston said, defending himself.

"Oh yeah." She had told him that, she remembered. And it was basically true. As a rule.

Bebe stared at her in disbelief. "I didn't mean that I never have a single drink. I just meant that I don't get drunk and drive." Now Langston was staring as well. "I'm not a saint," Reggie said in a small voice.

"Oh, I know that." Bebe said.

At the same time, Langston said, "Who is?"

"So shall we go get that drink?" Reggie asked, desperate to end the conversation.

"Sure," Bebe agreed. "Follow me."

Langston smiled and held out his arm. Reggie took it, glad to have gotten out of the spotlight without further discussion. As they followed Bebe out of the classroom, Langston said, sotto voce, "Are you just inventing these rules as you go along?"

"No," Reggie said between her teeth. "They are very sensible guidelines which I follow in order to keep from complicating my life."

"It all sounds pretty complicated to me," Langston quipped. "Maybe you should just write out a list."

"Just figure out what you would do in any given situation and you can pretty much guess it's against my rules."

"But you are going to have a drink with us now, right?" he asked.

"Definitely," Reggie said. "I earned it."

"I thought everything went pretty well," he said.

"It was fine. Better than fine," Reggie reassured him.

"Except for that stupid comment I made."

"It wasn't stupid. You just happened to say it to the wrong man. He lives for Black Studies. No one else would have even noticed."

"I've read all those people. All of them and more. I know that there is information about black history and the contributions African-Americans have made to this country. I just didn't think."

"It's not your area. But if you've read Turner and Dubois, and Hurston and Walker on your own, you've given yourself a course in black literature most professors would love to teach."

She could tell he was not consoled by her comforting words, but they reached the parking lot just then and Bebe turned and said, "Stop whispering, you two."

"We're not . . ." Reggie started to say, but she realized they had had their heads together while they had their rather private conversation and stopped.

"Langston, you come with me. I haven't had a chance to talk to you at all, and it's happy hour, so the bar will be too loud for intimate conversation," she wiggled a finger at him. "Reggie, you follow. Is The Plum okay?"

Reggie had known she was going to suggest their favorite neighborhood bar. "Sure."

"See you there," Bebe yelled, already walking away. Langston shrugged helplessly and trotted after her. Reggie watched them walk away, talking as if they'd known each all their lives.

Why was it that everyone she knew was so at ease with Langston, while she felt like she could barely let down her guard around him. He treated her just the way he did everyone else. She hadn't met many movie stars, but Reggie doubted that many were as down to earth and downright friendly as Langston was. He could be arrogant and conceited and vain. But he was also honest and funny and easy to be with, perhaps because he didn't try to hide his faults.

She liked him. Everyone liked him. Why couldn't she relax around him like her mother had, and Elaine, and Bebe, and everyone else they had met.

Reggie saw Bebe's black Jeep zoom toward the exit and a moment later heard the screeching of her wheels as she peeled out of the parking lot. If Langston thought Reggie drove too fast, he would love riding with Bebe, she thought, grinning as she pictured his expression. Heaven help him if he dared to comment on her old friend's skill behind the wheel. Bebe took any such remarks as criticism, and all criticism as a challenge.

When Reggie arrived at the bar, Bebe and Langston were already finished with their first round of drinks, as was evidenced by the two tequila shots and the beers that were waiting for her.

"You can catch up if you drink up quickly," Bebe said.

Reggie glared at her and said demurely, "I'll just have a beer since I'm the designated driver."

"I already called Neal and told him he might have to drive all of us home," Bebe shot back at her.

"That's all right. I don't really feel like drinking shooters." If she'd had the chance she'd have ordered something a little more sophisticated than beer on tap anyway, in order to demonstrate that she wasn't a complete reprobate. She didn't get drunk and act low-class every time she went out for the evening, despite the way she'd acted in the parking lot the night before.

She wanted him to know that that kiss had been an aberration. She didn't usually attack virtual strangers that way.

The beer did mellow her some. And the conversation—an exchange of jokes and personal information that couldn't possibly offend anyone—was guided by Bebe and interrupted by a fan or two or three who wanted to shake hands with Langston Downs. Most of the patrons kept a polite distance, although they were subjected to curious glances.

When Neal did arrive a couple of hours later to pick up his

wife, she was regaling Langston with stories of their misadventures in high school and since, and Reggie was trying to think of a painless way to shut her up. He really did not need to know how geeky she had been in school. The image she'd been trying to cultivate—as a responsible, knowledgeable, public relations whiz whom he could trust with his life—was nearly shattered.

Bebe had told him about Reggie's prom date, the president of the computer science club, who was a half a foot shorter than her and who insisted on dancing only the slow dances together. She'd also discussed Reggie's decision to leave teaching and go into business for herself, and the quandary it had put her in.

Bebe recounted the old war stories with pride. The computer science club president went on to build a very large, very profitable software company and he regularly phoned Reggie, either to ask her to lunch or to propose. "She lunches, but she won't marry," she said, shaking her head at Reggie reproachfully. "The girls who laughed at her at the prom would be green with envy if they saw them dating these days. Darrell's name was on *Fortune's* list of the highest paid CEOs in the country. And they're good friends. He offered to back her public relations company." Bebe also spoke like a proud mama about Reggie's business success. She bragged about how she managed some of the worst losers in the region, and always made them look good.

"I'm in good hands then," Langston said, winking at Reggie. When Neal half dragged, half escorted her out of the bar, Bebe was just warming up to the subject that was nearest to her heart these days—how perfect it would be if Reggie settled down and started a family. "Not with Darrell. She doesn't love him. But she needs someone to make her stop working all the time. Besides she should have kids." She raised her voice to be heard above the din of the crowd. "You should see her with her nieces and nephews." Embarrassed again, Reggie could only be thankful that she was gone.

But Langston was smiling. "She's fun," he said.

"Bebe's fun all right," she said somewhat sourly. "But for a lawyer, she's not very tactful."

"I've got the feeling she's a good lawyer—if she's as passionate about her cases as she is about her friends."

"She is a good lawyer," Reggie confirmed, feeling guilty already for her disloyal comment. "One of the best," she said with feeling.

"My sister Charlie's husband is a lawyer. He still works in the inner city in Detroit where I grew up." There was a wistful, admiring note in his voice that Reggie picked up on immediately.

"Do you think you might have been a lawyer if you hadn't become a football player?"

"I thought about it. I got in trouble enough when I was a kid, and a friend of my mom's who was a lawyer helped me. I wouldn't have minded being able to do the same thing for some of the boys I've met."

"But you're still able to help them. Providing a good role model for young black men is important. And you definitely do that," she reassured him, feeling protective again.

"I don't know. They see a guy like me, making a lot of money, and, let's face it, they don't see the work that goes into being a star. They see the fame and fortune and *that's* what they want."

"They see you: a successful, intelligent, caring man from the same streets they're growing up on. When they see all the negative images of African-American men in the media, they compare them to you. And believe me, they want to *be* you."

"I hope so," he said, his voice doubtful.

"You should know so," she remonstrated.

"Okay, Teach," he agreed, his mood suddenly changing. "I'll take your word for it that I'm a hero to black urban youth, despite all my negative publicity."

"Which you haven't had in . . . let's see . . . How long have I been working with you?" she teased in the same light tone.

"Oh!" he exclaimed. "So that's the way it's going to be, is it? You're going to take all the credit for my good behavior from now on?"

"Your good press," she corrected. "And only for as long as I'm the one in charge of your public relations. After that, you're on your own."

"You'd throw me to the wolves, then? Just like that?"

"Did you think I was going to give up all this?" With a wave of her hand she indicated the darkened bar, the wobbly bar stools, the flimsy, lopsided tables, scuffed floors, and stained walls. "Forever? Just for you?"

"Just for me? Some people think quite highly of me, you know."

"I know that."

"What about you?" He grabbed her hand and held it.

"What about me?" she asked, laughing.

"What do you think of me?" He squeezed her hand.

"I think we've already established that," Reggie said stiffly, suddenly remembering that this was Langston Downs she was joking with so irreverently, and not just, as he pointed out, anyone. He was her client. And this was her big chance. She didn't want to mess that up with some barroom banter. "Shall we call it a night?" she suggested.

"Not yet," he said. "You've had a few days to get to know me, now. We've been working closely together all this time, and I think we work well together." She nodded. "So, tell me, are you as attracted to me as I am to you?" She stopped nodding.

"I told you already that I don't get involved with my clients."

"I didn't ask you to get involved with me. I asked if you were at all *interested* in getting involved with me?"

She knew what he asked. She didn't want to answer him. "I don't think it's a proper question, given the circumstances."

"What circumstances?" he asked.

"We *are* working together."

"Then if we weren't working together? Would you or would you not kiss me again?"

"I thought we were going to forget about that," she reminded him. "There is no point to this discussion."

"The point is I want to know," he pressed.

"Why?" she asked, frustrated. "What difference does it make? If I tell you I am interested in you, we can't act on it, which will make things awkward. And if I say I'm not, I'll hurt your feelings, which will also—"

"Make things awkward between us," he finished for her. "Tell me anyway."

"Why keep pushing this?" she asked.

"I'd like to know where I stand with you," he answered.

"You are a client. Period."

"And a friend," he added before she could protest. "You said we could be friends. And I'm glad, because I like you. I can say that, can't I? It's not exactly an insult, Reggie. I like you a lot. So, now," he caught her gaze and held it. "How do you feel about me?"

"Langston, we are friends," Reggie stated. "I like you, too. But . . ." she continued, when he would have spoken, ". . . I don't think anything else is possible between us. I care about you and your success. Not just because it's my job, but because I do know you now. Our professional relationship is very important to me, as I hope it is to you. You can get any number of other women to . . . to have a personal relationship with. You don't need me."

"How do you know?" he asked, and this time he sounded very serious "I don't think you know what I need."

"Apparently you need a girl," Reggie said.

"We're not kids. I don't need a girl, I need a woman. You."

"You need me?" she said, incredulous. "A few minutes ago you wanted me. Which is it?"

"You know what I mean," he said intently. "There is more to it than that."

"No, I don't know. Are you going to sit there and pretend you've fallen in love with me?"

"I didn't say that," he backpedaled.

"Or is it just sex you want? Or need?" she said meanly.

"I'm not talking about sex," he protested.

"You're not? What was all that about attraction? About being more than friends? About needing a woman? Are you saying you're not coming on to me?" she challenged him.

"I didn't mean it like that. Do you honestly believe I'm just some horny bastard trying to get into your pants? Because if you do, if you really think that that's what I'm talking about, you don't know me at all."

"You're right. I don't know you and *you* don't know me. We've only known each other for a few days. What do you expect?"

"I don't know what I expected. An answer maybe. A simple yes or no. It's not that complicated. I met you, I liked you, and the more I've gotten to know you, the closer I felt. I was hoping you felt the same way. So do you?"

"What I feel is that . . . too much has been said. I don't mean to insult or annoy you, but I can't give you any other answer than the one I've given you. We're working together. Anything else would be impossible."

"What about later? After the film opens? When we're not working together?"

"Langston, what is wrong with you?" she asked, exasperated.

"With me? Nothing. I'm trying to say that I want to start a relationship with you, Regina Primm. Not just anyone with a pretty face, but your face. And everything that goes along with it."

"I think we should keep our relationship strictly professional. And I think it's time to go." There was no danger that she would kiss him tonight. She drove him home.

Reggie couldn't understand Langston's persistence. He knew she didn't want to pursue a personal relationship, so why couldn't he just leave it at that? Why did he have to keep pushing her and pushing her until she had to insult him. How was she supposed to look him in the face after she said those things to him. She really hadn't intended to imply that he was a skirt chaser. "Sorry," she said, when they'd driven a few miles in silence.

"Me, too," Langston said.

"It's not you. I've got . . . a lot on my mind."

"I understand," he said. They were both silent for the rest of the ride, and she dropped him off and quickly headed home. She had more important concerns than Langston Downs' libido. She knew he genuinely liked her. Unfortunately, that didn't matter. She couldn't believe he felt more deeply for her. Why should he? She was so plain compared to his usual companions. She was a fat, frumpy, ordinary woman who couldn't even apply her own makeup. He was a superstar. They didn't belong together. And her mother was in some kind of trouble. She called her as soon as she arrived at home. "Mom, what's wrong with your eyes?" she said, without preliminaries.

"I've got cataracts," Jennifer Primm said, calmly.

"Are you . . . ?" Reggie started, horrified. "Does that mean . . . ?" She couldn't finish the sentence.

"Eventually, I'll lose my sight. But there is nothing to worry about at the moment. I've lost some peripheral vision but I'm okay."

Reggie wanted to commiserate with her, and offer sympathy and help, but Jenny Primm wouldn't listen.

She insisted she wasn't ready to discuss it yet. "It's still too new. It's private. I'll talk about this with you and your brother and sisters when I've sorted it all out for myself."

Finally, Reggie gave in. "Night, Mom. I'll talk to you tomorrow."

"Night, Baby. Please don't worry about me. You have your business to take care of. That's where your attention should be."

"Okay, I know," Reggie said, but she couldn't help worrying. She was scared.

Nine

Langston couldn't believe Reggie accused him of pursuing a relationship with her solely because she was a female and she was there. In fact, if he understood her correctly, she didn't even believe he wanted a relationship. She thought all he wanted was sex. It was true that the idea of making love to Reggie had kept him awake for the past few nights, but that was because she was so sweet and smart and sexy. It wasn't because she was available. Far from it. He had never known anyone so unattainable.

There were women who were not interested in him, a few of whom he *had* been interested in simply because he couldn't have them. That was human nature. But that had nothing to do with his feelings for Reggie. She was beautiful. She was funny. She was caring. And she seemed to understand him. That combination was irresistible. He could fall in love with her quick mind and her sweet smile, if she would let him.

He did his hundred push-ups that night while his brain worked overtime on how to convince her that he wasn't some sex-starved beast waiting to pounce the moment she let her guard down. He truly was a friend. And he really wanted to be more. He didn't know how he was going to arrange *that* since Reggie was so dead set against it. But he still had hope. She hadn't said she *wasn't* attracted to him. She might have been trying to protect his feelings, or his fragile male ego, but he suspected she was aware of him as a sexual being and she didn't want to admit it because of her damn rules.

He just couldn't forget that kiss.

The next day they didn't have any scheduled appearances but Reggie had arranged a lunch with an editor from the weekend section of the newspaper, which would be reviewing the film when it opened. They were also supposed to drop in on another friend of hers who had videotaped the lecture at the university the day before. They were to discuss whether he thought they could sell some of the footage to the producers of entertainment news television such as *E.T.* or *Access Hollywood,* or even produce a short segment themselves.

It was a full day despite there only being two appointments on the schedule. Langston's job was to be as charismatic and charming as possible while Reggie "sold" him to her contacts. He enjoyed it. When he did the promotional tour for his first film, he'd been ordered about—politely, of course—and told where to be, sit, stand, when to smile, speak, sparkle. It was a strange, lowering experience to be treated in one moment as a demi-god whose wishes were assiduously inquired after and whose every whim was instantly granted, and in the next moment as basically a piece of furniture to be pushed, prodded, and properly lit so as to shine more brightly than the antiques and the objets d'art in the background.

This world of Reggie's, in which she determined the promotability of her particular product (him) and then pushed to get others to recognize and value it (him) as she did, was run by self-determination and the sheer force of her will. He never felt like an object, not even a valuable commodity, when she was selling his image. She saw him—his face and body—as an advertisement for his craft and work, and saw his personality—his words and actions—as an even more effective sales tool.

She was courteous and reserved with him, but toward everyone around them she displayed eager enthusiasm for the opportunity to show him off. He watched her until she caught him staring, and then he pretended not to have been absorbed in taking in every minuscule detail about her. He enjoyed the sway of her hips as she walked across a room, the way she tilted her head when she looked up at him so that she didn't look directly into his eyes, but sideways at his mouth and shoulders and chest.

By the end of the workday, as they drove back toward the

hotel at five o'clock, he was sure she was as aware of his physical presence as he was of her light feminine scent. They were alone together for the first time that day. She had not driven him to their lunch date. He had gone in a taxi straight from a midmorning meeting with his producer to his luncheon with her and the columnist. They walked from there to the meeting with the cameraman. Langston was sure she'd planned it that way. He was surprised when she offered to drive him back to his hotel. If Reggie thought he would refuse out of chivalry or out of embarrassment, she had not indicated it when he accepted. She just turned and led the way back to where she parked, near the restaurant. She hadn't said a word since, and he didn't know how to break the silence between them.

It wasn't as uncomfortable as he would have thought, sitting beside her, enclosed in the air-conditioned comfort of her Camry. He waited patiently, determined to let her pick the tone of their next conversation. Langston was no closer to knowing how to proceed with her than he had been the night before. He only knew he wasn't ready to give up on the idea that they could be something special to each other.

When they reached the hotel, they still hadn't spoken to each other. He thought she breathed a sigh of relief as she pulled up at the entrance, but he couldn't be sure. A bellman ran out to the car before he could open the door. When he tapped on the window, Langston depressed the button that lowered the glass.

"There's a whole convention of newspeople in there, Ms. Primm," he told Reggie. "They are waiting for someone else, so if you guys want to avoid them you can go down to the garage and come up on that elevator."

"I'll do that. Thanks," Langston said, slipping him a five-dollar bill before shutting the window.

Reggie drove the car down under the building and found a parking space not far from the elevators. "Here we are," she said.

"Come on up," he half asked, half ordered. "Just in case I meet those reporters in the elevator." She didn't move. "Please?"

"Okay, let's go," Reggie answered, throwing the car into park, then releasing her seat belt and taking her keys from the ignition in one smooth motion. She was out of the car and around it and moving toward the elevator in a minute and a half. He walked beside her silently, encouraged by the ease with which he'd gotten her to come up to his hotel room.

Once there he had no clue as to what he planned to say or do, but they were definitely headed in the right direction as far as he was concerned. He'd have bet a year's salary that she would not have agreed to come, *so far, so good,* he thought as the elevator doors closed behind them. They turned to face the panel that displayed the floors they were passing, and he let out a sigh of relief when the car didn't stop at the lobby. He didn't want to face the paparazzi at that moment. The reprieve was short-lived. On the second floor the elevators stopped for a group of people attending a convention at the hotel. They streamed into the tiny box, one after another, until they couldn't squeeze another soul inside. The businessmen and women chattered excitedly about the last meeting and the next, ignoring him and Reggie, whom they had barely noticed as they filed steadily in, piling into the confined space and forcing its occupants back into the corner.

He held her against him, not wanting to see the expression on her face, but knowing that she could feel his arousal. They were so close together, her back against his stomach, she could not fail to feel his erection against her buttocks, even through the clothes they wore. Langston could not have moved if he had wanted to. And he didn't want to. Reggie moved, brushing against him, and his hands went around her waist to hold her in place. He didn't want her to turn, at least not until he could get his body back under control. If Reggie saw the expression on his face at that moment, she would know just how much he really did want to make love to her. He inhaled deeply in an effort to get his breathing under control, but it was a mistake. Her scent, a light floral aroma that seemed to emanate from her brown skin, went straight to his head, making him feel more aroused than ever. The elevator stopped and the convention attendees got out. He closed his eyes, trying to block out the sensations he was feeling, but that just made them more intense.

He was so lost in the sensual haze that it took a moment for Langston to realize that Reggie hadn't stepped away from him.

Her hands rested on top of his, but she made no move to move out of his embrace or dislodge his arms from around her body. She was completely still. He tried to look over her shoulder, but her face was turned away from his. He heard her swallow and was suddenly aware that she was holding her breath. Langston slid his hands down to her hips. The elevator shuddered slightly as it stopped at his floor, and she gasped. He reached out to press and hold the door open button for her, enjoying the slide of her full backside against his sensitized flesh. He nuzzled her neck. She tilted her head, allowing him access to the tender flesh below her left ear, then suddenly she snapped to attention, her whole body rigid, and walked out of the door. He followed more slowly.

She stopped, her back still to him, and asked, "Right or left?"

"Right," he croaked, turning automatically in that direction as he took the card key from his suit jacket pocket.

He tried to catch a glimpse of her downturned face as they walked up the hall, but he couldn't. He stepped up to the doorway quickly and inserted the key in the lock, turning the handle the moment the red light turned green. Even so, he wasn't quick enough to stop Reggie from turning away before he could look back and see her expression.

Reggie had already taken a step back, in the direction of the elevator, when he reached out and grabbed her wrist.

"Wait!" he pleaded.

"I've got to go." Her voice was muffled and soft, and he could not tell if she was crying or if she was furious with him. She half turned back to him, but refused to raise her head as she said, "We'll talk later. Please?" She didn't sound furious, her voice was just barely louder than a whisper.

"I think we should have that discussion now," he commanded, pulling her gently but inexorably back toward him.

"Let me go," she said softly.

"Just come in. And I promise I'll let go. Okay?" At least she wasn't angry. He didn't want to scare her away, but there was never going to be a better chance than this to convince Reggie that what he felt for her was more than lust. "You owe me that much," he pressed. "Look." He let go of her wrist and raised his hands up in front of him, palms out, in a gesture of surrender. "I won't touch you again. We'll just talk."

She sidled through the door and into the living room of the suite, and headed directly for the bar. "I could use a drink."

"Me, too," Langston said, closing the door.

"What do you want?" she asked churlishly. He was relieved that the scared rabbit seemed to have disappeared and his Reggie was back again.

"Whatever you're having." He leaned back against the door and crossed his arms. He felt like a prison guard. In a way, that wasn't far from the truth, since he had no intention of letting Reggie leave until he had his say.

"Vodka on the rocks," she said, her voice almost even, though there was still a slight tremor to it as she cleared her throat. Langston couldn't help wondering if she was afflicted with the same lump in the back of her throat that he was.

"You wanted to talk?" It was more a demand than a question, but Langston wasn't about to complain.

"Last night was . . . well . . . last night. But today, just now, I think you answered my question."

She came toward him with both drinks in her hands. Langston prayed she didn't throw either one or both of them in his face, but he stood his ground bravely, arms across his chest. No matter what was said, he was determined not to touch her. Not now. Not until Reggie admitted that she wanted him to. From her chagrined expression, he guessed he would have quite some time to wait. Maybe even forever.

It was only when she said, "Do you want it or not?" that he realized she was holding out his drink to him. He was so intent on finally seeing her face that he hadn't noticed. She looked unhappy. He carefully extended his hand and took the glass from her. Reggie turned away and went to sit down on the couch.

"All right, so we're attracted to each other. So what. I don't see how that helps the situation."

"The working together thing," he said instantly.

"Yes. That. I gather this is a new concept for you?" she said wryly.

"Well, in the league, there weren't a lot of women I considered to be actual colleagues—aside from the odd towel girl. I've been in the movie business for less than two years, and I didn't meet that many single women. So you could say it hasn't come up before now."

"What about the bimbo in New York? Or doesn't she count?"

"What bimbo?" he asked, completely confounded.

"The assistant you told me about the first day we met. The one you assumed I was replacing."

"Oh yeah. She . . . I . . . We didn't get together in the end," he stammered. She had been too much of a groupie for Langston to take her seriously, but now that he thought about it, he supposed a number of women he'd had casual affairs with over the years had, in one form or another, worked for or with the same people he did. "Okay, I grant you that there may have been a couple of women—"

"A couple?" she interrupted.

He ignored her. "In my past whom I met through my work, but I didn't harass them or anything. Half the time, they asked me out. You have to meet people somehow. And get to know each other. Working together is one way to do that."

"Sure it is. That's why it's important to keep your personal life separate from your professional relationships. It's very easy to get caught up in a relationship with a person with whom you work. But it's a bad idea. One's work tends to suffer, maybe not yours, but for a lot of people, it's hard to make a good, clean business decision when personalities are involved. Then there's the relationship itself. If you're indiscreet, then everyone around you knows you're sleeping together—bosses, colleagues—and people get jealous. Not to mention the discomfort of having to continue to see someone you've broken up with, or get a new job."

"All right. I understand. But we don't have to worry about any of that stuff," he said mildly. "We don't exactly work in a small office."

"Are you out of your mind? You're a celebrity. Everyone would be watching us. Whether it works out or not, my private life is going to be exposed for the whole world to see. You may have to live with that, but I don't." She drained her glass.

"So what are you afraid they'll see?" Langston asked. "Would you like another drink?" He trusted himself to move away from the door, finally. Reggie was comfortably ensconced on the couch and he could take the chair facing her. Now that they were talking, he didn't think she'd run out on him in the middle of the discussion.

"Sure," she said, holding up her glass. "The same." She seemed pretty relaxed, and Langston hoped she felt safe enough to tell him her fears so he could reassure her that they could not come true. He wouldn't let them.

"What are you afraid of?" he asked again when she still hadn't answered his question a few moments later as he handed her her drink.

"I just don't think I can stand up to that kind of scrutiny," she said. "And I don't want to."

"Dating is not, as far as I know, against the law."

"Sex sells," she said woodenly. "Your sex life is definitely news."

"We are two consenting adults. We don't have to answer to anyone."

"What about your fans?" she asked bitterly.

"My name has been linked with other women's," he pointed out.

"I know that," she said. "That's why I know how this is going to go."

"So what can they say?"

"What does he see in her, for one thing?"

"That's crazy. Obviously. I see a beautiful, intelligent, successful woman."

"Oprah is a beautiful, intelligent, successful woman, but you don't see that on the front page of the tabloids. All they care about is her weight, her hair, alleged affairs, and the fact that she's single."

"And her production company," he countered.

"The beef producers lawsuit," she shot back.

"The books she reads."

"Whether she really threw a hairbrush at her makeup woman."

"So you're worried that they'll make up stuff about you?" he asked, trying to understand. He knew he was missing something here, but, try as he might, it still eluded him.

"They won't need to. They've got plenty to work with already."

"Like what?" he asked, baffled.

"Look at me, Langston. I'm overweight. I don't exactly wear designer clothes, and I haven't seen the inside of a fashionable night spot, ever!"

"And that's it. That's why you won't go out with me?" He couldn't believe she was serious. But she hadn't cracked a smile since she'd arrived. Not even during the ridiculous debate about the tabloids. "Oprah!" he snorted.

"No that's not the reason. That's an . . . illustration. I don't want to get involved with you because of who you are and who I am. We lead very different lives, Langston. You've been in the spotlight since high school. I'm as ordinary as they come. You probably *hang out* with Oprah."

"Not her again."

"Forget Oprah then. What about all the famous women you've dated?"

"I never dated Oprah."

"Fine, but you live in L.A. for Chrissakes."

Now she had really stumped him. "What's wrong with L.A.? Lots of people live there."

"Not like you do. You know what I mean. You're a star. The Sexiest Black Man in America. I'm not even the sexiest woman in this hotel."

"You are to me," he said sincerely.

"That's not true," she said, sounding annoyed, though why she was irritated with him when he was the one who kept getting shot down, he didn't know. Her argument made no sense. If he was so all-powerful and sexy and she wasn't, why was he the one standing there virtually begging her to go out on a date.

"Yes it is." His voice emerged in a deep growl that surprised him as much as it did her.

"It is?" she said doubtfully.

"I should know," Langston responded, still feeling abused and frustrated.

"You haven't seen every woman in this hotel," she said. Then she smiled.

Langston slowly made his way over to the couch. "I don't need to see them. You are the sexiest black woman in America to me."

"That's a little hard to believe," she said, but her voice had changed timbre. It was warm and soft and silky.

"Believe me. No one else could do what you do to me. No one ever has."

"That's good," she said.

"It's sort of scary," he joked.

"Tell me about it," Reggie said. He looked into her eyes and he knew she *wasn't* joking.

She was wearing a pastel pink suit, which outlined the shape of her body. The jacket was wide at the shoulders, tapered in at the waist, and then flared out over her hips. The pants were loose, flowing, pink linen. Langston was dying to know what she wore underneath, but, true to his promise to himself, he waited until Reggie made the first move. She leaned over and gently placed her lips against his, setting him on fire. He couldn't hold back. He couldn't bring himself even to take the time to bring her into the bedroom next door. He bent her back onto the sofa with his kiss, his hands traveling up and down her arms. The pastel suit he had thought was linen was actually raw silk. When he unbuttoned the jacket, he found only a lacy black bustier beneath it.

"Regina," he breathed. "You are beautiful." After that, he couldn't speak. He felt like he'd been waiting months rather than days for this moment, and his fingers went swiftly to the zipper at her right hip. He drew down the zipper and her slacks were off in one long smooth movement. He pulled away to look into her eyes and found the same eager anticipation that he felt within himself.

Her hands were busy, too. His suit jacket landed on hers on the floor, and his shirt, after some unsuccessful fumbling at the buttons, soon followed. She helped him remove his trousers, quickly and efficiently disposing of the unwanted item of clothing. She was as ready as he was. She hooked two fingers under each side of the elastic waistband of his shorts and pushed them down as far as she could reach and he kicked them off.

Langston looked down at her curvaceous body and felt again that surge of protectiveness she evoked in him. Clad only in silky black short shorts that were sexy as hell and a lacy, strapless bustier that supported her abundant breasts, she looked delectable.

He bowed his head and kissed the upper curve of her breast, working his way up to her chin, her cheeks, her lips. She arched her body up into his and he slipped his leg between hers and rolled her over on top of him. He couldn't get enough of the feel and taste and sight of her.

He groaned as she reached between their bodies and wrapped her soft fingers around him. "Reggie, I want to go slow, but you're driving me crazy," he said through clenched teeth.

"Slow?" She stroked him gently. "Like this?"

His breath escaped in a hiss. He pulled her beneath him once again and held her arms down while he caught his breath. She reached up and kissed his collarbone. "I don't think I can wait," she murmured.

He removed the last little scrap of silk between them and positioned himself at the warm, wet entrance to her body. She arched upwards to meet his first downward thrust, pulling him into her.

They moved together in a rhythm as old as time. Sighing, pulsing, writhing against each other, they sought release from the building wave of desire that sent his hot mouth in search of her full lips. The tension built within him, higher and higher, and he moved within her, faster and faster, until they both spasmed at once, clutching each other tightly and holding on for dear life as they rode the wave of heated blood to the crest and down again.

"We'll work it all out," Reggie whispered. "No one has to know. Right?"

Ten

The vodka and the unaccustomed exercise took their toll on Reggie and she couldn't summon the energy to protest when Langston suggested they retire to his bedroom. She couldn't picture herself sneaking out of the hotel like a thief in the night anyway. She made a quick visit to the luxurious bathroom where she avoided looking in the huge mirror until she'd wrapped herself in his voluminous white terrycloth robe. Langston was in the half bath in the other room. After removing her makeup, she beat him to the bed by minutes. She had enough time to discard the robe, put her silk and lace underwear back on, and slip between the cotton sheets before he came into the room.

She didn't have any more time to think about what she was doing there, in his bed, before he strode into the room, long and lean, his chocolaty brown skin taut over firm, well-defined muscles. She admired his body as one would a sculpture. Every inch of flesh, over his ribs, across his abdomen, on his thighs, moved smoothly when he moved. Nothing sagged or careened off in a different direction from the rest of his body. His perfection contrasted with all of her shortcomings, and she pulled the sheet up to her chin and held it there so that it wouldn't slip when he got into the bed.

Langston had no such inhibitions, of course. He smiled sweetly at her as he turned out the light and leaned over to kiss her gently. Then he stretched his full length out beside her. She felt his body all the way down the length of her side. He promptly began to snore. Softly.

Reggie laughed. Movie stars, moguls, or musicians—men were men. Her eyes slid closed and she burrowed down a little deeper under the covers.

She woke up briefly during the night with his heavy arm curled over her stomach, and thought, *This is real. I'm not dreaming. I am actually in bed with Langston Downs.* She didn't feel uneasy or uncomfortable or out of place. It felt right. It felt better than she ever could have imagined when he was a big beautiful image in celluloid. Then he seemed too good to be a real man. Now, he was real, and he was hers. For the moment, this was where she was supposed to be. Whatever came after, she had this night. Reggie was too sleepy to think about it any more than that. She retreated back into slumber.

She didn't stir again until morning when she awakened slowly, keeping her eyes closed against the bright sunlight streaming through the windows, enjoying the feel of it on her face and shoulders. She still didn't feel bad, although the beginning twinges of guilt were knocking on the door. People did this all the time, she reasoned in an effort to forestall the inevitable recriminations of her overactive conscience. It was a vain attempt, she knew. Reggie had had her share of relationships at thirty-three years of age, but she didn't just jump into bed with guys she barely knew. Sex wasn't something she treated particularly casually. In Langston Downs' case, she felt like she did know him because of his celebrity—his face, his smile, his eyes, his lips, were all so familiar.

Langston had her bustier half unhooked when she realized he was no longer dozing next to her.

"Stop that," Reggie ordered, her voice sharper than she intended.

His fingers stilled. "What?"

"Hook it back up, please?" she requested more gently. "I should probably get going."

"It's early," he argued mildly. "Very early. Don't go yet. Have breakfast with me, Reggie." He kissed her neck while his hands went back to releasing the second of the five eyehooks that held her bustier in place.

"Don't, please," she pleaded. That worked. He stopped.

"Is everything all right?" he asked. "If you're upset about last night—"

"I'm not," she reassured him. "I'm fine. I just don't want you to do that." She should leave, Reggie knew that, but she couldn't fathom how she could get out of the bed, the room, or the situation with any part of her dignity intact.

"Okay, but . . ." He pulled her over, onto her back, so she was looking up at him as he leaned over her, propped up on an elbow. ". . . Will you stay?"

She slid back to sit up against the headboard, bringing the sheet with her so it covered her to her shoulders. She reached behind her and refastened the two hooks.

Langston watched her curiously. "What's the matter?"

"Are you going to order breakfast?" She tried to divert him while she cast about in her mind for an exit line.

"Yeah, sure," he said in answer to her question, but he didn't look away. He gazed at her so intently she began to think he saw right through her cool facade to the panic and desperation beneath.

So she was shocked when he asked, plaintively, "Why won't you let me look at you?" He gently tugged the sheet down, inch by inch. Reggie was mesmerized by the way his heated gaze traveled over the flesh he uncovered. The sheet fell to her waist, and he left it there. "You look great," he said, his voice hoarse with suppressed excitement. His obvious desire to make love again did not leave her unaffected. Reggie was pretty sure she should not allow herself to be seduced. Last night she had succumbed to an irresistible impulse. Even the prude within her could understand how she might lose her head after the excitement of the last few days. To consider repeating her mistake was something else again. In the cold light of day, the only sensible course of action was retreat. She should be gone already, but she couldn't turn and slide out of bed and walk away. She wasn't a good enough actress to pretend that sleeping with him was no big deal. She couldn't help it if he discovered she wasn't experienced at this kind of thing, but she was determined to show him that she could handle it gracefully. Her only recourse was to brazen it out.

In the spirit of her decision to be as detached and yet as true to herself as possible, she confessed in a self-effacing tone, "It's embarrassing wearing this thing." The black lace and silk covered a reinforced framework of wire that held her bust up like a ball gown from previous centuries. It left bare a large expanse of skin above her decolletage. Reggie felt self-conscious enough having him see her with the undergarment on. Without its support, she sagged, and she definitely didn't want him to see that.

He looked up into her face. "What's embarrassing about it?" he asked.

"I'm . . . It's so big." She started to cross her arms over her chest, but he took her hands in his and held them down. He leaned over and kissed her right above the swell of her breast. "I'm certainly not complaining."

She took advantage of their linked hands to pull him closer and kiss him. "I appreciate that. But some of us are not as . . . sure of ourselves as you are. There's this little thing called modesty. You may have heard of it."

"The Puritans invented it, right?" he teased.

"They perfected it, but it was around before that," she said determined to hold her own in this sophisticated word play.

He pretended to think about it for a moment. "I don't think I believe in it," he announced finally.

"You don't believe in modesty," she said dryly. "Why am I not surprised?"

"That wasn't nice," he said.

"You said it," she defended herself.

"I admit I'm not the most modest guy in the world, but it so happens I wasn't talking about me. You're a beautiful, sexy girl. You should flaunt it." Right then, she knew she was lost. When he turned that devastating charm on her, she could not resist him. Not in the cold light of day—or any other time.

"Hmm, flaunt it," she said thoughtfully.

"Flaunt, you know, show off. You may have heard of it."

Reggie shook her head. "Sorry. Don't think so. That's more your style."

"Woman, what am I going to do with you?"

"You could feed me. Like you promised."

"All right. I'll order breakfast." He telephoned room service and ordered two of everything on the breakfast menu.

"They said it will be half an hour to forty-five minutes. Any ideas on what we should do while we're waiting?" He grinned wickedly at her. Her resolve to keep her cool was abandoned. There was no way she could rebuild their friendly but distant former relationship. She didn't have it in her.

"Kiss me, you fool," Reggie said. "I always wanted to say that," she murmured against his warm mouth. Then she didn't say anything for quite some time as he explored her mouth thoroughly with his own. The heated rush of their lovemaking the night before had been a combustible force, beginning with a flaming match and ending in an explosion that left her breathless. This time Langston wooed her with his lips and teeth and tongue. And his hands. They were so big and hard, it was amazing that they could be so gentle and probing. He caressed her back, her stomach, her thighs. He touched her all over and she quivered in anticipation as he explored every inch of her body thoroughly.

She was gasping for breath when he raised his head and said, "I love kissing you, Reggie." His lips moved over her chest and down, where he nipped at the edge of the bustier with his teeth. "I want to kiss you here, too." He suckled her through satin and lace and the feel of his hot mouth combined with the heat of the fire he was stoking within her melted her resistance.

She couldn't believe that they were making love in the full light of day, with the curtains open and room service on the way. But his magician's hands played over her sensitive flesh and she was lost.

"Please?" he pleaded.

"Yes," she murmured.

He made quick work of unhooking and freeing her from the garment. While his lips moved over her face, her shoulders and, finally, her chest, his hands returned to her hips. He slid one hand between her thighs and found the most sensitive spot of all. He brought her to the brink of ecstasy with his skillful fingers and then filled her with himself and began the slow dance of passion with the intensity of the previous night. This time his controlled, deliberate movements kept her joined to him in passion for what seemed like forever.

Room service knocked at the door while she was still trying to catch her breath.

"One minute!" Langston called out. He rose, then went to the door and spoke through it. "Come next door to the other room." He left and closed the door between the adjoining rooms.

Reggie got out of bed and scooted into the bathroom, with his robe and her underwear in her hand. She wanted to take a quick shower and cover herself up without an argument from him.

She made her shower a quick one, covering her hair with the shower cap the hotel had thoughtfully provided. She emerged fully refreshed and revitalized, though she suspected she owed the surge of energy and her ravenous hunger more to Langston's mastery than to the water's powers of rejuvenation. She caught a glimpse of herself in the rather large mirror that covered the wall opposite the shower, but unfortunately, she didn't share Langston's ability to appreciate her nude body. To Reggie, her breasts, hips, and thighs looked flabby and unappealing and she quickly slid into the flattering underwear, which hid the worst of her flaws. She considered going out into the other room dressed only in the provocative lingerie, but decided she would feel more comfortable eating in front of him in the robe, which covered her from her neck to mid-calf. When she left the bathroom, she was surprised to find the bedroom empty and the door into the sitting room still closed. Even more curious was the low murmur of Langston's voice coming from the other room. She listened for a moment at the door, but couldn't hear anyone else in there. She assumed he was on the phone, but since she didn't want to intrude on a personal conversation, even a one-sided one, she only opened the door a few inches and peeked around it to get permission from Langston to enter.

Looking straight at her, from her seat on the couch, was an attractive older woman who, from the resemblance she bore to him, Reggie guessed must be Langston's mother. Mrs. Downs' mouth formed an "o" of surprise and Langston dropped his head into his hands.

"You might as well stop skulking behind that door and come out and meet me," the older woman said.

Langston came over and pulled the door from her nerveless fingers and ushered her into the room. "Mama, I'd like you to meet Regina Primm. Reggie, this is my mother, Tricia Downs." Mrs. Downs bent her head in a regal nod of greeting.

Reggie finally found her tongue. "It's nice to meet you, Mrs. Downs." She walked forward and, gathering her shattered dignity about her like a cloak, she offered the woman her hand.

"Reggie?" She looked surprised and somewhat pleased as she shook Reggie's hand. "My son told me about you. You're the publicist?"

"Yes, ma'am." She held the robe closed at her throat, wondering whether to excuse herself from the room and return dressed. Maybe she could just sneak out the bedroom door and forget the whole embarrassing scene.

"Tea?" Mrs. Downs offered.

"Mmm, sure." Reggie sat down very carefully so that the white terrycloth robe she wore wouldn't expose a millimeter of skin. Room service had delivered their breakfast while she was in the bathroom, and she couldn't keep her eyes from straying to the heavily laden table while Mrs. Downs poured the tea. Langston and his mother had apparently already partaken of the spread. Her stomach rumbled embarrassingly loudly and Langston's mother asked, "Would you like a bit to eat with that?"

"Oh, I—" Reggie began to protest.

"Please do. There's plenty here. My son seems to have quite an appetite this morning."

Reggie didn't know how much he told his mother about his love life, but Mrs. Downs didn't seem shocked to find a woman in his hotel suite dressed only in a robe, so she wasn't exactly a prude. Whether that note of levity in her voice was aimed at Reggie or her son, Reggie couldn't know.

Langston didn't look at either of them.

"Thank you," she said to the elegantly attired woman. Mrs. Downs had a high forehead, like her son, which gave her a patrician air, and a long square face which was almost as attractive on her as it was on him. She was tall and very large-boned and wore a beautiful caped dress in a bright turquoise and teal print material. She had to be in her late fifties or early sixties, since Langston's oldest sister was in her early forties, but Patricia Downs didn't even look fifty. Her smooth café au lait skin was only complemented by expensive, tasteful makeup that Reggie envied and admired.

"A croissant? And some fruit perhaps." She didn't wait for an answer but put a portion on a small plate and handed it to Reggie.

"So, you're the one who's arranged all the interviews and the seminar at the university. Langston said it went quite well."

"It did," Reggie confirmed.

"I'm so pleased that you got him into a classroom again. I've been trying to convince him to go back to school, but . . ." Her voice trailed off when she looked up at Langston, but when Reggie followed her gaze, she couldn't see anything in Langston's expression that could have stopped Mrs. Downs in midsentence. He had an impassive expression that Reggie couldn't read at all. "Anyway," she continued. "I understand you've been trying to hold him off. Without much success, I see." Reggie choked on a bite of croissant. "Don't feel bad. He can be very persuasive." Langston coughed. Again his mother looked at him and subsided. Reggie met his conspiratorial gaze and raised eyebrows and could almost hear him thinking, *We're going to laugh about this later.*

"Umm, yes," Reggie stammered. Apparently, Langston and his mother were *very* close. She couldn't imagine telling her mother about the men she dated. At least, not since junior high school.

"I've embarrassed you. I'm sorry," Tricia Downs apologized. "It's just so refreshing to meet a woman who is more interested in Langston's mind than his body. Not that it's not a great body."

"Mom!" he exclaimed. He sounded as shocked by his mother's comment as Reggie felt, and he looked embarrassed for the first time since she'd come into the room. She was less surprised by the content of Mrs. Downs' speech than by the manner in which the older woman spoke. She casually mentioned her son's body as though it came up in conversation every day.

Perhaps when one's son was a sexy superstar, it did.

"How about changing the subject?" Langston requested, though his tone made it clear it was more of a demand.

"What would you like to discuss, son?" she asked.

"Something else. Anything else," he said. "How long are you here for?"

"I thought I'd stay a few days," she said. "Take in a few of the local . . . sights. Perhaps Ms. Primm will be kind enough to suggest an itinerary."

"Certainly, Mrs. Downs," Reggie agreed.

"Please call me Tricia. And I can't call you Ms. Primm. It sounds so old-fashioned."

"Regina or Reggie. Whichever you prefer."

"Good. Now that we've got that settled, I think I need to freshen up. Where is the . . . ?"

"Through that door there, Mama," Langston supplied. "It's only a half bath though."

"That'll be fine," Tricia said, and left them.

They stared at each other, Reggie in shock. "Did you expect her to visit?"

"Not at all," he said. "She doesn't usually jet in to see me. I wonder what she's really here for?"

Reggie had a sneaking suspicion that Patricia Downs might just have come out here to look her over.

"What did you tell her about me?" she whispered.

"Not much." He shrugged. "You know, just the usual."

"You usually tell your mother that you're interested in women that are . . . what did she call it . . . holding you off?"

"Well, not exactly." He thought back. "She said it sounded like you were a nice woman, and had I asked you out, so I told her about you not dating clients. She said that was sensible, and I said you were sensible, and she said I didn't know enough sensible women, and I think that was it."

It sounded innocuous enough. Tricia could not have thought Reggie was some kind of man-eater from whom she had to defend her son—not with that description. Reggie didn't imag-

ine the woman would fly halfway across the country just to see
a sensible woman who, as far as she knew, was *not* sleeping
with her son.

Mrs. Downs was probably accustomed to seeing Langston
with his lovers anyway. She had barely raised an eyebrow when
Reggie emerged from his bedroom, although she seemed a little
cold at first. But it didn't take her long to drop the formality
and speak to Reggie as if she'd known her for much longer than
just the last few minutes. Reggie found it endearing.

Reggie wondered what her mother would have said if Langston walked out of her bathroom for breakfast dressed only in
a robe. Jenny Primm was quite earthy. Reggie didn't think her
mother would have been quite as nonchalant as his mother was
about finding her daughter in the robe of a man she barely knew,
but Jennifer Primm was no prude. She might lecture and advise,
but she didn't preach. She did believe in speaking out and being
honest. She would never say anything to intentionally wound
someone else, but other than that, she didn't censor herself. She
spoke very frankly to Reggie and her siblings about her sex life
with their father and her children all knew they could speak with
her about every intimate detail of their lives. Reggie never really
discussed sex with her mother, except in general terms. Neither
did her brothers and sisters until they had children, at which
time, they told Reggie, it became so difficult to find the time
and energy for sex that *any* advice was welcome, even if it came
from Mom.

If she had to make a guess about her mother's possible reaction to this situation, she supposed Jennifer Primm would be
tolerant, if somewhat shocked. She might even be amused, just
as Tricia appeared to be. In fact, Langston's mother's urge to
feed her, the tone of voice Tricia used, even the forthright comments about her son, all reminded Reggie of her own mother.

Mrs. Downs emerged from the bathroom already talking.
"Langston, I like this hotel, but you should really tell the front
desk you are not to be disturbed when you have overnight guests.
I could pop up anywhere." Reggie couldn't help it. She liked
the woman.

"Next time I will, Moms," Langston assured her. "More coffee?"

"No, thank you, son." She turned to Reggie and said conspiratorially, "The best thing about being ah hem . . . over fifty, is having grown children who can wait on you hand and foot, if you need them to. Or even if you just want them to. It's wonderful."

"I can see how that could make it all worthwhile," Reggie said, smiling.

"Don't let her con you," Langston warned. "She has kindly allowed us to wait on her for as long as I can remember."

"It's a good thing I did, too. I trained all my children to treat their loved ones right. This one left home so young, I wasn't sure it would stick, but he never got too full of himself to listen to his mama. So I must have done something right. All those people fawning over him, and those football players trying to lead him off the straight and narrow, and he's still a good boy. Don't you think I trained him well?" she asked Reggie.

"I'm not sure I—" Reggie spluttered.

"That's okay," Tricia said gently. "I didn't mean to put you on the spot."

"Thank you."

"Yes, thank you, Mama. Now, why don't we change the subject," Langston suggested.

"Okay," Mrs. Downs agreed easily enough. "My son tells me he enjoys working with you," she said addressing Reggie once again. "You own your own company?"

"Yes." Reggie breathed a little easier. She liked to talk about her work. "Langston has been a joy to work with."

"Um hmmm," Tricia murmured encouragingly.

Reggie tried, and failed, to detect any sarcasm in the sound. "He is used to appearing in public, unlike a lot of my clients."

"Who do you usually work for?"

"Writers. And it's a funny thing about that," Reggie said, warming to her theme. "Most authors are not used to selling themselves. It's easy to understand . . . their work is done in private, and most have to struggle to find the time and the solitude—get away from their family and friends—to work in peace.

It's a paradox. They need an audience to whom they can communicate their thoughts and feelings and experiences but in order to create, they are constantly turning off the phone and hiding away from everyone. It makes a lot of my clients seem a little neurotic, but I guess you need to be a bit neurotic to think people will be interested in what you have to say anyway," Reggie finished, a bit breathlessly.

"Ah ha," Tricia said, nodding. "Funny." But she didn't sound like she got the joke.

"My mother is a writer," Langston announced.

Reggie winced. "I didn't mean to imply . . ."

"No, no. It's true." The older woman waved her hand, negating her apology. "I never thought of myself as neurotic, but I suppose you could say . . ."

"It explains a lot," Langston chimed in.

"I spend a lot of time with authors, and I don't mean to say that they are all—"

"Nuts?" Tricia finished for her. "Why not? Most people are."

Reggie looked helplessly at Langston, hoping he could dig her out of the mess she'd landed herself in, but he was barely suppressing his laughter at the situation. She glared at him.

"Reggie is an expert on Seattle, Moms. Why don't you get her to suggest some places you might like to visit while you're here?" he finally managed to add to the conversation.

"Thank you, son." Her reply was dignified, but if Reggie didn't miss her guess, Langston was going to be punished for his levity. She felt a twinge of satisfaction at the thought. He had gotten her into this.

If she had to break her own rule about sleeping with a client, and if she had to break it with the most important client she ever had, and if she had to make this choice after knowing the man only a few days, and if she had to be discovered the morning after by his mother, in his robe—at least she was grateful that his mother was someone she liked and respected. But when Reggie was alone, on her way home, that was the only positive development in the whole affair.

Reggie didn't even tell Bebe about her lapse, and she always told Bebe everything. But she couldn't confide in her friend about this. She was too unsure of her own thoughts and feelings. Being with Langston was great. Not because he was a movie star, or because he was so beautiful, but because Langston acted as though being together was the most natural thing in the world. Reggie had to admit she felt the same way. It was as if she had found the exact person she'd been intended to make love to all along. They fit.

In a way it was a revelation. She had never been so comfortable with anyone before. But it was also disconcerting. He was so compatible in some ways, but so completely unsuitable in every way that counted. Maybe every woman who slept with him ended up feeling exactly like this? She had never been with anyone really famous before, so she had no basis for comparison. On the other hand, this was a first for her and that was valuable. Wasn't it? The way he made her feel, these sensations, were so rare and different from anything she had felt in the past. Perhaps she owed it to herself to find out what came next.

Reggie argued with herself all day, but in the end, she knew it couldn't go on. It just didn't fit her picture of her life, her image of herself, or any of her plans. She couldn't justify the risk she would be taking if she pursued a relationship with a man she barely knew. She didn't even know if he was interested in a relationship. If he were, she told herself, she would find out soon enough. They had work to do, together. And there was his mother, and her promise to call her about sight-seeing. He was well and truly ensconced in her life. Reggie wasn't sure at the moment if that made her happy, or sad.

Eleven

Langston had only one desire, which was to make love to Regina Primm until neither of them could move a muscle. Unfortunately, his mother's surprise visit had put an end to that little fantasy, and try as he might, he couldn't figure out a way to recreate the intimate atmosphere Mama destroyed with her unexpected entrance—especially not while she remained in town, in his hotel, only a few doors away. A repeat of Friday morning's awkward encounter seemed all too likely.

Reggie left on Friday morning shortly before his mother did, but she had already promised to call Tricia as soon as she got home to discuss which sights were most worth seeing. His mother made a date to meet her that afternoon, to go shopping and sight-seeing and it was through Patricia Downs that Reggie sent the message that she would not be accompanying him to the screening of the film for the regional distributor that afternoon. That evening, too, she left him alone with the co-producer and the director of *Under His Skin* for a charity dinner. She met them there, but she refused, straight out, to sit at their table. When he insisted, she said she felt guilty sitting in one of the thousand dollar a plate seats the production company had purchased.

"We don't even have ten people in our party. There are extra seats," he tried to convince her.

"Better to give the money and not eat the meal, and then that much more will go to charity, right?" she said brightly, then slipped away. He couldn't complain that she wasn't doing her job—there was a limo waiting for him when he was ready to go home.

He confronted her every chance he had. The moment they were alone—which in his opinion was any time they weren't actively engaged in conversation with a third party—he tried to force her to discuss the incredible encounter of the night before. But Reggie wasn't talking. She kept agreeing that they needed to discuss what had happened, but she didn't share his view of the proper time and place—which was wherever they were together and as soon as possible.

"When!?" he asked each time.

"Later," was all she would answer.

He couldn't even accuse her of neglecting him. The producers had arranged an interview for him with a morning television show before they'd even hired Reggie, which was a large part of the reason he'd been brought to Seattle in the first place. That interview was scheduled for Saturday morning. Originally, he knew she'd planned to accompany him to the studio where they broadcast the program, but since it hadn't been made through her contacts, Reggie asked him if he could handle it on his own. Langston couldn't very well say that he didn't think he could. He wanted to impress her with his ability to satisfy her every desire, not to make her life more difficult and certainly not to convince her that he was a complete imbecile.

Reggie spent Saturday giving his mother the grand tour of Seattle including a ride home for him. Then she offered to drive them to her mother's barbecue the next day. It was on Sunday afternoon at her mother's barbecue before he had his first real chance to pull Reggie aside and talk with her, but not until he'd spent a good two hours speaking with her mother, her brother Johnny and her two sisters, Virginia and Olivia, and meeting their children. Not that he didn't enjoy meeting her family. Tricia and Jennifer Primm hit it off right away, and huddled together talking quietly while their children got acquainted. He found them an unassuming, loving, entertaining lot.

"Wow! You look even better in real life than you do on the screen. Reggie, I can't believe you brought Langston Downs to our house," Virginia gushed. She was a slimmer version of her sister, who was only a couple of years older than her.

"Whose house?" asked her husband Manny. He was a football fan and was eager to sit and talk with Langston, but not, apparently, under false pretenses.

"Mom's house," she clarified, adding, "but I grew up here, so I can call it mine."

"Sure, hon," Manny said, sharing a look of amusement with Langston. But when she ordered him to take their toddler to the bathroom, he obeyed her without a moment's hesitation. Although they were clearly not newlyweds—with a two-year-old, Ginnie, toddling about—their devotion to each other was apparent. He watched them and imagined how it could be between himself and Reggie.

He was so excited by the thought, he actually whispered to her. "That could be us."

"Virginia and I only look alike," was her bland response.

He guessed from that that she identified more with her older sister, Olivia, who also had a husband and two children, although her kids were not there. "I love my girls," Olivia said. "But we didn't bring them—for your own safety. They are entering that obnoxious prepubescent stage when they'll do anything for attention, especially from a handsome older man who also happens to be a movie star. It's an awkward age, twelve to twenty-two."

"I told her you were probably used to it, bein' a football hero," her husband Evan drawled. He had a thick Southern accent, and didn't seem to fit in with the family really. "But it's mainly boys that follow football, right?" he asked, starting off a round of debate about girls and boys in which he was the lone advocate for the theory that the sexes were equal but different. Langston kept his mouth shut, as this was obviously an issue the family often debated.

Reggie told him that John was a civil rights lawyer, his wife Lucy proudly proclaimed herself a homemaker, Virginia and Manny were accountants who shared their high-paying job so they could share the child-rearing duties, and Olivia was following in their mother's footsteps as a social worker. Evan was a shipbuilder, and the blue-collar job, combined with his accent and his old-fashioned viewpoint, put him in a different category, in Langston's mind, from the rest of this middle-class black family. But he and Olivia seemed perfectly content to agree to disagree. Though she joined in the argument against her husband, she clearly felt he had a right to his opinion, making her the only member of the family who thought so. Langston hoped Reggie did identify more closely with Olivia than with her younger sister. As well-matched as Virginia and Manny appeared to be, Langston would rather have Reggie treat him with the tolerance Olivia had for Evan than with the air of satisfied ownership that Virginia displayed toward her husband.

Johnny's marriage to his high-school sweetheart, Lucy, was as traditional as could be, and they had a cute little five-year-old, Freddy, who was as big a fan as his father. Langston enjoyed getting to know the little boy as much as he enjoyed meeting the older members of the family.

"Are you going to marry Aunt Reggie?" Freddy asked, his mouth full of hot dog and dripping ketchup.

"Wahoo, Freddy boy," his uncle, Evan, exclaimed, as he actually slapped his knee. "That's not somethin' you ask a man— 'specially not in front of the lady in question."

"Why not?" Freddy asked, as he'd been doing for the last hour.

"It's what's known as a delicate subject," his uncle tried to explain.

"It's grown-up talk," Olivia interjected. "And none of your business, young man."

"But Mommy and Daddy were talking about it," Freddy piped in his high little voice.

"Go play with your cousin," Lucy commanded. Freddy took one look at his mother and quickly obeyed, his little legs pumping away.

"Sorry about that, Mo," Manny said, embarrassed. "Where do kids get these crazy ideas?"

His wife wasn't as tactful. "From their parents, apparently," Virginia chimed in.

"We didn't say you were getting married," Lucy said defending herself.

"You told him we were just working together, right?" Reggie asked her sister-in-law with a martial gleam in her eye.

"Not exactly," Lucy answered. "I told him what you always tell me. His Aunt Reggie isn't interested in getting married."

Evan tried to change the subject. "Look, honey, Freddy's trying to give little Ginnie a piggyback ride. Isn't that cute?"

"Forget it," Manny advised his brother-in-law. "The kid could be playing with a gun and they wouldn't notice. The three of them have been on the phone every day since Reggie got this gig, speculating. They're not about to let her out of here without some answers—or at least the benefit of their advice."

The women ignored their husbands. "What does Darrell think about you working with Langston Downs?" Lucy asked.

"I don't know. I didn't ask his opinion," Reggie said soberly. "Can we drop this?"

"Does he know about it?" Olivia probed.

"I doubt it. I haven't talked to him lately," Reggie said. "I'm serious now, it's time to change the subject," she added with an air of finality.

But her sisters were not finished. "What *are* you going to say to him?" Virginia pressed.

Reggie kept her cool. "About what?"

"You and Langston," Lucy said impatiently. "He's bound to wonder how he measures up compared to a movie star."

"There is no comparison to be made. Darrell is an old friend. Langston is a client. One thing has nothing to do with the other."

"Take it from me, he won't see it that way. His fragile male ego will be threatened by this," Virginia insisted.

"Reggie, you better come up with something better than this 'strictly business' routine for him," Olivia said.

"I don't have to explain myself to Darrell Hunt or anyone else," she said, looking pointedly from one sister to the other. "I don't owe him anything."

"After fifteen years of even the most casual dates, I think the man feels a little more than friendship," Olivia opined.

"I'm sure it will be fine, thanks," Reggie dismissed her concern. "Now this subject is closed."

Langston was amused, but he had one thing on his mind, and one thing only. He wanted to be alone with Reggie, even if it did start more talk about the two of them among her siblings.

After a lively debate about who was going to clean the grill, which Reggie's mother won by refusing all insincere offers of help from her loving children, in what was clearly a family tradition, Reggie ended up following Jenny into the kitchen. Langston gathered the bowls of leftover food and said to no one in particular, "I think I'll help clear. Shall I take these inside?" He trailed after the other two women, his arms full in a transparent attempt to hide his true purpose in following her, which the others acknowledged by ignoring him completely.

He was in time to hear Reggie say to her mother, "Maybe you should go to a specialist, Mom?"

"My doctor sent me to an ophthalmologist and a special surgeon," Jenny said. "I will be going to a nutritionist in order to re-evaluate my eating habits, which may be helpful, but otherwise, there is nothing to be done."

"What about surgery?" Reggie asked.

"It's not operable, yet. The new laser surgeries could be used, but not unless . . . or until . . . it gets worse."

"Mom, I can't believe you're so blasé about this. I'm sorry, but I'm terrified."

"Don't worry, baby. It's not as if I'm going blind. Changing my diet should help a lot, the doctor said. That's not so terrible. I feel fine."

"All right," Reggie said.

She hugged her mother, who kissed her on the cheek and said, "Langston Downs, stop lurking in that doorway."

He stepped into the room. "Hey, Jenny, how's it going?"

"Fine, just fine. You can help this one here with that disgusting grill. I'm going back outside to find your mother and have a nice little chat." She winked at him. "I'll keep her out of your hair."

Reggie was quiet, already at work covering the bowls of food he had brought in with him when the older woman left.

"Finally, I've got you where you can't run away, and we won't be interrupted," he said.

"What makes you think that?"

"No one else is going to come in here," he said definitely. "In case you haven't noticed, they've all got us paired off already. Even Freddy."

"I noticed, but that doesn't mean we need to confirm their suspicions by hiding here in the kitchen."

"We're not hiding. We're . . . uh . . . cleaning the grill."

"Ha!" she snorted. "They'll never believe that one."

"We'll just make it true then," he said. He put the heavy iron grill in the sink, poured soap over it, closed the drain and started the water running. "We should probably let it soak for a few minutes, don't you think?"

She shook her head at him, reprovingly. "Langston."

"Let's sit. And talk," he said. "While we wait."

"All right, you've got it. Let's."

Although she seemed a little distracted, he was surprised at how easy it had been, in the end. Then Langston realized he had only one thing to say to her, and it wasn't, he didn't think, what she wanted to hear.

Since she was sitting, silent and motionless as a statue, he jumped in anyway. "Reggie, Thursday night was incredible."

"Uh huh," she said impassively, as if he had just commented on the weather.

"I know you didn't think it was a good idea, but it felt right to me. And I think we should start seeing each other. If not now, then maybe when you're no longer working for Spirit Productions. I don't want to walk away from this."

"This what?" she asked.

"This. Us," he answered, waving a hand between them as if tracing an invisible thread connecting their bodies.

"There is nothing between us but one night. We've known each other less than a week," she said gently. "And we have nothing in common. A week from now, you're going to be going home to Los Angeles. How exactly do you propose we 'see' each other then?"

"I don't have to get right back to L.A. I can stay for a little while. After that, we can work it out. Lots of people have long-distance relationships. Won't you at least think about it before you shoot me down?" Langston was encouraged by her calm, considering expression. He had expected her to be angry or resentful because they broke the rules. He thought she would blame him for that. But apparently, she didn't.

She was talking logistics, and that was something he could deal with. He hadn't been a quarterback for ten years without figuring out how to tackle a problem, even a seemingly insurmountable dilemma. If he'd gotten through her defenses, he could handle the rest of it.

"Langston, I know you think I'm unreasonable, but I don't really see this going anywhere. Great sex is great, and that night with you was a fantasy come true, but it wasn't reality. I can't pretend it was, or that it ever could be. Do you really think we can build on what is only, if you face the facts, a passing attraction between two virtual strangers?"

"Why not? Doesn't almost every relationship develop from a mutual attraction between virtual strangers?" he said, a little hurt that she would reduce one of the greatest nights of his life into just another one-night stand. For her, as she made clear, it was a night with a movie star. But he supposed that jumping into bed with someone after only four days made the lovemaking, technically, less than loving. She couldn't be blamed for thinking that that was what he wanted. She probably thought he did things like that all the time. True, she'd been the one to initiate the encounter, but he definitely talked her into it. "It's getting to know the person that makes it more than just sex," he said to himself as much as to her. Once she knew that he wasn't just some horny sex symbol who couldn't sleep alone, she would understand that they meant more to him than a casual fling.

"We're working together for the rest of this week. That's the end date on my contract with your production company. I'll think about it," she conceded. "Will that satisfy you?"

He had to restrain himself from answering with some sexually charged innuendo. She already thought he was controlled by his hormones. "How about this for a deadline?" he proposed. "A date, Friday night. You and me. Dinner? A movie? Bowling? Whatever. We can decide then."

"Do you think that's necessary? I already know what your decision will be," she said, smiling wryly.

"You never know," he teased. "I've been pumping your family for information, and they've told me some very interesting things about you. I'm not at all sure anymore that my mother's right."

"Why?" she asked. "What did your mother say?"

"That you're a doll, and I should snatch you up before you get away."

"Oh . . ." she mused. "So that's why you've been doing all of this. Just following orders."

"She trained me well," he retorted. "Between my sisters and my mom, I've been pummeled like a steak till I'm tender, molded like dough into the perfect gingerbread man, and stretched like a worn pair of jeans so I'm capable of a far more comfortable fit than women generally expect from the average man.

"Nice analogies. Did you just make that up?" she asked, smiling.

Actually his sisters had spent last Thanksgiving tormenting him with these and other reasons why his fame really belonged to them. "No," he admitted. "I just thought you might enjoy it."

"I did."

Her sister Lucy's son, Freddy, came into the kitchen just then. "My mom said you'd play catch with me," he announced. Then he remembered to add. "Please?"

"Sure," Langston agreed, laughing.

When they rejoined the others outside, Lucy said, "Sorry, he got away from me. I hope he didn't interrupt anything."

"That's okay," Reggie said, glaring at her.

"No problem," Langston assured her. "I like to play catch. Especially when I'm asked so politely." He winked at Freddy, who laughed and then ran straight into him. Langston caught him and swung him up into the air, which made the boy scream. The adults winced, but the other two children came running up or, in the two-year-old's case, toddling up.

"Can I have a turn?"

"Me, next."

"No, me."

While he played with the children, Virginia made up with Reggie. Langston watched them and eavesdropped from a distance. "You have to be careful what you say, because they always repeat it at the most awkward times," Virginia said. "This morning in church, Ginnie said a very bad four-letter word in front of the pastor. She didn't know what it meant, and everyone laughed, but I never even realized I said that word in front of her."

"That's because maybe y'awl didn't say anythin' like that," Evan drawled. "They get a lot of that stuff from television."

Olivia joined in. "I remember one time when the girls were three and four, they decided to run out in the front yard naked and scream every naughty word they ever heard."

"I remember that," Reggie said, nodding. "They didn't know what the words meant so they ran around yelling damn, dooty, pee pee, kaka, effing . . ."

Virginia was laughing, "That was mine, effing, back when I wanted to be a good example for my big sister's kids."

"Me, too," Reggie said. "But we weren't fooling them. The funniest thing was that mixed up in the expletives were a couple of words that they thought were obscenities which were just ordinary words. Sugar was one, I remember—I guess because Olivia didn't want them eating it. I don't remember all of them, but my personal favorite was 'wearsvemoteuntol' which meant 'where's the remote control,' which somebody yelled a lot in their house." She looked at Evan, who grinned back, shrugging.

Everyone was laughing, and Olivia took advantage of the bonhomie to ask, "So what is the story with you and Langston?"

Virginia and Johnny gave each other a look anyone with siblings could interpret. Langston read it easily even from a few feet away. "Goodie, they're at it again, and we didn't even have to do anything."

Manny, Lucy and Evan just looked on as Reggie shot a glance at Olivia that could have leveled a redwood. "Langston is a client."

"And . . ." Olivia pushed it.

"Doesn't your work provide enough opportunities to butt into other people's private lives?"

"Sure, but you need more help than they do."

"Okay, now," Evan said soothingly. "Olivia, do you want a drink, honey?"

She refused to be diverted. "No, thank you."

"I think Langston and I should be going now," Reggie said.

"Oh don't go, Reggie," Johnny said. "Livy will shut up now, won't you?" He looked threateningly at his younger sister.

"Okay," she agreed grudgingly.

"O-kay!" Virginia echoed, more enthusiastically.

"No more questions," Reggie warned them.

"No problem."

"I'll keep 'em out of your hair," Johnny promised.

The kids kept them all busy for a while after that, and when the sun started to go down, everyone started to get ready to go. Langston took advantage of the parents' preoccupation with collecting their children's baggage to murmur in Reggie's ear, "They know you're hiding something."

"It's none of their business," she said without rancor.

"You shouldn't lie to them. They're your family," he warned.

"I wasn't lying. You are a client and that's all," she said firmly.

"I thought we were friends," Langston replied.

"We are," she said, flustered.

"We are what?" he prompted.

"We are friends." She smiled. "Just friends," she added.

"So far," he said and winked.

Twelve

Although Reggie had given them a ride to her mother's house, it was her brother John who took Langston and his mother back to the hotel. She gratefully accepted his offer when he said he had to go that way anyway. Reggie took the opportunity to stay with her mother that evening, waiting for her sisters and their families to leave so that they could speak further about her medical condition without fear of interruption. Her mother hadn't told the rest of the family, and Reggie didn't want to betray her confidence, but she also wanted to know more so she could do something. She felt impotent and confused, and she hated it.

The situation with Langston didn't help her mood. He was trying to manipulate her and she couldn't seem to outmaneuver him. She gained a little time with their chat that day, but all she really did was to delay a future confrontation. At least she didn't have to deal with it until the end of the week. She had five more days to dazzle Seattle with Langston Downs' charm and charisma. Meanwhile, hopefully she could inure herself to it. Perhaps exposure to him would cure her of the absurd feelings she had for him. He seemed determined to get to know her. She would get to know all about him as well. Once she knew all his faults and foibles, she hoped he wouldn't be so attractive to her. Or maybe she could just wait him out. She didn't think he'd keep this up for long. It was not exactly a foolproof plan, but it was the best she could come up with.

Her mother interrupted her musing. "Reggie, you really have to stop worrying about me. This isn't the end of the world. It isn't even a real emergency. It happened so gradually, I didn't even notice it until the doctor checked my eyes. I am very lucky. I still have over eighty percent of my range of vision."

Reggie needed glasses from the time she was five years old. She still resented wearing contact lenses. She couldn't truly comprehend her mother's acceptance of this catastrophe. She could never accept losing any more of her sight. But Jennifer Primm made it clear that she didn't want any sympathy.

"Is there anything I can do?" Reggie asked, trying a proactive approach.

"No, but thank you. You will just have to accept this, baby. I have a great life and no regrets. This couldn't be helped."

"I want to grow up to be just like you," Reggie said, only half joking.

"I hope you will." But there was a note in her mother's voice that Reggie hadn't heard before. A trace of doubt.

"I'm working on it, Mama," she assured her.

"Langston seems like a good man. He seems very down to earth."

"Earthy. That describes him all right," Reggie said sarcastically.

"Why are you being so hard on him?" she questioned.

"I guess it's because I'm off duty. I don't have to wax poetic about the man on my own time."

"It seems like more than that?" she probed.

"Everyone likes him. My friends, my family, everybody we meet. Which is great for business, but it makes me feel like I have to provide some balance. Remind myself that he's not really *all* that."

"Why? What can it hurt to think of him as exactly what he seems to be?"

"Well, umm," Reggie stuttered. "He'd be too perfect. Too hard to resist."

"So why resist?" her mother asked.

Reggie's mouth dropped open. She was shocked. "You would approve?"

"I've always encouraged my girls to go after what they want.

That includes the men they're interested in. Why should this be any different?"

"Because he's different. He's . . . Langston Downs." She was stammering again.

"There's some strong chemistry between you two."

"You never pushed me about Darrell or any of my other boy-friends. Why now? Why Langston?"

"You didn't return Darrell's feelings. I can think of a few men who have been interested in you, but you never really seemed to reciprocate. This one you care for."

"What woman wouldn't want him? Of course I'm interested. But you, of all people, can't expect me to . . . to . . . have an affair with him."

"I don't see why not," Jenny said, as unexcited as if they were talking about which color sheets Reggie chose to put on her bed rather than the man whom she would be sharing that bed with. "You obviously like him. I like him. As you said, so does everybody else. And he likes you. What's the problem?"

"I can't even think where to begin," Reggie said, deflated. Even her own mother was on his side. What magical power did this man possess?

"We know every skeleton in his closet and there's nothing there that can't be excused. I think he has potential."

"Potential for what?" Reggie asked.

"Son-in-law potential."

Reggie stared at her in disbelief at this bombshell. "You think he wants to get married? To *me?*"

"Of course not. He's only known you a week. But he's clearly infatuated. He can't take his eyes off of you," she said with the blind faith of a proud mother.

"But, Mama, men like Langston do not get serious about women like me," she argued.

"Of course they do. They love women exactly like you. Don't sell yourself short, Reggie," was her motherly counsel.

"I'll try not to," Reggie said faintly. "I should probably get home now. Tomorrow's going to be a busy day."

"All right, baby. I'll talk to you in the morning," Jenny said complacently.

Reggie left her mother's house in a haze. She didn't even remember driving home. She got ready for bed automatically. But once between the sheets, she couldn't sleep. Her thoughts ricocheted between Langston's proposition and her mother's unexpected advice.

Why not? they had both said, more than once.

Why not indeed? she said to her ceiling tiles. But the reasons were myriad. Langston Downs was rich and famous and sought after by the most beautiful women in the world. She couldn't compete with that, even if she wanted to. On the other hand . . . it didn't seem like she had to worry about that. For some unknowable reason, he wanted her. And if eventually he missed seeing a beautiful face staring back at him from across the breakfast table, she could handle that. It wasn't as if she were in love. She had only known him for a week. But she did like him a lot and that was a decent basis for dating a guy. For all she knew, they might only have the one "date." He said he could stay, but she didn't know if he would. If he did stay, perhaps the attraction would fade. Maybe he would turn out to be the kind of guy who had to have every woman he met. Or maybe he would turn out to be the man of her dreams, and he would make her fall in love with him and then leave her. Maybe, maybe, maybe.

Reggie had a lot more questions than answers, but three hours later she had decided to go out on the date with him on Friday, despite all her reservations. The only question that remained when she woke up in the morning was whether to wait until Friday to let him know, or to tell him right away.

It was probably a good idea, for the sake of her business, to avoid even the hint of impropriety until her contract with Spirit Productions ended. But then she would have to be with him all day, every day, with no outlet for her pent-up emotions. Then again, anticipation was a great pleasure. Reggie was the kind of woman who bought her Christmas tree weeks before the event, and then saved every present she received under the tree to open on Christmas morning.

On the pro side for playing a waiting game was Langston's very good suggestion that they actually get to know each other. She didn't have to commit herself, yet. Perhaps more importantly, Langston was willing to wait, and that had to mean something. She hoped it meant that he understood her reservations, even if he didn't share them. That would be nice. It would be even better if it meant what he said it meant—that he didn't see her as a one-night stand, but as a girlfriend. She giggled as she got dressed. Langston Downs' girlfriend. Whoever would have thought that she, Porky Pie, could grow up to date the sexiest black man in America. Reggie wasn't sure she could wait.

She waited until that evening, after work. He had done the Morning Show without her as she requested, but she was waiting for him when he finished up, and she took him to dinner.

"This is a nice surprise," he said as he looked around at "their" coffee shop.

"You seemed to enjoy the cuisine here," she said, waving airily at the paper-plate specials still pasted on the wall opposite the counter. "I thought you might want to come back and try something new, or eat the pig-out special again."

"I think it's romantic," he said.

Reggie nearly spit out her coffee. "Romantic?"

"You could say we had our first date here," he pointed out casually.

"I hadn't thought of it like that," she replied. One of the reasons she brought him back here was because this was the spot where she'd first felt they were going to be friends.

"Of course not," he said knowingly.

"Really," she insisted.

"Okay, okay," he said, but she could tell he didn't believe her. She decided right then and there to let him wait until Friday before she told him her decision. It might make him a little less arrogant if he had to wait.

"So what looks good to you?" she asked.

After they had ordered, they talked about work, the film, and the past week. He was so attentive, and his eyes were so beautiful, that Reggie was starting to feel she might have been a bit hasty in making her decision when Langston asked, "Are we anywhere near the Blue Room?"

"No," she said, then asked suspiciously, "Why?

An important message from the ARABESQUE Editor

Dear Arabesque Reader,

Because you've chosen to read one of our Arabesque romance novels, we'd like to say "thank you"! And, as a special way to thank you, we've selected four more of the books you love so well to send you for only $1.99.

Please enjoy them with our compliments, and thank you for continuing to enjoy Arabesque...the soul of romance.

Karen Thomas
Senior Editor,
Arabesque Romance Novels

SPECIAL OFFER!
4 BOOKS FOR ONLY $1.99

ARABESQUE
A PRODUCT OF
BET BOOKS

Check out our website at www.arabesquebooks.com

3 QUICK STEPS
TO RECEIVE YOUR "THANK YOU" GIFT
FROM THE EDITOR

Send back this card and you'll receive 4 Arabesque novels!
These books have a combined cover price of $20.00 or more,
but they are yours to keep for a mere $1.99.

There's no catch. You're under no obligation to buy anything.
We charge only $1.99 for the books (plus $1.50 for shipping
and handling, a total of $3.49). And you don't have to make
any minimum number of purchases—not even one!

We hope that after receiving your books you'll want to
remain an Arabesque subscriber. But the choice is yours to
continue or cancel, anytime at all! So why not take us up on
our invitation to receive 4 Arabesque Romance Novels, with
no risk of any kind. You'll be glad you did!

Call us
TOLL-FREE
at 1-888-345-BOOK

THE EDITOR'S "THANK YOU" GIFT INCLUDES:

- 4 books delivered for only $1.99 (plus $1.50 for shipping and handling)
- A FREE newsletter, *Arabesque Romance News*, filled with author interviews, book previews, special offers, and more!
- No risks or obligations. You're free to cancel whenever you wish... with no questions asked.

BOOK CERTIFICATE

Yes! Please send me 4 Arabesque books for $1.99 (+ $1.50 for shipping & handling, a total of $3.49). I understand I am under no obligation to purchase any books, as explained on the back of this card.

Name _____

Address _____ Apt. _____

City _____ State _____ Zip _____

Telephone ( ) _____

Signature _____

Offer limited to one per household and not valid to current subscribers. All orders subject to approval. Terms, offer, & price subject to change.

Thank you!

AN060A

...keeping the four introductory books for $1.99 (+ $1.50 for shipping & handling, a total of $3.49) places you under no obligation to buy anything. You may keep the books and return the shipping statement marked "cancel". If you do not cancel, about a month later we will send 4 additional Arabesque novels, and bill you a preferred subscriber's price of just $4.00 per title (plus a small shipping and handling fee). That's $16.00 for all 4 books for a savings of 33% off the cover price. You may cancel at any time, but if you choose to continue, every month we'll send you 4 more books, which you may either purchase at the preferred discount price. . . or return to us and cancel your subscription.

THE ARABESQUE ROMANCE CLUB: HERE'S HOW IT WORKS

ARABESQUE ROMANCE BOOK CLUB
P.O. Box 5214
Clifton NJ 07015-5214

PLACE
STAMP
HERE

"I was hoping we could extend this trip down memory lane . . . in the parking lot," he joked.

He deserved to suffer, she thought. She definitely wouldn't give him the satisfaction of knowing he had won up until the very last minute.

That afternoon, Elaine had a book signing at a local mall, at which Reggie decided Langston would make an appearance. It worked. She watched proudly while he flirted with teenage girls and little old ladies and the women who threw themselves at him, and he did it with just the right note of disinterested charm. He was even more comfortable with the boys who came in to ask him questions about football, after the management added his name to the posterboard out front.

He had infinite patience, and they stayed until the last copy of Elaine's book was sold. Reggie spent a good deal of time talking to the store's manager, who was a business acquaintance she always meant to get to know better. The woman, Angela, was very knowledgeable about books, and they found they had read a lot of the same material and shared many of their views on the publishing industry. She was curious about black books. Before she met Reggie, Angela never bought self-published books, but she said again, as she had so many times before, that it was amazing how many copies they could sell of a local author, regardless of the publishing house.

"Readers don't know about vanity presses," Reggie reminded her.

"What is a vanity press?" Langston asked, joining them.

"They are publishers who publish books at the author's expense. Regular publishers pay for the right to license the book, and pay all the expenses of producing and distributing the books. Black authors self-publish a lot more, and black bookstores don't generally have a problem selling their books on consignment, so that's where the bulk of their books are sold. But bookstores that are franchises of major chains, like this one, don't usually buy books that are self-published. That might be changing, because computer bookstores like Amazon will take self-published books."

"And so do I," Angela chimed in. "Ever since Reggie and I

met. But I still don't get a lot of African-American customers in here, and I know that's a huge audience. I've thought about hiring Reggie here to promote this place to the black community. A number of my customers have told me that they came to me to buy a book because Reggie's publicity lists include my store as one of the outlets that sell it."

"I can definitely recommend her," Langston said.

Elaine joined them, looking exhausted. "I second that."

Reggie was embarrassed, but pleased. Already Langston had gotten her a new customer, and one she never thought of as a potential client, despite the rapport she shared with the woman. She counted Angela a friend and had never pitched her. *That's what happens when you hang out with the rich and famous,* she thought as they left, Langston's hand behind her elbow. *Their good fortune rubs off on everyone around them.*

But it wasn't business she was thinking about as she drove him back to his hotel. It was his dark, intense eyes, which had burned into her each time she looked at him that day, and his full lips, which tempted her anew with every smile he aimed her way. When they reached the hotel she didn't stop at the front entrance but drove around to the parking lot. "Are you surprised? I am," she babbled nervously. They did jump the gun once, it was true, but that didn't mean they couldn't behave like adults now that their hormones were back under control. "I don't know if this is a good idea or not."

"It's a great idea," he answered. "Trust me."

"I don't even know you. I can't believe I'm thinking about this. You're a client and a celebrity, and I have no idea what I'm doing." She sounded to herself like a record being played at too high a speed.

He leaned over and kissed her cheek. "Are we going to sit in this car all night, or are you going to come up to my room?" he inquired.

"I don't know," she answered, feeling torn.

"What is it about you and parking lots?" he asked.

Reggie laughed. "I think it has something to do with you. Parking lots never turned me on before."

"That's very interesting. Is there anything else I should know about you?" he asked, sitting back as if they had all the time in the world. Which, she supposed, they did.

She didn't answer his question. Instead she told him, "I don't want to go home. But I can't seem to get out of this car. I feel like the minute I open this door, I'm doomed."

"Doomed?" She thought he was going to be offended by the turn of phrase she used, but he just seemed amused. "Every time I talk to you, we end up discussing your vocabulary. It's very . . . colorful. I like the way you talk."

"Thanks," Reggie said, feeling the tension slowly seeping out of her as she realized he was perfectly content to sit there waiting for her to decide what she wanted to do. "That's sweet."

"I'm a sweet guy," he replied. "Ask anyone."

"I was going to ask for references," she joked. "Is there anyone special I should call?"

"You could get the dope on me from my mom. You met her," he added, when she looked at him dubiously. "She's a tough critic, but I think she'll give me a fair recommendation."

"What about an ex?" she suggested.

"You want me to remember a name?!" he said as if shocked.

"Just tell me there aren't thousands of them."

"Thousands?" He looked at her quizzically. "Really, Reggie, I think you overestimate me."

"Ditto," she replied. "What is it about me that you can't resist? I'm not glamorous or sophisticated or anything special. So why me?" It was a question that she couldn't wait to have answered.

"I don't know, Reggie," he said patiently. "Because I like you. You make me feel good. You're funny and smart and cute and you speak like someone out of the nineteenth century. How's that?"

"Good answer," she said, thinking about all of the reasons why she shouldn't believe him. But she wanted to believe.

"So what do you want to do now?" he asked.

"Let's go upstairs," she said.

"Are you sure?" he asked, smiling widely.

"No, but let's do it anyway." Reggie opened her own car door, but he was at her side in seconds.

* * *

She thought it would be awkward, seducing him. But it was incredibly easy. "I love your body," Reggie said after she had ravaged him. She ran her hand across his washboard stomach.

"Same here." He kissed her shoulder.

She made a sound between a sniff and a snort. "You don't have to say that. We both know it's not true," she said without rancor.

"What are you talking about?"

"Your beautiful hard abs, and my soft squishy tummy," she explained.

"This tummy?" He pulled the sheet out of her hands, uncovering her from her neck to her toes. His eyes swept down from the top of her head to her feet, then came up again to her breasts and stomach. Where his gaze touched her skin, she burned in renewed excitement. And shame.

"Didn't your mother ever tell you it's rude to stare?" she tried to joke, one hand sneaking down to grasp the top of the sheet and pull it up over her to her waist. When she would have pulled it farther, he covered her hand with his own, stopping her.

"Don't you know how exciting it is for me to be able to look at you like this? To touch you?" He brushed her nipple with the back of his hand, sending a shiver through her. "Like this."

She knew what it did to her, but she couldn't believe it was the same for him. "Men," she said weakly. "You're all alike. Women are just body parts to you."

"I like *your* body parts, individually and as a whole." He took her chin in his hand and turned her to face him. "These eyes are beautiful. He kissed her eyes, then waited for her to open them again. He held her gaze as he continued. "This mouth is beautiful. Luscious lips," he touched them lightly with his own. "This chin is beautiful." His lips trailed lightly downwards, followed by his fingertips. "This neck is exquisite. And tasty." He nipped her there. "These breasts are fantastic, and so is this soft round tummy." He nuzzled her stomach. "And this is wonderful." He stroked lightly between her legs. Then he did it again. She sighed, as his hand drifted lightly over her hip and down

her thigh and up again. "And your smooth, soft legs." His me-
lodic baritone washed over her. "The dimples in your knees are
delicious. And your big, muscular calves are so round and
strong. And I adore your perfect little feet."

"Langston," she said breathlessly as he raised her leg and
kissed her instep, then slid his hand down and down until he
reached her backside. He placed her foot on his shoulder and
reached behind her to caress her bottom. "That is not my foot,"
she commented, not so much in complaint, but as a simple statement of fact.

"But it is one of my favorite parts," he said.

"I like your butt, too." Reggie mentioned, wanting to contrib-
ute to this litany of extravagant compliments before the desire
evoked by his words and his actions overwhelmed her.

"Women," he said in the same tone she had used a few moments before when she castigated his sex. "They're only after
one thing."

Thirteen

Langston thoroughly enjoyed the newfound intimacy between he and Reggie, except for one minor annoyance—her insistence on keeping it a secret. He understood her reservations, he thought, about exposing herself and her life to the media, but he thought the chances small that anyone would even pick up the story.

Besides, as he pointed out to her, he was going to be asked, point blank, if he was involved with anyone once the national promotional tour started for *Under His Skin,* which was only a few weeks away.

"Lie," she advised.

"I'm not going to lie," he protested. "I want to tell people about you already, and they're not even asking. I'm not going to tell a bald-faced lie when I *am* asked."

"Then go ahead and say you're dating, like always. But don't mention my name. I'll deny it if anyone asks me," was her firm response.

Other than that one small bone of contention, each day that week was better than the next. And Friday night, they went bowling just as he'd planned. She was a better bowler than he expected, and they had a good time, but the real excitement began when they reached home.

They went to her place, finally. And she had the supper table set, with a big brass candelabra, gleaming china and polished silver. She popped a casserole in the oven, and pulled out bread, soft cheese, salad and fruit, to warm to room temperature. They had just enough time to shower before the dinner was done. They didn't dress for the meal. She wore a long T-shirt, and he wore her terrycloth robe. He was tempted to delay dinner until his other appetites had been satisfied, but she insisted they eat and his protest ended with his first bite of the delicious spicy main dish.

"I didn't know you could cook like this," he said, savoring the shrimp, corn, and rice, dripping with a cheesy white cream sauce with flecks of hot red peppers.

"Just like Mama used to make," she said lightly.

"Not my mother. We ate everything out of boxes and cans. With two jobs and four kids and her writing, there wasn't a lot of time for cooking. It was never her favorite thing anyway. The turkey at Christmas and the ham at Easter were about her only two fancy dishes."

"This isn't fancy. It's quite simple to make, but you have to spend a little time at it," she told him.

"You'll have to give me the recipe," he said seriously.

"You cook?" she asked, amazed.

"I like to make a nice dinner when I'm home," Langston said. "I spent so much time on the road, and I didn't want to lug around a bunch of stuff, so cooking became a way of providing some of the comforts of home. Hey, with a mom like mine, it was a necessity." He leaned forward. "Actually, I enjoy it," he confided as if it was a deep dark secret.

"I like cooking for people. I'm not into it for the sake of the art. When I eat alone, I tend to pick up fast food," Reggie confessed.

"So you enjoyed cooking this meal for me, did you?"

"I like my men well-fed and grateful. It tends to make them more . . . malleable."

"You can maul me any time," he promised.

"We'll see," she said darkly.

The whole night was a sensual delight. After dinner Reggie served fruit and cheese and sorbet. And the entire repast was just the beginning. She lingered over her wine, and then poured herself coffee, letting the sexual tension build. At first, he was impatient, but then he began to anticipate the pleasure that was to come, and he found himself enjoying it. He sat back and had a second cup of coffee himself, this time laced with brandy.

"I should not be so happy that this job is over," she said, shaking her head.

"I'm the client, and I'm happy."

"Technically, my client was Spirit Productions," she reminded him.

"And they're happy, too," he pointed out.

"Which is good. But it would be better if they were so happy with my work that they decided to . . . oh, I don't know . . . suggest I take over all their publicity, at least here in Washington."

"All right, I can see that. But I can't help it. I'm glad we're not going to be working together anymore. I feel like celebrating."

"So do I, but I shouldn't," she said.

"I've waited long enough." He finished off his coffee and stood, then bent and picked her up in his arms. "Let's go to bed."

"Langston, put me down. I'm too heavy. You're going to drop me."

"I will if you keep wriggling around like that. Just put your arms around my neck," he commanded. Then he carried her into the bedroom.

He put her down gently in the middle of the bed, and spread out next to her. "So, shall we start the celebration?" he asked.

"I thought we already did," Reggie said.

"Then let's call this the second phase."

"Just so long as you don't forget what you promised," she agreed, tugging him up into a sitting position opposite her by the lapels of the robe he still wore.

"Never," he avowed, kissing her. "What promise was that?" he asked a minute later.

"You were going to show me your appreciation for the meal, remember."

"Mm hmm," he murmured. "Now I wonder how I can best do that," he mused aloud.

* * *

The next morning, the sound of the television woke him up. Reggie had gotten up and showered already and she was wearing that long T-shirt again. He found it amazing that she was still so uncomfortable about her body despite the time and attention he had lavished on every inch of her chestnut skin. He found most women were like that. She'd just have to get used to having him around, then maybe she wouldn't always drape herself in extra-large T-shirts and other baggy clothes.

"Look, Linda Hayes is on Regis. And they're talking about you," she said.

"How did Regis Philbin get to be such a celebrity?" Langston said. "He annoys me."

"Aren't you going to be on his show next month?" she asked.

"Yes. But I can't help that," Langston said.

Regis was currently asking Ms. Hayes what she thought of Langston, so Reggie shushed him and turned up the volume.

"You worked with him on his first film just last year, Linda," Regis was saying. "Are you surprised that he's starring in a major release so soon? Most actors wait for years before getting that kind of a role."

"That's true. I am one of them. But Langston has natural talent. I'm not at all surprised that Hollywood recognized that immediately. He is very easy, very real, and he was a pleasure to work with," the actress answered graciously. "And it didn't hurt that he was already a national celebrity."

"So who did you enjoy kissing more, Langston Downs or Laurence Fishburne?" Regis asked with his smarmy laugh.

"They are both so handsome, you know. I couldn't really say," she giggled.

"Did you keep in touch after you made the movie?" Reggie asked Langston, feeling a little jealous.

"No," he said. "We were friendly, but we didn't become friends. She was nice, and she helped me a lot, but it was hard work, and we didn't really have time for socializing. I was pretty freaked out about making the movie in the first place, so I wasn't really looking to make friends, just to get through it."

"So you're saying you were never even tempted?" she teased.

"Not you, too. Even my own mother doesn't believe me. I

guess I'm a better actor than I thought, because we never even considered it. First of all, she's very happily married. And she's an exercise nut. She works out five hours a day. Starting at five in the morning. There's something creepy about it."

"I've heard she's really smart. And look at her. She's flawless. You two looked so perfect together." She looked from the television screen to him, and back. "Perfect." She wasn't joking.

"So what? You saw her. She's a good actress, but her personality is a little . . . bubbly for me."

"It's just hard for me to believe you would want to be with me when you could be with someone like her."

Langston thought about arguing with her. He wanted to explain that he had not been attracted to the woman, despite her beauty, because he and Linda just weren't compatible like he and Reggie were. But he decided to keep it light. "It never even crossed our minds. How can you think I'd want to be with anybody else but you after that marathon last night. How many times did we make love? Eleven? Twelve?"

"Four," Reggie said, looking more confident.

"That was a lot of moaning and groaning for just . . . how many?" he asked skeptically.

"Four," she insisted.

The phone rang just as he was about to suggest they try to break the record.

"Hi, Mom," she said as soon as she put the receiver to her ear.

Langston went to the kitchen and checked the refrigerator for the ingredients for eggs Benedict, or something equally impressive, so that he could prove his claim that he could cook. She didn't have any meat, but she had cheese and spinach, so he made eggs Florentine and brought it into her in the bedroom.

"Wow!" Reggie said. She took a bite and sighed blissfully. "This is amazing. Where's your plate?"

"I thought we could share," he said.

"No way. Get your own," she ordered.

Langston couldn't help laughing. He stole a forkful of her food and then went back into the kitchen to make himself another omelette.

He felt very comfortable in her little house. Reggie told him it was the house her parents lived in when they were first married. They used her father's G.I. benefits to get the mortgage. When her mother was pregnant with Reggie, they moved into the larger house in which Jennifer Primm currently resided, but they kept their first home and rented it out, mainly to faculty members at the nearby University of Washington. When Reggie started teaching at the university, she took over the lease, and eventually she bought the place from her mother.

The house had two floors. Her bedroom and the guest room were located upstairs as well as a bathroom, and on the first floor was a small room she used as a den, another smaller bathroom, a large living room, and a relatively large dining room and kitchen, separated by a half-wall covered with glass-fronted cabinets full of crockery, china, silver, candlesticks and vases. All of the rooms were painted off-white. A rug or carpet gave each room a predominant color which was echoed in the curtains and some of the furniture. Reggie liked country-style wooden furnishings best, and old-fashioned homey knickknacks adorned the windowsills and shelves. Simple prints and photos of relatives adorned the walls. It was a charming little place with a cozy feel to it, and Langston liked it a lot.

That afternoon, they decided to go to the International Food Festival. Reggie drove Langston back to his hotel so he could pick up some clothes, and she waited for him in the sitting room while he changed. He put on his disguise in preparation for their outing.

"Ready?" he called before he emerged from the bedroom.

"Sure," Reggie answered.

He stepped through the door. She took in the outfit and laughed. He knew how ridiculous he looked in his skull cap, dark "Aviator" glasses, football jersey—on which, perversely, he wore his own number, although it had the colors of a different team—and, most laughable of all, gangsta jeans which rode so low that his neon underwear with the palm trees could be glimpsed when he crossed his arms. The finishing touch had been when he'd cut the jeans off, mid-calf, and added golf socks with Tiger Woods' name on them, tucked into his Air Jordans.

"Do you think anyone will recognize me?"

"No, but they'll all be staring anyway," she said, grinning widely as she walked around him.

"This won't blend in here in Seattle, huh?" He'd perfected the disguise over the last year in Los Angeles.

"Not exactly. But, hey, you'll be bringing big-city fashion to the kids here," she said encouragingly. "Let's go."

He followed her to the door, where she stopped so abruptly he nearly walked into her. "You did bring a change of clothes, didn't you?" she asked.

"Of course," Langston said.

The food festival was on the grounds of Westlake Center and featured dishes from all reaches of the globe. They strolled through the booths, stopping occasionally to nibble on some tasty tidbit, talking about everything from cooking to their favorite books and movies to their families. Reggie was much more relaxed than she had ever been before, and he enjoyed her laid-back attitude and mellow wit.

They rode the Ferris wheel together, and did some serious necking when their seat halted at the top of its arc.

"Do you think we've got time to do it?" Langston said into her ear.

"No," she replied. "And there definitely isn't enough room."

"Oh, I think we could manage," he said, stretching his arms wide. "See."

"Forget it," she admonished. "I'm not athletic enough for that."

"I'll take care of it," he said, standing up and causing the car to careen back and forth.

She let out a little shriek of alarm. "Sit down, you fool."

"You just lie down and make yourself comfortable. You won't regret it. I promise."

"You are out of your mind," she said, but she laughed.

"I'm just feeling good," he said. "Really, really good." He sat down beside her. "Because of you."

"Me, too," Reggie said.

Fourteen

Reggie hated having to wake him up on Monday morning. Langston was asleep on his back, one arm stretched across her pillow. As gorgeous as he was with his eyes wide open, he looked even more beautiful when he slept with his long black lashes fanning his cheekbones. His jaw relaxed in sleep and his mouth was soft, like a child's.

She leaned over and kissed him gently. "Langston?" she whispered in his ear. His lips parted slightly and Reggie couldn't resist touching her mouth to his twice more, first catching his top lip between hers, and then the fullest part of his bottom lip. Still he didn't awaken, but she was enjoying this experiment. She slanted her mouth over his and dipped her tongue in the sweet honey pot just inside.

She felt it immediately when he woke up—first, just an indrawn breath and a quick touch of his tongue, then a hand behind her head stopping her when she would have drawn away. He drew her deeper into his mouth to explore further. His mouth pressed upwards as his tongue met and dueled with hers, and his eyelashes brushed against her cheeks as he opened his eyes.

"Good morning," he said, smiling happily. "That's a nice way to wake up."

"Good morning. It's Monday. I have to go to work," she announced. Their wonderful weekend was over. "What are you planning to do today?" she asked as she began to get dressed.

"I hadn't thought about it." Langston stretched languorously. Reggie could almost see the energy flowing from his shoulders to his biceps to his strong forearms, and all the way out to his fingertips. "Can I stay here with you?"

"During the day?" she asked incredulously. He nodded. "Why would you want to?"

"Why not?" he replied.

"I have to *work!* What would you do?"

"I don't know. Watch you?" he said, eyeing her speculatively.

"Not a chance," Reggie said. "One, I'll be too self-conscious; two, I need to concentrate; three, you'll be bored, so; four, you'll distract me."

"I won't. I promise," he vowed, sounding just like her five-year-old nephew Freddy when he tried to con his mother into buying him a forbidden piece of candy.

"Forget it," Reggie said.

"Don't you trust me? I'm a man of my word."

"Don't bat those big brown eyelashes at me, Langston Downs. I know that trick," she warned.

"Just until lunch time," he said, trying to bargain with her.

"This is not negotiable. No," she stated firmly.

In the office later that morning, she looked over at Langston as he pretended to read his newspaper, and she cursed the soft heart which made her her nieces' and nephews' favorite aunt and a complete pushover for an experienced con artist like Langston Downs.

Reggie had enclosed the porch that ran along one side of the house in order to create her home office. It was much wider than it was long, eight feet across and some thirty plus feet from the front of the house to the back, but it was a comfortable space. In the outer walls, she'd replaced the old wire screens with windows, and painted the waist-high oak panels white. The inside wall she'd covered with bookshelves. When she sat at her desk those shelves were behind her, and she faced outward, toward the house next door, which was barely visible over the high shrubbery between them. The rest of the furniture consisted of two waist-high lateral files with flowerpots under the central windows. Next to a narrow table on which she collated her publicity packets was a small unit on wheels containing her "media center," otherwise known as her old television, video cassette recorder, and a large boom box with a tape-to-tape recorder. At the front end of the room, a comfortable couch with short square tables on either end faced a couple of chairs for when clients came in to work with her, or just to chat.

It was chilly in the winter, but now, in late spring, it was quite comfortable. The sun streamed in through the windows. Langston was camped out on the couch, almost twenty feet away, and yet she was just as aware of him as if he'd been standing at her shoulder. He hummed tunelessly under his breath while he tried not to look too pleased with himself. He did not speak to her, which was smart, because Reggie still didn't think this was a good idea.

She had been puttering about for the past hour, checking her computer-generated to-do list without actually getting anything done. It did indeed make Reggie feel self-conscious to have Langston watching her, or even pretending to read rather than watch her, flip through the files on her desk, reshuffle the papers in her in and out boxes, and move documents about.

She reached for the phone, withdrew her hand, and reached for it again. Finally, she dialed a client's phone number. She got the answering machine and left a message for him to call her, so aware of Langston's listening ears that she kept replaying the simple message in her mind over and over again, wondering if she sounded as unnatural as she felt.

"This isn't going to work, honey," she said. "I feel like the place is bugged by the F.B.I. or something."

"What did I do?" He sounded aggrieved.

"You didn't do anything wrong. I'm just not accustomed to being monitored," she tried to explain. "It's making me jumpy."

"Try to relax," he suggested.

"I have a desk full of work to do, and I can't do it with you sitting there. Why don't you go out shopping or something, and come back for lunch? You can use my car."

"I don't want to go shopping. I want to hang out with you."

"Langston, I'm sorry. Just let me get started. Once I'm in the swing of things, you can come back."

"Maybe I can help you with that." he said.

"I don't want help with it. I am just not used to having an audience. I'm preoccupied and can't concentrate."

"All right," he finally gave in. "I'll go."

"Thank you," Reggie said, relieved.

"You're welcome. But I hope I get a better reception when I get back."

"You will. I absolutely guarantee it."

He gave her a kiss and left the room, and Reggie got to work. Currently, only one of the books she was promoting was actually published. The other two were in production. That was why she'd had the freedom to put everything on hold while she spent two weeks concentrating on Langston Downs' regional publicity campaign. Now she had some makeup work to do, and she was completely immersed in it until Langston returned at lunchtime.

"Did you have a good time?" she asked, logging off her computer.

"It was okay," he said, disgruntled.

"Where'd you go?"

"I tried to go to the store, but I didn't have my disguise," he said, disgusted.

He looked so despondent, she couldn't help feeling a little sorry for him. "Which store did you want to go to?"

He mumbled something unintelligible.

"What?" she asked. "I couldn't hear you."

"The grocery store."

Reggie couldn't help laughing at his crestfallen expression, but he was so pitiful, she did feel for him. "Poor baby," she crooned. "This might make you feel better." She pulled him into the office and led him to the couch, then sat on his lap. She framed his face with her hands, one hand on each side of his face, and leaned over to kiss him lightly, gently, just above his right eye. His eyes closed and he lowered his chin so she could kiss him again and again, moving slowly down to his cheekbone, and his chin. A breath of laughter escaped him.

"Better?" she asked.

He opened his eyes. "Much." He moved his head out of her

grasp and then took her face in his hands, just as she had done. But he didn't kiss her forehead, but stared deep into her eyes for a long moment. When she thought she would drown in those deep black pools, he lowered his eyelids and slanted his mouth over hers, his full lips opening slightly to catch her bottom lip between them and suck on it softly as his tongue grazed hers. It was a sweet, sexy, gentle kiss that moved Reggie to her toes.

She opened her eyes as he opened his, and she smiled at what she saw there. His answering smile was too big a temptation to resist. She wrapped her arms around his neck, slanted her mouth over his, and caught his upper lip between her own, sucking on it as he had done. She slid her tongue into his warm moist mouth. He opened wider and drew her in, tangling his tongue with hers.

"I wanted to make you a nice dinner," he said against her mouth.

"I have plenty of stuff here," she said. "You want to take a look in the freezer?"

"Not right now."

That afternoon, he disappeared into the kitchen while she got back to work, and, other than the occasional query concerning the location of a cooking implement or spice, he didn't bother her until six o'clock. Then he came into the office and announced that it was time for her to get ready for dinner.

"You want me to dress?" she asked.

"I like you naked, but that's up to you," he said. "You can come as you are or whatever . . . just come on."

"I meant dress up," she tried to explain, but he was pushing her out of the office.

"Dinner's ready."

He had prepared a fantastic meal of chicken marsala, asparagus tips in a lemon cream sauce, and wild rice, with sweet potato pie for dessert. It was delicious. It was also sinfully rich.

"How can you eat like this and look like that?" Reggie complained.

"I get a lot of exercise," he said. "Lately, I've enjoyed a nightly regimen as well as my daily workout. Coffee?

"Yes, thanks," she said. "I wish I had a body like yours."

"Not me," he said. "I like you just the way you are." She shot him a wry look. "It's true," he insisted. When she didn't respond, he let the subject drop, but when they were in bed later that night, he came back to it. "I like the way you feel. It's not a body like mine I want to feel against me," he whispered in her ear.

"No one ever said you had good taste," Reggie said self-deprecatingly.

"Why do you do that?" he asked.

"You're so perfect, and I'm . . . fat," she said.

"I like a girl with a little meat on her bones. I hate those skinny girls who exercise all the time."

"Lucky for me.

"Anyway, you want to talk about imperfection, look at this." He held up his beautiful brown leg, and Reggie examined it with enjoyment. "See there, that's where I had to have arthroscopic surgery."

She looked closer until she found the tiny scar. "That, there?" She touched the spot with the tip of her finger.

"And here," he showed her his hands. "This finger's disjointed it's been broken so many times, and these two are crooked."

"Is that all?" she asked wryly.

"You're right, it is ridiculous," he said. "You don't like me any less. So why do you think I'm so shallow as to care what you look like?"

"Uh huh," Reggie grunted.

"That didn't come out right," Langston said. "It's not that I need to overlook your flaws, because as far as I'm concerned, your weight is not a flaw. It's part of what makes you you, and it's part of why I feel so comfortable around you, and . . ." He caught sight of her expression and stopped speaking. He shook his head. "Reggie, I know I'm saying this all wrong, but I think you're really beautiful."

"I believe you," she admitted. "You've convinced me that you really do think *this*"—she gave her ungainly thigh a whack—"is beautiful. And I think you are enjoying the novelty of being with a woman who would rather read a book than jog five miles every morning."

"I hate to break this to you," he said mournfully. "But you're not the first imperfect woman I've slept with."

Reggie's heart leapt in her chest. "You slept with someone else who was fat?" She was thrilled. "Who? When? How much did she weigh?"

"Reggie," he said, laughing and pulling her into his arms as he fell back onto his side of the bed. "You'll never change."

"Do you want me to?" she murmured against his chest. When he didn't respond immediately, she advised, "Think carefully before answering that one."

"You're exactly what I want," he said.

"Good answer."

She looked up at his face to see him smiling down at her. There was something in his eyes, a question perhaps, or a desire that she couldn't understand. "Langston?"

"Yes?"

"What is it?" she asked.

"What?"

"Is there something bothering you?"

His eyes moved beyond her, beyond the bed, then up at the ceiling, but he only shook his head. Then he refocused on her. "No."

He was lying. She knew it. "Really?"

"Right at this moment, with you and I here, in your house," he smiled wickedly, ". . . in your bed . . ." He slipped his hand under her silky nightshirt and cupped her shoulder. Her chin came down automatically, and she kissed his wrist. "I'm the happiest guy in the city."

She still didn't believe him, not completely. Reggie didn't know if he was worried about the same things she was. Was Langston nervous about what would happen tomorrow? Did he also wonder whether this whole lovely dream would end as suddenly as it had begun?

She put the morbid thought from her mind as he pulled her up to him and kissed her. She didn't want to think about it. She knew this couldn't last forever, but while it did, she wanted to enjoy it the way he did, with his whole heart and soul. There would be time for regret later. Much later. And even if it was over tomorrow, she didn't think she'd ever regret this moment.

Fifteen

Reggie clearly had every intention of keeping their relationship a secret, despite all of Langston's efforts to convince her, by word and deed, that this was definitely more than a one-night stand. He didn't know if it was because she didn't believe him, or because she did. Was she afraid to let people know they were together because she was afraid she'd look foolish or pitiable or something when the relationship ended? Or was she afraid that he was right, and she'd gotten more than she bargained for when she became involved with him.

"I want to go out with Bebe and Neal," he said when she asked what he wanted to do on Thursday night. It must have been at least the fifth time he'd made that particular request during the past week. "I heard you talking with her, and I know she asked you to meet her."

"How do you know that?" she said obtusely. "You could only hear one side of the conversation."

"I know," he told her. "What I don't know is why you don't ever tell anyone that I'm standing right here in the same room with you, or that we're going to dinner together, or anything else about us?"

"As the song says, it's no one else's business what I do," she answered calmly.

"Does that include me? Because I disagree with you, there. It is very much my business," he argued.

"Langston, we're having fun together, why complicate things?" she asked sincerely.

"We could have more fun if we didn't have to hide out here," he commented. "Ever since I checked out of the hotel, I've dropped off of the face of the earth. No one knows where I am. I feel like I've done something illegal."

"People know where you are," she said wryly.

"My agent has my number. My mother guessed where I was when I spoke with her. But that's not because we told her. We're acting like criminals, and we haven't done anything wrong."

"I just don't need my life exposed to the whole world," Reggie said. "You're used to being the center of attention, the star, but I don't think I'm ready to have my personal business made public."

"So how long will it take?" he asked, frustrated. "A week, a month, a year? At some point, we have to start going out in public together."

"Why?" Reggie asked. "You'll be going back to L.A. in a week or so, right?"

"That's exactly why we need to get this out in the open now. People are going to start asking questions when I fly to Seattle every weekend to see you."

That surprised her "I didn't know you were planning to do that."

"What do you think? I'm going to go home next week and never call you again? Is that why you want to keep our relationship so quiet?"

"I am glad you'll be calling. You know I'll be happy to see you. But what makes you think that that's all there is to it? Langston, you've done this before. You know what the media is like. They'll never leave us alone. Especially when they find out you've chosen to see a woman they never even heard of. I don't want to be the subject of the *National Enquirer's* research. And I really don't want my clients, friends and family to be bothered with this. It's not their fault I'm . . ." she stopped, mid-sentence.

Langston jumped on that moment's hesitation. "You what? What crime have you committed, Reggie?" he asked, and then he knew. She felt and looked so guilty because she'd made the error of caring for him.

"It isn't their fault that I'm dating someone famous," she said hurriedly.

He didn't for a moment believe that that was what she had been about to say. "You're in love with me, aren't you?" he said triumphantly. "That's what you were going to say: 'It's not their fault that you're in love with me.' " It made sense. Reggie acted as though getting involved with him was a sin.

"Don't be so smug. For your information, not every woman you grace with your favor falls for you."

"But that is what you were going to say, wasn't it? Admit it, Reggie," he said triumphantly.

"Fine. Maybe it was. But I didn't mean it. I may be falling in love with you, who knows? That doesn't mean I want photographers following us around, trying to find out how serious we are, or are not." He wanted to grab her up in his arms and kiss her until she couldn't breathe, but Langston Downs knew better than to act cocky when he was in sight of the goal line. His instinct was to push the salad she was making out of the way, clear off the countertop with a sweep of his arm, throw Reggie onto the cool surface, and make love to her until she begged for mercy. But the conversation was far from over. He could tell that just by looking at her. She wouldn't meet his gaze.

"I think I may be falling in love with you, too, Reg," he said.

If he thought she looked surprised before, it was nothing compared to the expression she wore now. Disbelief warred with confusion. "You what?" she exclaimed.

"You heard me," he said, unable to keep from grinning.

"Where did that come from?" she asked, sounding like his mother had when he'd announced he was forgoing college to play in the pros.

"The same terrifying, wonderful place you're in," he said confidently.

"Oh no," she said, shaking her head. "That's not where this is coming from. This is just . . . just that thing you do, that same thing that makes you so convincing as an actor. It's easy for you to say something like this, because it doesn't mean anything real. You're just acting. Saying lines," she accused him.

"This is not an act. Look at me, Reggie. You know I'm not putting you on."

"You want to get your way, so you're outmaneuvering your opponent. You don't care who you mow down on your way to the goal line. You'll do anything to win."

"I like to win. Who doesn't? But in this case, I'm not playing a game. And I'm not playing a part. I care about you. I believe you care about me. I happen to think that's not such a bad thing. If it is, I'm willing to risk it."

"Risk what?" she challenged. "Losing?"

"Exposing myself. To you. To the world. I want you in my life. And I don't care what I have to do to convince you that I am serious about you, us, this relationship. This isn't just a fantasy, or something that you made up in your head. It's real."

"I know that," she said dismissively.

"I don't think you do. Why does it have to be such a big secret?"

Reggie stood motionless, regarding him seriously. "Even if we are . . . I don't know . . . going somewhere with this. Don't you think that's something we should handle alone, between us, before we expose ourselves to public scrutiny."

"If?" he echoed.

"What have we got so far? A new friendship? A very new relationship? All we know about each other so far is that we enjoy each other's company. It's easy."

"If you would just let it happen, we could go out and do other things, see what we have beyond the bedroom. Don't be afraid, Reggie. If you give it a chance, you'll see that we've got a lot more going for us than great sex."

"A lot of ifs. Not just from me, but on your side, too."

"How about it? We can start with your friends. The paparazzi aren't going to fly up here just because I had dinner with my publicist and a couple of her friends."

"I'll think about it," Reggie said, which was the best he had ever gotten out of her. At least she would consider his suggestion. That was progress. Langston didn't push it anymore that night, or the next. A couple more nights at home just being together couldn't hurt. But by Sunday, she still hadn't said anything more about it.

He wanted to go out with her. It was such an odd situation to be in. Women he was interested in usually weren't loath to accompany him anywhere—some had been embarrassingly eager to be seen with him in fact. He was glad that Reggie wasn't like that, but she was taking it too far. She acted like she was ashamed of their relationship.

"Are you ashamed of me?" he finally asked on Sunday afternoon as they sat in her kitchen drinking tea.

"Of course not," she exclaimed. Too quickly.

"Why?" he asked.

"I am not ashamed of you, Langston. I wouldn't be with you if I were."

"Then what is it?" he demanded. "What is so terrible about us being seen together?"

"It's not you. It's me."

He was stunned. "What?"

"Face it, Langston. They're all going to want to know what you are doing with me? What are you going to say? That we have great sex?"

"I'll say what people usually say. You're a wonderful woman, and I'm lucky to have met you."

"I'm sure they'll be very happy with your stock answer," she said.

"Who is this 'they' that you're so worried about?"

"The people who decide who's hot and who's not. And all the people who believe them."

"You're kidding, right?"

"No, I'm not kidding. It's not you they'll be criticizing, it's me. I do not look like one of the beautiful people. You do."

"That's crazy!" He strode over to her and grabbed her by her arms, forcing her to look up at him. "There's nothing wrong with you. I thought we already settled this." She was a clever girl, so how could she be so foolish about this one thing?

"I don't think you're seeing things clearly," she said.

"Me?! You think I'm not seeing clearly." He would have laughed at the irony of it, but it was obvious that she was completely certain she was right. "You are completely blind to the truth. All that talk about the press invading your privacy and not wanting to live in a fishbowl was a lie, wasn't it?

"No it wasn't."

"An excuse then. You don't care if they follow us around and take pictures of us together, you're just worried that the photos won't be flattering. All this week we've been playing hide and seek, making me think it was my fault that you didn't want to be seen with me, and it was just vanity." She looked away, unable to meet his eyes, and Langston knew his accusation was true. "I thought you were honest and principled and didn't care about appearances, but you're really just as shallow as those women who spend all their time exercising themselves into oblivion."

"Let me get this straight. You think I look this way to prove some point to the world? You think this body is some kind of political statement?" She didn't look guilty anymore. She looked angry.

"No, not exactly. I just figured you had your priorities straight."

"Because I'm fat?" she spat.

He winced. "I don't think of you as fat, I think of you as strong, healthy, and beautiful. So what if you're overweight. What's the big deal? It's just a number. One hundred pounds, two hundred pounds, what difference does it make?"

"It makes a big difference to me. I would do anything to weigh one hundred pounds. And apparently if I were some hundred-pound lightweight, you wouldn't have been interested in me."

"It's not as if I was attracted to you *because* of your weight," he said, defending himself. "And it wasn't in spite of it, either. It's part of you and I liked the whole package. How often do you think I meet a woman with brains and beauty who's as interested in me as I am in her? I'll tell you. Never. It *never* happened before I met you."

She seemed to relent somewhat. "All right. But you have to understand that all this is new to me, too. I never intended to give the impression that I was ashamed of you, or make you feel insecure."

"Me, neither." Langston suddenly realized that Reggie felt as vulnerable and uncertain as he did, and their fears about each other fed right into those insecurities. They shared the same feelings, but despite their closeness they hadn't recognized it at all.

"So how about if we try to help each other through this instead of treating each other like adversaries," he suggested.

"Does this mean you'll get off my back about going out together?" she asked, only half joking.

"No. I'm going to help you get over this complex you have about your weight." She laughed. "You don't think I can do it, do you?"

She managed to stop laughing, but she was still smiling widely as she shook her head and answered. "Hey, I wish you luck. If you can make me feel better about *that,* I'll love you forever. But you're taking on a problem that's suffered by every woman I know. No matter how thin or how old or how gorgeous they are, they see themselves as needing serious improvement. You figure out how to fix that and you can write a bestselling book of your own."

"I like that 'love you forever' part," he said, which made her smile disappear as she ducked her head. He raised her chin again with one finger and looked into her eyes. He was encouraged by the shining glow of emotion he saw there. It was hope. The same hopeful optimism he felt. He kissed her and took her to bed.

The next morning, Tommy showed up at their door.

He would have preferred that his agent meet Reggie when she was dressed for her role as publicist, since that was all he had told his best friend about her. That the man was surprised was evident. That Reggie took it the wrong way was equally clear.

She nearly ran back to the bedroom, and didn't emerge for nearly an hour. Then she barely said hello before she locked herself in her office.

"This is not exactly your usual style, Mo," Tommy Ray chided.

"What do you mean by that?" Langston asked, his hackles rising.

"Disappearing right before the release of your first major motion picture?"

"My bad," Langston said, embarrassed not because of the breach in his usual professional behavior, but because for a moment, he'd allowed Reggie's paranoia to affect him. He thought Tommy was referring to her when he mentioned Langston's behavior being out of character.

He soon discovered that Tommy had in a way been talking about Reggie. But not because of her appearance. "So, who is she? And how has that little honey managed to do what no other woman has ever done to Mo Downs?"

"She was the publicist they put in charge of the regional promotion for the film. You remember?"

Tommy nodded. "Sure. I remember." He waited expectantly, but Langston didn't know what more he should tell his old friend. "So what are you doing here? Playing house?" Tommy asked acerbically.

"I'm not playin' anything," Langston replied. "This is more important than anything I need to do in Los Angeles."

"Damn, she must be something special. You've never put a woman before work."

"I haven't?" Langston asked, genuinely surprised. He never thought of himself as particularly obsessed with his professional life. It had required a certain amount of devotion and had probably gotten in the way of a relationship or two with women, but he had never made a conscious decision to put his work before anything, or anyone. "It isn't as if there were any women who wanted me to—"

"Right." Tommy laughed. "What about Vanessa Longtree?"

Langston had forgotten all about his short-lived but tumultuous relationship with Vanessa. She was the ex-wife of one of the other players who had come up with him through the league, and the three of them were friends for years before the breakup of her marriage. The three of them remained friends even as the marriage dissolved, and Langston and she became lovers. But

Vanessa wasn't just interested in changing partners. She was interested in changing her life.

"That was doomed from the beginning," Langston reminded him. "She had an irrational attitude toward pro ball." She thought when she chose him, she wouldn't have to live the life of a player's wife anymore, and when Langston chose football, as she saw it, over her, she felt it was a repeat of the problems she had with her ex-husband.

"What about Jalisa." His high school sweetheart had come back into his life when she visited him in the hospital when he was injured, but she couldn't understand why he felt compelled to try to finish the season. That relationship hadn't even outlasted his physical therapy.

"That wasn't really—"

"And there was Brenda," he reminded Langston. "And Sammy—"

"Okay, okay, I get the point," Langston conceded. "I never realized I did that. Anyway, Reggie *is* special."

"I guess she must be," Tommy said, grinning. "I can't believe this. Mo Downs finally falling for a woman."

"She's smart and she's funny and she's independent—very independent."

"So why are you keeping it a secret?" Tommy wondered aloud.

"That's . . . sort of . . . a problem. I can't explain right now, but maybe we can talk later. Did you come here for any particular reason?"

"Nope. Just wanted to see what was happening with you. And I wanted to talk a little business. You've got a two-week tour coming up to promote the movie, and then we've got some scripts to go over. And you should probably schedule that meeting with Scott that you've been putting off." Tommy Ray was an old friend of Scott Peterson, his business manager, and they ran his professional life very much as a team. At least it seemed to Langston that they ganged up on him whenever he decided to diverge from the path they advised him to take.

He explained it to Reggie at dinner that night, after driving his friend the airport. "They are very efficient, and I'd trust them both with my life. They are two of my oldest friends as well as business associates, but they always think they know what's best for me."

"I don't think Tommy approved of me. He barely said two words to me." Langston didn't bother to point out to her that she spent the whole day avoiding the man.

He shook his head vehemently. "No, no. He was surprised to see you because I never mentioned that I was staying with anyone, but he liked you a lot." He wasn't about to mention that Tommy did comment on her appearance. Apparently he, too, thought Langston looked better with models.

"Umm hmm," she murmured skeptically. "That's why he hightailed it out of here five minutes after I joined you."

"He had a plane to catch. And you were the one that suggested I use your car to drive him. I swear, Reggie, he liked you just fine. I mean, he didn't really get to talk to you, but he congratulated me on finally finding a woman like you."

"I heard him. I believe his exact words were 'a woman of substance.' "

"You have to believe me, he didn't mean that the way you think he did. He was surprised by my behavior, not by you. We spent the whole afternoon talking, and he's looking forward to getting to know you when you have more time. You heard him."

"He did say that," she said.

It sounded to him as if she wanted to be convinced. "Reggie, I wouldn't say it if it weren't true."

"Okay," she relented. "I'll take your word for it." But he could tell she still felt some doubt.

"He was more surprised that he hadn't heard about us than anything else," Langston explained further.

"You know him better than I do." She shrugged.

"We're going to surprise a lot more people when we start going out," he pointed out. "You'll have to get used to it."

"I will. Just give me time." Reggie asked. "If your friend's surprised at you, he should try talking to me. I still can't believe you turned out to be so incredibly sweet."

Sixteen

It happened just the way she thought it would. Reggie didn't know how the tabloids got wind of it, but the paparazzi found them. It might have happened because she and Langston went out with Bebe and Neal to dinner Tuesday night. She made the mistake of telling her oldest friend that Langston's agent had found them together at her house on Monday.

"His friend gets to see the happy couple, but we don't? That's not fair," she whined.

"It's not like we invited him. He just showed up," Reggie tried to explain, but Bebe wouldn't let it go.

"Is this what it's going to be like now?" she asked. "Him or us?"

"Of course not," Reggie said. "It's not a competition."

"So when do I get to see you again?" Bebe asked.

"Langston's leaving at the end of the week."

Langston was just as bad. "How long is this going to go on?" he wanted to know.

"We'll see," Reggie said noncommittally. She suspected the problem would be solved after he went home. He wasn't likely to continue dating her when they lived so far apart.

But he didn't see it that way at all. "Are you planning to go into hiding every time I come to visit?" he asked.

"I don't know," Reggie said wearily. She would have been happy to stick to her plan to wait and see what happened, but between Langston on the one hand and her old friend on the other, she finally gave in. They were both equally accustomed to getting their own way and she couldn't stand it when they became impatient with her.

They were their usual cheerful selves at dinner of course. In the restaurant at the top of the Space Needle, they acted as if they'd been friends all their lives. Reggie, on the other hand, couldn't relax at all, and her nervousness transmitted itself to Neal, who couldn't fully abandon himself to the pleasure of dining with a celebrity while she was suffering from her paranoia. People stared at them, especially at Langston, but no one intruded on their evening out. Reggie did have to admit to him later that night that their dinner out did not seem to activate the paparazzi's radar the way she thought it would.

But two days later, the vultures descended.

It started innocently enough. *USA Today* left a message on her answering machine early Thursday morning asking her for a quote about the film she'd been hired to promote. Then her mother called and told her that a reporter called to ask if she knew her daughter was dating Langston Downs. She didn't give them any information of course, but it didn't stop the press from finding Reggie's address and phone number and beginning a campaign of low-level harassment that included everything from calling her over and over to ask for interviews to sending a photographer to her house who snooped around outside until she called the police and reported a trespasser.

The following morning, they took pictures of Langston when he emerged from her house. Unfortunately, he was only wearing a towel at the time because he didn't bother to get dressed to retrieve the newspaper from the porch.

"It begins," she said unhappily.

"No problem," Langston said. "They'll get tired of this and go away."

But they were more persistent than he expected, and he and Reggie were shadowed everywhere they went for the next few days—including the supermarket, the bank, and the Plum Bar. Luckily, her family didn't mind their sudden popularity, but Reggie hated seeing herself in the tabloids. They took pictures from every angle and invariably caught her double chin, and her big stomach, and her huge legs and butt. She dreaded even more the escalation of their press coverage, which was inevitable once Langston's film opened at the end of the month.

Even more than the paparazzi, she hated the idea that she might have to face them alone when he left to go home to Los Angeles. She tried to ignore them, but they had no regard for privacy or courtesy, and the only reason she hadn't started screaming at anyone yet was because Langston kept her calm. He was so rational and reasonable and protective.

He kept saying, "They'll go home soon."

"I hope so," Reggie said on the third day. "I'm afraid to go back to the supermarket.

"Ignore them," he advised.

"How can I? They're right in my face," she argued. Anyway, I don't want to see my photo on the cover of the *Star*. Bebe's secretary bought the last article and she read it to me, and the things they said were not kind."

"You should read what they say about me," he said.

"They *were* talking about you," she retorted. "They suggest that, after a long career as a ladies' man, you are scraping the bottom of the barrel with an unknown publicist."

"That's not too bad," he said. "If I wasn't able to take a cheap shot or two by now, I'd never have made it in the pros. They're always trying to dig up dirt on drug use or gambling or anything that reflects badly on the players in general. They wanted to know about me and everyone else on the team, and what they couldn't find, they made up."

"This doesn't bother you at all?" she asked, incredulous.

"Of course it's annoying, but it goes with the territory. My family and friends know better than to believe any of these stories, and that's all that matters to me. The people who respect me don't care about rumors and lies."

"What about the people who don't know you?"

"When we meet, they learn the truth. You, for example, know that I'm not at all the way they portray me."

"But a lot of people believe everything they read in the news. And if they don't believe every word, they do think there's no smoke without fire."

"There's nothing I can do about that," he said fatalistically.

"I get madder about other people than I do about myself. Especially when they lie."

"You don't seem to get angry at all."

"I don't sweat the small stuff, but I get upset when they lie about something important. For example, they accuse a lot of black men of beating on women, and they seem to love reporting when a black woman gets victimized. Not that they don't victimize everyone, regardless of color, creed or religion, but the racism really gets to me."

"But you're so patient with the photographers."

"I've had my moments."

Reggie couldn't imagine him losing his cool, but she did know how passionate he could be. While she knew him as a gentle, controlled lover, she supposed that that passion could manifest itself in more violent ways. She did know he'd been unstoppable on the football field.

"You can probably intimidate these little weasels pretty easily with your height and width, when you want to."

"I try," he said mirthlessly.

"I'm glad you're on my side," Reggie said.

"You know I am," he said, sweeping her into his arms and off her feet.

Sunday morning, he took her shopping for groceries, which was fine until she saw the *National Globe.* It was horrible. Langston looked familiar. She had seen him first in newsprint. But she wasn't used to seeing herself in a full color spread on the cover of a gossip sheet. And the photo was truly repulsive. The headline was the worst part. "MO GETS MO," it screamed. The caption proclaimed Ms. Primm was not very proper.

She bought the rag. She couldn't help it. She read every word with a kind of sick fascination. They waxed eloquent on the subject of her obesity, starting with her birth weight. Then they cast aspersions on her single status and recapped relationships she had had, especially the one with Darrell—the inference being that she was a money-grubbing golddigger who had kept her prom date enthralled for years until she cast him aside in favor of another rich, equally successful, more handsome man. The crowning insult was that her appetite for sex was as voracious as her appetite for food, which was what kept these eligible bachelors coming back for mo'.

She read it aloud to Langston, who only replied that they'd be writing their garbage about someone else soon. "Wait it out," he said.

"People are going to read this. Clients and potential clients are going to form an opinion of me based on this article."

"Don't let anyone see it upsets you. Don't lend credence to these ridiculous accusations. Believe me, I know. If you try to fight them, you just end up looking worse."

"I have to do something," Reggie said.

"I don't think there's much you can do. Let's go out tonight to somewhere really nice, and have a great time. As they say, living well is the best revenge."

"I would rather make them retract this nonsense about Darrell and I," she said. "But I guess I can't. So let's do it. Let's go out and have a ball. I'll invite Mama and the rest of the family. They deserve it after all we put them through."

"Sounds good," he said.

That night they all went out dancing with her mother and her sometimes beau, Pastor Johnson, and her sisters and brother and their spouses. It was the first time that Reggie had invited the whole family out with a male friend, and there was a lot of teasing, as well as congratulations, about her relationship with Langston.

Lucy was in good spirits, pleased to see her with Langston, and as self-satisfied as if she'd arranged the match herself. Which she probably thought she did. "When we went to the grocery store, Freddy saw pictures of you and Langston and he wanted to know why you were in the paper," she said mischievously. "We said you were on a date."

"Thanks," Reggie said wryly.

"He wanted to know if Darrell and Langston and you were all on the date together." She was smirking. "He was in the picture, too."

Virginia was also watching for Reggie's reaction. "I spoke to Darrell. He's fine with it."

"You did?" Olivia said.

"He is?" Lucy exclaimed.

"There, now, honey. I told y'all nobody reads those newspapers," Evan said, pleased.

"Of course they do," Lucy informed him.

"Obviously Darrell doesn't," John chimed in, shooting a quelling look at his wife.

"His secretary does. But he doesn't pay any attention to them," Reggie said. "He says he learned to ignore them during his fifteen minutes of fame when his company first took off." Maliciously, she added, "He's been a rock through all this." She watched as her sisters' enthusiasm visibly deflated.

"Okay?"

"Yeah," Olivia grumbled.

Langston charmed everyone with his quick wit and sweet smile, and he danced with all the women, including Jenny Primm. Reggie had a good time, too, but at the back of her mind two thoughts kept chasing each other around. He was leaving soon. And all she'd have left were some less-than-flattering clippings from the tabloids and plenty of bridges to mend with Darrell, her other friends, and of course her clients.

Reggie managed to put those negative thoughts aside and concentrate on the pleasure of dancing with Langston, who made her feel light and graceful as a feather on the dance floor. When a photographer showed up and started taking photos, she grew tense and awkward. He just wrapped his arm tighter around her waist and dipped her way back, until she felt sure he was going to topple them both over onto the floor.

"Langston!" she cried, but she had to laugh at the reckless romantic gesture.

"Relax, I've got you," he said. His strong arms held her gently but firmly, and the muscles of his back moved smoothly beneath her fingertips. Reggie loosened the death grip she had on him, and he swung her back on to her feet. "You can trust me," he said, smiling. "I wouldn't hurt you for the world."

A lump formed at the back of her throat, as it always did when she became emotional. She was going to miss him. Unshed tears stung her eyes, and she closed them so he wouldn't see.

They kept dancing.

It wasn't until they were back at her place, getting ready for bed, that Langston brought up the subject of Darrell for the first time. "Who is that guy?" he asked.

"Who?" Reggie inquired, putting on her nightshirt behind the closet door. No matter how many times he said he loved her body, her natural instinct was to cover it up whenever possible.

"This rich millionaire who's been in love with you for years," he clarified.

"Darrell Hunt? He was my prom date," Reggie explained, touched by the hint of jealousy she thought she heard in his voice. "Bebe told you about him, remember?"

"And . . . ?" Langston prompted.

"And he's a good friend," Reggie said. "We go out every once in a while for lunch or dinner. He takes me sailing on the sound occasionally."

"Is that all?" he asked around a mouthful of toothpaste.

"Sometimes he calls me when he needs an escort for a business function in the area," she went on. "I love him like a brother."

"Your high school sweetheart?" He waved the toothbrush at her.

"I wouldn't exactly call him that," she started to explain.

"You did date in high school?" She put toothpaste on her own brush.

She was sure now that he was, indeed, jealous. "We were friends, then. We went to the prom together, that's all," she said soothingly.

"I don't know about you, but for us that was a big date," Langston said. She paused in her teeth cleaning.

"Us?" Now she felt a little jealous herself. Who was us? He and his prom date? His first love? She brushed a bit harder and faster.

"We're talking about you and this Darren guy," he said just as she was about to ask for more information.

"Darrell," she corrected. "And there's nothing to talk about. Not really. He's just a friend. I told him that was all we could ever be."

"When was this?" he asked.

"Don't worry about it," she reiterated.

"I'm not worried. I'd just like to know more about the man you've been dating for the last ten years," he pressed.

"Fifteen," Reggie told him. "But we don't date. We see each other occasionally." Langston didn't look satisfied. "Aren't you the one who said these specious newspaper articles wouldn't matter to the people who know and respect you? What happened to my respect?"

"Yes," he said reluctantly. "I don't believe the reporters, but your family . . . ?" She climbed into bed and patted the space beside her invitingly.

"They were joking," she explained patiently.

"Okay, I'm sorry," he said.

"No, I'm sorry. You can ask me anything you want," Reggie told him.

"Thanks," Langston said and kissed her cheek.

"You're all right, right?" She didn't mind his jealousy, in fact it felt like a compliment, but she wanted to put him at ease.

"I'm fine. As long as we're okay," he said. "Are you going to be able to put this behind you."

"I'm certainly going to try," Reggie assured him.

It was very hard. The tabloids had a field day with their relationship and especially, it seemed to Reggie, with her appearance. It wasn't a blatant attack, just snide comments here and there about why they were hiding out. Then there was the article about the upcoming movie and Langston's beautiful co-star, and how Reggie compared to her, or rather didn't compare.

"Ugh," Langston growled after he read the headline SHE SHOT MO DOWN. DOWNS IS OUT. He threw the newspaper on the table, almost knocking over his coffee cup. She knew his indignation was more for her than for himself. That he was truly upset that she was hurt by these insinuations, she didn't doubt.

"I told you this would happen," Reggie said, depressed but trying to hold it in, since it seemed pretty shallow to cry over some stupid comments made by the jerks who wrote for the tabloids. Try as she might, she just couldn't help feeling demoralized by the whole ugly business.

"It won't be much longer," he said.

"What makes you say that?" she asked.

"Some juicy scandal will come along and they'll lose interest in us."

"You've been saying that all week. I don't want to sit around hoping some other poor slob draws their fire with some stupid indiscretion."

"That's about the size of it," he said.

"And what makes you think that will be the end? They've been chronicling Oprah's diet habits for years." He shot her a look that almost made her laugh. "All right," she acknowledged, "It's not just Oprah, though. They did it to Muhammad Ali, too. And what about Liz Taylor? She's one of the most beautiful women in the world, and they can't leave the subject of her weight alone, either."

"You're not them. Or Oprah. Your only claim to fame is your relationship with me."

Reggie wasn't sure she liked the sound of that. "My *claim* to fame? I never wanted any of this—"

He cut her off. "I'm not saying that you asked for it. It just . . . comes with the territory, that's all."

She stood. "And you're the territory? Well, that makes the solution simple, doesn't it? All I have to do is stop seeing you." She started to clear the table.

He stood and helped her. "That's not a solution."

"Funny, it sure seems like one to me," she said, miffed.

"Reggie, get serious. You're not going to let a little thing like this ruin everything." He picked up the newspaper. "Are you?" He carried it over to the trash can and threw it away. "It's garbage. It has nothing to do with us."

"Except that we can't seem to get away from it," she said sadly. "It is ruining things between us. This breakfast, for example, is ruined for me."

"I can fix that," he said, coming up behind her and wrapping his arms around her. "Just give me a chance," he murmured in her ear.

"That's your answer to everything." She put her hands over his arms and leaned back into his strong body. "How many times do you think that will work?"

"As many as it takes." He nuzzled her neck.

"Making love won't solve the problem," she said. "What if it never ends."

"All good things must come to an end," he quipped.

"This isn't a good thing. It's a bad thing."

He looked into her eyes. "I was talking about my solution."

"I know. But I was talking about the press. They're getting worse. I'm starting to think they'll never go away."

"They will."

"I hate to contradict you, but—"

He cut her off. "Then don't," he commanded. "Don't contradict me," he whispered in her ear. "Just repeat after me. I want you."

"But—"

"No," he shook his head. "I want you."

She played along. "I want you."

He turned her around in his arms and kissed her, long and slow, as he backed her toward her bedroom. "I need you."

"I need you," she echoed.

The debate was at an end, for the moment. Reggie couldn't resist his slow, skilled seduction, and she knew it. But when they lay in bed, sated, entwined in each other's arms, she had to ask, "That is your answer to everything, isn't it?"

"Until I can think of something else that works as well."

"To shut me up?"

"To distract you. I can't control what they say about you in the tabloids, but I can make a pretty convincing argument about their credibility."

"What argument?"

"They keep implying that you're not attractive. To me, you are. Ergo, they've got their heads up their butts."

"They're not implying anything. They say it straight out."

"Who cares if all they see is your dress size?"

I do, Reggie thought.

He continued. "They don't see what I see in you."

"Obviously," she said dryly.

"So as long as we're together, we're showing everyone that they have their heads up their butts," he finished triumphantly.

"As long as we're together?" she repeated faintly.

He didn't seem to hear her. "They'll get the message. In the long run." He kissed her shoulder.

"If there is a long run," Reggie said. "Or we'll prove them right," she commented philosophically, "if there isn't."

"If there isn't what?" he asked, puzzled.

"A long run. We've only known each other a few weeks. This could be over tomorrow. Anything could happen between us. And if we don't stay together, the paparazzi will think we broke up because I'm fat," she said. "Which is better than reporting that your inability to lower the toilet seat split us up, I suppose," she said fatalistically.

"First of all," he started, sounding annoyed. "What is this about splitting up?" he asked. But before she could answer, he went on, "And why would that prove *them* right? They don't know us. They don't know anything about us. They're just making stuff up to sell newspapers, for Pete's sake!"

"I'm not saying they *know* anything. They're saying I can't compete with your beautiful on-screen love interest, and they'll think they're right when this relationship ends, and so will their readers, I guess."

"I don't want to talk about readers or gossip magazines or any of that," he said, frustrated. "I want to talk about us."

"What about us?" she asked blandly. It was strangely satisfying to see Langston acting nervous for a change.

"We have a future," he stated definitively. "I don't see anything ahead of us that could change that."

"You are going back home next week," she pointed out.

"So what? That doesn't change anything between us," he said.

"We don't know what will happen. I certainly wouldn't make any predictions," she said reasonably. "We barely know each other. And we're very different."

"I know you," he argued. "You're a bright, loving woman. I know this is new and scary and difficult, but I think we can make it work. I believe that. Why can't you?"

"I don't know, but just at this moment, I think the odds are against us," Reggie said unemotionally. She thought now, just as she had at the beginning of their relationship, that it was unlikely that Langston Downs was going to settle down with a woman like her when he could have his pick of all the beautiful, talented women in his world. She planned to enjoy their affair for as long as it lasted, but she didn't expect it to outlast his trip home for very long at all. "You are thirty-five years old, extremely successful, and the most charming man I have ever met. I like you a lot. So, I assume, did the other women you've dated."

"What other women?"

"You've been involved with half a dozen women that I've read about."

"Where?" he interrupted. "In gossip columns?"

"Touché. Are you going to sit there and try to tell me you never cared for anyone else?" she asked.

"No, but—"

This time she cut him off. "Why aren't you with one of them now?"

"Different reasons," he shrugged.

"Exactly. People split up. I don't know how long you're going to want to be involved with me, or if I'll meet someone else, or if one of us will get hit by a truck tomorrow. The truth is, you could decide just like that that we don't have a future." She snapped her fingers.

"This is different," he said. "From the beginning, there's been something special between us."

"So what?" she said contentiously. "That isn't any guarantee that things will work out."

"Maybe not, but why assume they won't? Why not hope they will?"

"I do."

"Stop right there," he said before she could argue further. "Stop saying it won't work. Didn't you ever hear of a self-fulfilling prophecy?"

"Sure."

He explained as if she hadn't answered. "If you keep saying something is going to happen, it will."

"I've heard of positive thinking, too," she countered.

"Do that," he said. "Think positive, Reggie. Because I want us to be together."

"Forever? Are you proposing marriage?" she asked wryly.

She expected him to immediately reject the idea, or at best to hem and haw until she let him off the hook, but instead he looked straight into her eyes and said, "Are you?"

"Of course not," she said instantly.

"So what are we talking about?" The question was obviously rhetorical, so Reggie didn't answer it. But she did think, *We're talking about the end of this relationship.*

For all Langston's assurance that they had something special, she still didn't think they had a snowball's chance in summer of surviving the tabloids, the upcoming separation, or any of the other hundred things that could go wrong between two people who were so much more different than they were alike.

It was a shame, really. Because she agreed with him to a certain extent. She, too, felt that there was something really special between them. *Of course,* Reggie thought. *That's why they call him the sexiest man in America. Any woman he wanted would feel like she was special.*

She had fallen under his spell. Luckily, she didn't mind at all, right then. When it was over, she might feel differently. But until then, Langston Downs made her feel wonderful. If her unwelcome notoriety was the only price she had to pay for that, then it was definitely worth it. She wouldn't let it bother her anymore, Reggie vowed to herself. At least, not today.

"Let's go out, Mo. I feel like eating some fried oysters."

"Oysters? What are you trying to do to me, Reggie?" he groaned.

"It's only an old wives' tale, Langston. But if you want to believe in their miraculous powers, you should know that the myth is they only make you horny when they're raw," she assured him.

"What's the point of eating them fried then," he said, grinning wickedly.

"They serve the best ones in a tourist hangout down on the

Pier. I want to go because I don't want to hide from anyone
anymore."

"Congratulations, Teach! But you don't have to prove anything to me."

"I want to," she persisted.

"Are you sure it will be worth it?" he asked.

She pretended his question was about the oysters. "Come and
taste them and find out," she suggested, starting to get out of
bed.

"Wait a minute," he said, pulling her back into his body. "Just
let me get a little bite of you first." He nipped her ear and then
her neck, which made her jump.

"Langston," she said warningly.

"I have something to prove, too," he said, pressing her back
into the pillows.

"We have plenty of time for this later," she told him.

"Just relax. This will only take a minute," he said, disappearing under the covers.

Shivering as his lips moved slowly down her body, she decided not to argue with the man, since he was so intent on prov-
ing himself. "No rush," Reggie said. "No rush at all."

Seventeen

Langston couldn't believe that Reggie brought up getting married, just to dismiss the idea. He had achieved star status before he hit the legal drinking age, so he knew that the outrageous propositions and marriage proposals he received weren't real. However, he didn't think it was outside the bounds of possibility that a number of women would seriously consider a proposal of marriage from him, no matter how impromptu, to be quite flattering.

They probably weren't particularly well-suited. They might end up finding they couldn't be together because of their different lifestyles, but he wanted to try to explore the possibilities. He loved talking to her. He thought he made her happy, too. He didn't want to leave her.

He understood her reservations about their relationship, even though he didn't agree with them. They were, as she said, two very different people, and his approach to life was much more adventurous, more reckless and unthinking. She was cautious with him, keeping more of herself to herself, while he was out on the line, leaving himself open and vulnerable to rejection because that was the only way he knew how to win. He had spent most of his life trying to win, and more often than not, he did win.

But it was almost time to go home. He was going to have to leave her house, her bed, and get back to real life. The problem was, life felt more real with Reggie around.

He didn't call Tommy Ray about his flight home until Saturday evening.

"Langston, I made the same arrangements as last time. You've got an e-ticket waiting. Just pick it up at the airport," his agent said.

"Okay, thanks," Langston said.

"You lookin' forward to comin' home?"

"Not particularly. We start that promo tour right away, so I'll only be home for a day or two."

"That was your choice, buddy. You could have come home last week and gotten a little rest. But I don't suppose it's the rest you'll be missing," he joked.

"Why you have to play that way, Tom?" Langston said, only slightly irritated at his old friend's gibe, but responding out of habit and a sense of inevitability. He was going to have this conversation with all of his friends at one time or another. He might as well start now. "Reggie is a lady, and I don't want you talkin' trash about her."

"Yessir, boss. But can you just tell me one thing?"

"What?" he asked warily.

"What's a lady like that doing with a dog like you?"

"Just lucky, I guess."

It was a standard joke among his friends and family that the women he chose were so skanky he couldn't bring them around, which was why they never met the women in his life. It started years ago when his teammates asked him where he kept his girls, when they didn't see him with any groupies. It caused less grief to let them create the fantasy that he kept a secret harem than to explain that he didn't want to be with any woman his mother wouldn't have approved of. Tommy and the guys couldn't resist carrying the joke one step further. They told the few dates he did bring around about it. Regina was in for a dose of the same medicine if she came to Los Angeles to see him. He didn't think she would appreciate the guys' references to other women.

"I don't want you talking that way to her," he told Tommy, who was his best friend and his agent and would be seeing a good bit of Reggie.

"I never pictured you with a woman who didn't have a sense of humor."

"She has a great sense of humor, Tom. What she doesn't need are your and Scott's comments about her 'pretty boy,' etc."

"I'm sure she can take a joke, Mo," he said.

"Sure she can. But not about what a slut I am, or about the sluts I usually sleep with. You're going to have to wait until she gets to know me, and you, a little better before you start ripping us apart, okay?"

"Sure, sure," he agreed. "I wouldn't want to do anything that would mess you up, bro. Don't worry. I'll talk to Scott."

"*I'll* talk to Scott, thanks," Langston said. "You try to keep your mouth shut about Reggie as much as you can. I'm sure you already got it out on the grapevine."

"Hey, when you get a new lady, that's news we all like to hear," Tommy said in his own defense.

"Fine. There's nothing I can do about that. But we're already being hounded by the tabloid photographers, so please try not to add to the rumors that are already circulating."

He also called home, and warned the family about making remarks about his love life. "She already thinks I date supermodels," he told his sister, Zora.

"You do," she said.

"But she thinks that means I can't be serious about her because she's . . . because she . . . doesn't look like a model at all."

"I see." He believed she did. Zora was the oldest and wisest of his sisters, and the most understanding. She married his best friend and fellow quarterback, Frank, who loved to give him a hard time, and she was the only one who might persuade Frank not to tease Reggie, which was one of the reasons he had called her.

"Why don't you tell her that you're not really the hound that the tabloids paint you. She should understand that, after what she's gone through with them."

"Why should she believe me?"

"Maybe because it's the truth? She knows you well enough to know you're not a liar, doesn't she?"

"I came on pretty strong when I met her. She naturally as-

sumed the stories about me were at least partially true, and I
didn't try to counteract her impression."

"Why not?" Zora asked, confused.

"There is nothing more pathetic than a guy trying to get over
on a woman by saying he's got no past. Besides, I want her to
like me in spite of my reputation."

"Well, then, maybe you deserve whatever Frank dishes out,"
she said unsympathetically. Langston could just imagine Reggie's reaction to Frank's taunts. And Tommy's. As well as his
business manager, Scott, and the others. She wouldn't be
pleased, that was for sure. Nor would she enjoy the attention of
the reporters who flocked to Malibu to catch sight of his famous
neighbors.

Still, he couldn't wait for that first visit. Maybe once she met
his friends and saw that their snide comments were aimed at
him, she would understand. All of it was created to humiliate
him, not her. They just happened to be using Reggie, but he was
the one they knew, and he was the one they were making fun
of, but not because of Reggie's looks. They had followed his
career and nosed into his personal life for years, and no one
expected him to get serious about anyone, let alone a former
college professor who was currently the proprietor of a small
public relations firm. But Langston had a feeling he would never
be able to get Reggie to believe that the paparazzi, like his
friends and family, were surprised by the fact that he was involved in a serious relationship at all, and not because it was
she he was involved with. They marveled at his relationship with
her because she wasn't an actress or model, it was true, but only
because she was a woman of substance. She was the kind of
woman men dated when they wanted to settle down and get
married.

They decided to have a quiet dinner at home on Sunday, since
it would be their last night together.

"I don't want to leave you," he said.

"You have to go home some time," she said as she served
him his pasta.

"This feels like home," he answered.

"And you have the tour," she continued. "You'll be in fifteen cities during the next two weeks promoting *Under His Skin.*"

"Maybe you could meet me in New York next weekend."

"I might be able to manage that," she said, but he didn't know whether she was serious or not.

They had been very careful of each other over the last few days. She seemed now to have a new tolerance for the ever-intrusive press, which was an incredible relief to him since he had run out of new ways to convince Reggie that she truly was beautiful to him. The constant commentaries in the papers continued, but, though he knew they probably bothered her, she didn't mention it, and he wasn't about to bring it up.

He wanted her to spend the next few weeks thinking only of how much fun she had with him, how great they were together, and how much she missed him. "We could have a good time, darlin'," he drawled.

"You don't need to sell me," she said. "I'd love to go to New York with you, if I can get away from my work."

"That's up to you, isn't it? I mean, you're the boss."

"Yes, I'm my own boss, but I don't control how much work I have. If I have a lot to do, I'll have to get it done. As you know, I haven't been working my usual seventy-hour week lately," Reggie said.

"Oh, right." Langston looked into her eyes, but he couldn't tell if she was just humoring him, or if she really would consider flying to New York City the following weekend.

"Let's worry about it later," she said. And then he knew. She had no intention of flying across the country to meet him. She was just trying to avoid an argument.

He had been doing the same thing lately. Any potential problem that came up between them was ignored, or at least put on hold. But he suspected her reason for putting off the difficult discussions was different. He planned to return and work all these problems out slowly, over time. But he knew she didn't really believe he'd be back. Well, he'd prove her wrong. And there was only one way to do that.

The end of the meal came much too quickly, or excruciatingly slowly, Langston couldn't decide which. Reggie cleared the table while insisting that he sit and drink his coffee. He watched her, all out of things to say about leaving or returning. She bustled back and forth from the dining room to the kitchen, taking their dishes and utensils, then putting the candlesticks and napkin holder in their places in the cabinets. He felt his heart breaking in his chest, the pain almost physical. This was the end of their beginning. This was the last time they would be here in her home, their relationship still new enough to make his blood sing with every move she made.

Her uncertainty added a bittersweet note to his musing. From tomorrow on, he'd be fighting a different battle. When he got on that airplane and left her, she would say her good-byes. Then she would receive each phone call, every visit, in expectation of repeating that final moment. But it wouldn't be over. Not tomorrow, and not, he thought, for a long long time after that. This was just the beginning of a new phase of their affair. No more hiding out from real life, for her or for him. They would both emerge from the cocoon they'd woven around themselves, and anything they did together would be a part of that life that included work, family, friends, and all the normal interaction with people that they had been avoiding.

She finished clearing the table and wiped it off with a wet rag, then took the rag back into the kitchen. She came back and leaned against the doorjamb, drying her hands on a dishtowel. He stood and she looked over at him, and then around the room, which was clean and neat and back in order, except for the chair he pushed out from the table when he rose. He pushed it in. Then he took a step, then another, toward her, and she brushed past him lightly and picked up his coffee cup to bring it into the kitchen and rinse it off at the sink. He followed. It was only a couple of feet and he sidled up behind her while she washed the china cup.

She sighed audibly and leaned back against him. Langston took the saucer from her fingers and put it in the drying rack, then he reached around her to turn off the water. She reached back behind herself and splayed her hands on his thighs. She let her head hang down, exposing the nape of her neck. He kissed the sensitive skin there, and she raised her head and turned her face to him, eyes closed, searching blindly for his kiss. He turned her in his arms and pressed her backwards over the sink before he finally kissed her, deeply. His arms slid around her to pull her as close as he could into his body.

Their lovemaking was bittersweet. They walked into the bedroom hand in hand, like children. They undressed each other, taking their time, savoring every moment, every glimpse of newly exposed flesh, every sensation. For once, Reggie didn't rush to hide under the covers or turn out the light. Naked, she came to him. He drank in the sight of her until she took his face in her hands and raised his eyes to her face. She placed a kiss right next to his lips, then whispered past his mouth to kiss his other cheek in exactly the same spot. Then she put her lips over his and kissed him as deeply as he had her. Langston drank in that kiss eagerly. He brought one hand up to the back of her neck while he deepened it, drawing her tongue into his mouth as far as he could and exploring the inner warmth and texture of her mouth.

They fell onto the bed together and entwined their arms and legs around each other. Langston couldn't get enough of her. He traced every line and curve of her body with his hands, and worshiped her with his mouth. When she was panting, begging for him to fill her with himself, he circled one nipple with his tongue and one with his fingers. He wrapped his free hand over her hipbone to guide her back and forth over his hard flesh in a rhythm that was as slow and sweet as an old song. He brought her slowly just to the summit of desire, then he withdrew and calmed and soothed her until she was ready to begin again, and again, and again. Finally, he couldn't bear the sweet torture for another second. He buried himself to the hilt inside of her, and felt her velvety warmth contract around him. He let go his iron control and waves of pleasure broke over him and through him and to her body, joined with his.

After she fell asleep he whispered in her ear, "I'll be back soon. Don't worry, Reggie."

Eighteen

Reggie awoke with a start, as if a giant hand grabbed her and tugged her out of her dream. It was just as well. Though she couldn't remember it, the dream left her with a vague feeling of unease. She lay quietly in the bed, deriving comfort from the rumble of Langston's snoring, and trying to remember what she dreamed.

She felt terrible. Whatever her subconscious had come up with during the night, it hadn't been pleasant. And emerging from that state into consciousness had not helped. Langston's imminent departure hung over her head like a dark cloud. She got out of bed, sat in the chair by the dressing table, propped her feet up on the bed and watched him sleep, trying not to think.

She had to be cool about his departure. She knew that. She talked to Bebe the day before and told her friend how nervous she was about seeing him off.

"Try to be cool," Bebe advised.

"I know. I haven't known him long enough to go all melodramatic on him."

"That's not what I meant," Bebe said. "I don't think the man would mind if you collapsed on him, sobbing. He might even like it. But I was thinking of those nasty little photographers who follow you around lately. You don't want to give them any chance to make a soap opera out of this."

"That's another good reason not to take him to the airport,"

Reggie said. "Do you think it would be too obnoxious if I didn't take him to the airport?"

"I, uh, guess not," Bebe said. "But you're missing a great chance to indulge in a public display of affection. If you're into that at all."

"I suppose I have my exhibitionist side, but that doesn't mean I want my mother seeing me doing anything. It sort of takes the fun out of it when you know that your exploits will end up being read at the supermarket the next day. Like you said, I don't think I'll give the sleazy photographers any more opportunities."

"I didn't mean you shouldn't give them something to write about. I just meant that you shouldn't give them a drama. Show them up in a big way. Hot photos of you and Langston saying good-bye could get them to ease off on those stupid headlines they keep writing."

"Long Kiss Good-Bye is a headline that fits right in with Sleazing In Seattle." That was the caption Reggie hated most.

"Not if it doesn't look like good-bye," Bebe said. "A sizzling hot kiss is a long way from a kiss-off. You know how to do it. I know you do. You kiss him like . . . well, like someone who can't wait to get him alone. I guarantee he'll respond in kind. Those maggots from the tabloids won't be able to deny the heat between you." Reggie was glad they were on the phone. She was embarrassed at being told that the sexual tension between Langston and herself was so evident.

"I don't care what they say," Reggie lied.

"Right." Bebe said sarcastically.

"I'll think about it some more," she promised. Inwardly, though, she already knew she was going to bug out on him. She didn't want to say good-bye at all, and she especially didn't want to do it in public.

But that was yesterday, and when she looked at him in the cold light of day on their last morning together, she couldn't deny him her company for his last few hours in Seattle. She couldn't bring herself to go without his, either. He woke up at seven, and they got ready for the day together.

He was very quiet. Reggie was, too. His plane left at nine thirty, so she planned to drop him at Seattle-Tacoma International Airport at eight thirty. After he showered and dressed, he had just enough time to pack, which he had, of course, left to the last minute.

"We can grab a quick breakfast after you check in at the airport," she said.

"I thought we were going to go to our coffee shop," he said.

"We won't have time, Mo."

For a moment he looked disappointed. Then his expression cleared. "Next time," he said.

"Sure," Reggie agreed. "Are you finished with that bag? I'll put it by the front door." She leaned down to pick it up, but he intercepted her hand and raised it to his lips.

"I'll get that," he said. He turned her hand over and kissed her palm.

"We'd better get going," Reggie said.

"Okay." He let her go.

They drove to the airport in silence, immersed in their own thoughts. She didn't know what he was thinking. She thought about everything that had happened between them. She never expected to care about him so much. Certainly not when she first heard she would be working with him. Even less after she first met him. And even when it became apparent that he was interested, Reggie would not have predicted that she would fall for him. He was Langston Downs. Football defined him. His life was an endless radiant adventure, filled with grace and magic. Everything he touched turned to gold. Except her. She stayed the same: an ordinary, dime-a-dozen, workaday woman.

But commonplace or not, he liked her. A lot. She loved seeing herself through his eyes. He changed her perception of herself. In fact, he had changed her life. She was going to hate to see him go. She knew this day was coming. She tried to prepare herself for it. But he kept insisting this wasn't good-bye, and she really wanted to believe him, despite the sane, rational portion of her brain that kept reminding her that they couldn't possibly have a future together.

At Sea-Tac, she parked in the short-term parking lot, and they walked into the terminal together. Reggie was accustomed to being stared at after the last couple of weeks, but under the harsh terminal lights, it felt different. She felt exposed, vulnerable, while Langston didn't seem to feel any discomfort at all. He smiled at the people who happened to catch his eye, made jokes with the girl at the ticket counter, and just generally accepted the attention as his due.

She chose a table against the wall of the airport café for their breakfast, while he went to get them coffee and bagels. Once seated at the wobbly little table, his wide shoulders and sexy smile filled her vision, and she forgot about anyone who might have been watching them and concentrated on enjoying her last twenty minutes with him.

"I'll miss you," he said.

"I'm sure you will," Reggie tried to joke. He gave her a look of reproach and she answered more seriously. "Me, too."

"Would you ever consider moving to L.A.?" he asked.

Her mouth dropped open, and she shut it quickly. "Are you serious?"

"As a heart attack."

"I thought you said Los Angeles wasn't someplace you wanted to stay in permanently."

"I don't," he said. "But I'm living there now, and I'm not sure how smart it would be to move. For my new career," he explained. She nodded her understanding, but she wasn't sure what he was talking about. "Maybe you could come and stay for a while, take an extended vacation so we could figure things out together."

"Where is this coming from?" she asked, bewildered.

"I don't want to say good-bye," he said sincerely.

"Neither do I, but Langston, people don't just uproot themselves overnight to live with each other in Hollywood. At least not the people I know."

"I guess it sounds a bit nuts the way I said it. But I've been thinking about it for a while now. Ever since you said that long-distance relationships rarely work out."

"Did I say that?" she asked.

"I think so," he replied. "I heard it, anyway. And I want us to be together. I can't imagine my life without you now."

"You'll get over it when you get back home," Reggie said

calmly, though her heart was beating a mile a minute. He genuinely wanted this. She could tell. "Anyway, I couldn't get the time off. I have a business to run."

"You've got a fax, modem, laptop, and all. The move wouldn't require you to stop working. And a different town might just give your company a shot in the arm," he offered.

"Even if I could just pick up and move, I don't think I'd feel comfortable," Reggie said gently. "We country bumpkins aren't like you jet-setters," she joked. "We're sort of rooted in the community."

"Are you calling me rootless?" he asked in the same tone.

She sighed in relief. He was dropping it. "Whatever you want to call it, you do tend to spend a lot of time on the road. You shot both of your films on location, and you're about to head out for a fifteen-city tour."

"And then back to L.A."

"You don't even know *what* you'll be doing after that, let alone where. Besides, my business, my friends and family are here, and I like it here. It just doesn't make any sense to talk about this now." If he were really serious, Reggie thought, he'd be talking about moving to Seattle.

"It was just a thought," he said.

They finished their breakfast, and she walked him to the entrance to the gates. "Your flight is leaving in twenty minutes, so . . . " She let her voice trail off.

"I guess this is it," he said. "Say it again, Teach."

"Say what?" she asked.

"Kiss me, you fool."

She kissed him on his sexy superstar mouth. "It was your turn," she explained. That seemed to satisfy him. He kissed her, too. Passionately. Just the way Bebe had suggested they kiss—as if they couldn't wait to be alone together.

He let her go slowly, reluctantly. Reggie stood back and took one last long lingering look. "It's been real." She managed to make it sound like a pert, offhand remark.

"I'll call you soon," he said.

She gave him a little salute. "Talk to you soon, then." She pivoted on her heel and walked away. She didn't look back until she was sure he must have gone through the metal detector. Then she slowed and turned around. He was standing there, staring after her, and he waved. She waved back and quickly walked away.

To her surprise, she didn't cry. Not even when she was alone in the car, driving away from the airport. She tried to think of the phone calls she had to make, but his casual question about whether she would ever consider moving to L.A. kept coming back to her. She should have said yes, she thought. If she were totally honest, she would consider it. She might even jump at it.

She didn't feel like going to work after all. She felt disheartened and unsettled. So she drove over to her mother's house to derive comfort from being in the presence of the wisest, most stable woman she knew. Jennifer Primm was gardening in the spring sunshine. When her daughter came into the yard, she looked up, shading her eyes from the spring sunlight.

"So he's gone?"

"Yes," Reggie reported, trying to sound nonchalant, but not at all sure she succeeded.

"He's a sweetheart. When are you going to see him again?"

"I don't think I will. It's over," Reggie said. "Why torture myself? It's better to end it clean."

"Yeah?" her mother said wryly.

"Yes, it's time to get back to real life, now."

"Did you tell him that?" she asked.

"Not exactly. But I'm sure he got the message. He asked me to come to New York for the weekend."

"Well, what are you doing here? Why aren't you at home packing?" Jenny asked, surprised.

"I can't go to New York," Reggie said, shocked at her mother's reaction. "I've got responsibilities here, and work to catch up on, and I can't just drop everything like that. Besides, I'm not sure I should drag this thing out any further. I already care about him so much. More than I should."

"How do you decide how much you *should* love someone? Is there a rule book somewhere?"

"It's just common sense, Mom. I don't want to risk too much on a gamble that isn't going to ever pay off."

"I have no idea what you're talking about," Jennifer Primm said. "You love that boy, and he loves you," she continued. "You find something like that, you don't throw it away."

Reggie wasn't going to argue with her about how much they loved each other. Not when her mother sounded that definite. Leaving that issue aside, there was still a big hole in her mother's reasoning. "But you know as well as I do you always risk getting hurt when you love someone. We talked about this when Daddy died. I know you think the risk was worth it—so did I, for you and Daddy—but we're not in the same situation that you were."

"Of course you are."

"Mama, the times have changed. Women today don't just throw away everything they've worked for to chase a man."

"I didn't say anything about chasing him. He invited you to come. Why not accept the invitation?"

"I don't want to get hurt."

"Baby, you're already hurting," she said wisely. "You might as well stay with him as long as you can."

"You think I should move to Los Angeles?" Reggie couldn't believe it.

"I thought we were talking about a visit to New York City. Where did moving to Los Angeles come in here?"

"He is talking about it. It was just something he said in the heat of the moment."

"You don't know that," Jenny said. "What if he really meant it?"

"If he thought this was more than just a casual thing, he'd consider moving here. He has a lot less reason to stay in L.A. than I do to stay in Seattle."

"He could have been afraid of being rejected. He's just as frightened of his feelings as you are of yours. He was probably making the invitation in order to see what you would say."

"What do you want me to do, Mom? I can't change who I am."

"I'm not suggesting you change. I know you're proud of your independence and your achievements. I'm proud of them, too. But you don't measure yourself solely by your success in business. Being there for your family and friends is equally important to you. Your ability to give to the people you love with your whole heart is a part of who you are as well. I'm not suggesting you change at all. I respect you so much for being such a giving, loving woman. Why can't you treat this man the way you treat the other people you care about?"

"It's like you said . . . I'm afraid to. When it comes to relationships, Langston Downs has even less experience than I do. He's only had brief flings and short-term affairs."

"You can teach him. You were always a good teacher."

"What if all I can teach him is what not to do. Then I'm out of the picture and he's on to someone new. This is better. At least I've still got my dignity."

"Dignity doesn't keep you warm at night," Jenny advised her. "If you don't at least take a shot at this chance, you'll regret it. I guarantee you that."

"I'm not so sure," Reggie said. "And anyway, I was pretty happy with my life before Langston Downs ever showed up. I've got work I love, a business that's in the black, and good friends I enjoy. Anything more than that would be icing on the cake."

"Go for the icing," Jenny urged. "It's the best part."

"As a calorie counter from way back, I don't think it's worth it," Reggie said, trying to sound perky and failing. "It could never work between us," she said, resigned.

"It can't if you're not willing to try," her mother said. "Work can be postponed. Life can't."

She was almost home when the car phone rang. She figured it was probably Bebe, calling to find out how things went at the airport after their telephone conversation the day before.

But it was Langston. "They're going to make me hang up any minute," he said. "We're taxiing down the runway now. But I couldn't wait until we were up in the air to tell you about my surprise." The tears finally came, silent and heart-burning.

"What surprise?" she asked.

"Look in the glove compartment," he said. She pulled over and put the car in park, then did as he asked.

"Oh my God!" Inside the glove compartment were airplane tickets. "There must be a dozen tickets here." She flipped through them. Seattle to Los Angeles, they read, and back to Seattle, over and over again.

"You have to come see me at least twice a month. I don't need them for anything. Yet. If you turn me down, of course, that will be another story. I'll have to get them changed from your name to mine and come back up here to put you on the plane personally."

"This is crazy, Langston," she said, laughing through her tears.

"What is crazy about wanting to see as much as possible of the woman that you love?" he asked matter-of-factly.

"I can't believe this," she said. One of the tickets was for a trip to New York the following weekend.

"Believe it, Teach," he commanded. "It's true."

"But—" she started.

"I've got to turn the phone off now," he said quickly. "The captain just said so."

The next thing Reggie heard was a dial tone. Still frozen in shock, she just sat staring at the receiver. "I'm going to have a martini at lunch," she promised herself.

When she arrived home, she went straight into her office and started to plan her day. She considered asking Bebe to meet her for a liquid lunch, but dismissed the idea. Bebe was just going to give her the same advice her mother had.

She finished printing out her phone log and reached for the telephone. But instead of dialing the first name on her list, she found herself punching in Langston's home phone number.

His machine answered.

"I can't get away this weekend to meet you in New York City," she said. "But call me later. I'll be here, getting my office in order so I can take that extended vacation you suggested . . . down there in the city of angels."

Nineteen

He met her at the airport, looking more delectable than she remembered, if that was possible. He was much calmer than she expected, not as charged up as he seemed in Seattle. Perhaps that was because L.A. contained a kind of palpable energy she never felt at home. It felt like a big city while Seattle did not. Especially the highway, where they zoomed along at seventy, as did everyone around them.

She visited Los Angeles before this, once on business and once on vacation when a friend who relocated got married. She enjoyed the city both times, but found it so spread out and difficult to navigate that she didn't think she got a real feel for the place.

"I've been to Venice and Santa Monica," she told Langston as they passed the road signs reminding her of her previous visits. "But I'd like to spend more time on the mall in Santa Monica and on the beach in Venice. And I only drove through Beverly Hills once, so I definitely expect you to show me the hot spots in that part of town."

"Done," he said. "Anywhere else you want to go, Teach?"

"Hollywood didn't look so great. I think one visit to Grauman's Theatre was enough to satisfy me. But I went to a very cool restaurant up there. I don't know if it was in Hollywood, but it wasn't too far from that really great bookstore on Sunset Boulevard."

He smiled and shook his head. "You come in for a weekend and find the best bookstore in L.A. on your own. I can't even

get my friends to go there with directions and my strongest recommendation."

"Everyone knows people in film only read coverage," she
teased.

"Hey, we read *Variety,* too," he joked.

"It was business. Elaine did a signing there. It was the first
time we came to Hollywood to talk to the movie people. She
didn't think they'd actually do the deal, so we figured we might
as well do some P.R. while we were here."

"I'm going to have so much fun showing you all my favorite
places. I've only lived here a year, so I haven't had time to get
jaded yet. You'll love Tommy's house. He lives in Long Beach,
where the hip people hang out."

"Your agent?"

"Yeah. You remember him. He's from New York and he says
it reminds him of the city."

"I thought I detected an accent," she said.

"He's a great guy. And you'll love his new girlfriend. She's
a . . . V.P. of development at some independent film company, I
think, and she's really nice."

"What's her name?"

"I don't remember," he said casually. She wondered how nice
she could be if he remembered her job description but not her
name, but Reggie kept the thought to herself. This was Lalaland,
and she didn't know how it worked yet.

They got off the freeway onto the Pacific Coast Highway, and
rode alongside the Pacific Ocean, which gleamed blue-green
and shining in the afternoon sun. "I've never been to Malibu
before," she said. "Elaine says it's *the* place to see the stars at
home, if you can get in. Is it very exclusive?"

"The houses are expensive, so that makes it exclusive, but
they're worth what they cost. They are right on the beach, and
other than Malibu Colony, there are no other towns for miles
except some big compounds in the hills that aren't visible from
the road, and a ranch or two. It's only an hour from L.A., but
it's completely residential—a small beach community. It's like
a different planet. But it's not very snobby. It's where the stars
actually let down their hair. They walk on the beach and wash

their cars in the driveway and play with their kids. Just like real people. Everybody is friendly. I lived there all year, but most people use the houses there as vacation homes."

"I hope I don't make a fool of myself," Reggie confided.

"You couldn't do that," he said confidently.

"I can be as star-struck as the next person," she confessed. "Believe me."

"I'm sure you'll be fine. I can't wait to show you off myself."

"Oh great," she said. "I don't own any designer gowns, remember?" she said, thinking of the argument she had with him on their first night together.

He smiled. "I remember. We can fix that."

Personally, she wasn't in any hurry to add haute couture gowns to her wardrobe, but she didn't contradict him because that wasn't a discussion they needed to have on their first day together again after three weeks apart. Besides, she was going to be flexible, she reminded herself.

"How was your tour?" she asked.

"Tiring. But I think it was good. Did you see me on the *Today Show?*" he asked.

"Yes, and you deserve a reward for behaving yourself. I know how much you were looking forward to chatting with Regis Philbin."

"I was good, wasn't I," he said smugly. "And I didn't even know I was going to get a reward."

"And your reward is the satisfaction of knowing you acted like an adult," she told him.

"Oh," he said, sounding disappointed. "When you said I deserved a reward, I thought maybe you were going to . . . I don't know . . . do something sort of special for me."

"Like what?" Reggie asked suspiciously.

"Whatever you thought was appropriate," he answered promptly, the soul of innocence.

"I'll think about it," she promised.

"We'll be home in fifteen minutes. Will you know anything by then?" he asked playfully.

"We'll see," she said. They had been speeding along a stretch of deserted highway for quite some time, the last of the houses

disappearing as the road leveled out. The ocean to their left was
relatively calm, and the beach was completely deserted except
for the occasional beachside eatery or pub where cars were
parked, but she didn't see any people. To their right, the terrain
was hilly and the vegetation sparse and brown. There were a few
small roads leading up into the hills, but they were marked private.

"I can see what you mean. It's hard to believe we only got
off the freeway a few minutes ago."

"It's a nice place to live," Langston said.

"Not that you're biased or anything." Reggie laughed.

"I hope you like it," he offered.

She was sure she would like his home, but when they arrived,
she was surprised by the relatively small house. It had a tiny
front yard, with a small garden surrounded by a five-foot fence
with a slightly lower gate covered with vines to ensure his privacy. All of the houses were built close to each other, and the
hidden turnoff and the narrow road into the Colony virtually
screamed "Keep Out." She wondered if he just didn't notice it.
This was the kind of place that people of color would have been
barred from just a few years ago—money or no money. Not that
Seattle didn't have its own snooty enclaves. She just wouldn't
have described any of them as nice, friendly neighborhoods.

Knock it off, girl, Reggie thought. *Give it a chance.* If Langston didn't see what she saw, he spoke from experience. She
was making assumptions she had no right to make.

He led her through the house, and as soon as she saw the
other side, she understood what he meant when he said the prop-
erty was worth it. They were halfway up the cliff side, and
through the wall of tall, arched windows lay a panoramic view
of perfect, clean white sand, and the ocean, pounding ceaselessly
against the shore.

"Wow!"

"It's pretty, isn't it?" he said proudly.

"That's an understatement. It's magnificent," she said. She
stood at the window taking it all in. To the left were some larger
houses, built a little further out on the rocks that made up the
cliff. They seemed to hover directly above the ocean like huge
fishing birds, and sunlight glinted off huge picture windows,

installed to bring the view of the ocean into the houses, she assumed. To their right, the small weather-worn houses of gray, tan, sky blue, pastel pink, and other muted colors seemed to fit the landscape perfectly, just as their little house probably did when seen from the outside.

"Could you get used to this?" he asked complacently.

"Of course," she replied. It was the first time she understood why he might want to continue living in the Los Angeles area rather than moving up to Seattle with her. It could be a hardship, giving this up. *He could keep it, as a vacation house, and move for your convenience,* the obnoxious little voice in her head rebutted. She ignored it. They weren't talking marriage. He hadn't even officially asked her to live with him, yet. They were just . . . trying it on for size.

"Welcome, Teach," he said, coming to her and taking her in his arms. "I'm very glad you decided to come."

"So am I," she said.

"What do you want to do first?" he asked. "Could it be the same thing I'm thinking of?"

"Not unless you're thinking of unpacking my bag while I scrounge around in the kitchen for something to eat," she said sternly.

"As a matter of fact, I was thinking you'd do the unpacking and I'd do the cooking. And there will be no scrounging in my kitchen. I've got enough groceries here to please even the most exacting gourmet. For tonight I have everything planned, including a lovely early supper."

"I'm impressed," she said.

"That's what I like," he teased. "A woman who has her priorities straight. Food first, then." He kissed her cheek and let her go.

She appreciated the thoughtfulness of the gesture, but Reggie wasn't sure she liked being classified as a woman who thought only of food. It came too close to the joking remarks she sometimes heard from her sisters and brother because of her weight problem.

"I want you to have plenty of energy for our reunion," he elaborated as he walked around the island between the dining area and the kitchen. Reggie relaxed and felt the tension leave her for the first time in days. She hadn't realized how stiffly she was holding herself until she untensed her shoulders and her back.

"I missed you, Langston," she told him.

"Me, too, Reg. The bedroom is through that door behind you."

She unpacked and laid out her lingerie, brought specially for their first night together in his house. After she unpacked, she decided to have a shower and dress in the revealing negligee.

Reggie stopped for a quick look in the mirror as she was leaving the room to check that no dirt spots marred the pristine white satin. But as she examined the negligee, she started to see herself, and it was as if it were the first time. She had taken out her braids during the last week, and her newly released hair was a riotous mass of soft black curls that framed her face and grazed her bare round shoulders. Two straps of white satin, an inch wide, framed her collarbone, accenting the dark chestnut hue of her skin and leading down to the deep V that formed the neckline. The swell of her breasts above the shiny white material looked inviting and—she had to admit it—sexy. White satin flowed down over her waist, hips and legs, and swirled as she turned toward the door.

She took one last glance back as she walked away and was amazed to find her backside looked good, too. The material clung to, and revealed, her posterior in all its rotund glory. Reggie had never expected in her life to enjoy the view of herself from behind, but even she could see that it was enticing. It had to be the negligee. She was going to have to buy more expensive lingerie, she decided. It was definitely worth the money.

His reaction was everything she could have hoped. "Are you sure you want to eat, before—"

"Before what?"

"Before your official welcome to my humble abode."

She looked at the delicious spread he had prepared of cold broiled shrimp, chilled asparagus in vinaigrette dressing, and simple but elegant butterfly pasta primavera, all of which had been beautifully laid out with glistening china and sparkling silver. The table was placed in front of another tall window that looked out over the beach and the ocean behind the house. "I could use a little sustenance," she said, unembarrassed by her appetite for the first time in her life.

"Your wish is my command," he said, then took her by the elbow to lead her to the table and help her into her seat.

"That's what I like to hear," Reggie said. "You have outdone yourself, Langston. This all looks so beautiful."

"Dig in," he ordered, and then proceeded to demolish half of the meal in no time flat. He always made her feel so dainty when they ate together, because he devoured so much more food than she did.

She was still enjoying the delicious meal when he offered her coffee. "I'll stick with the wine, for now," she answered. "It's lovely with the pasta."

He sat and watched her eat, which made her feel very self-conscious. "I'm so glad you're here. I love you."

"I love you, too," she replied after swallowing a morsel of tasty shrimp. "And I can tell you, I think you will be getting that reward tonight after all."

"Good," he said, looking extremely pleased with himself. "But we have to meet some people afterwards. Around eleven."

"Tonight?" she asked, flabbergasted. It was her first day here. She wanted to spend a few hours alone with him. "Do we have to go?"

"We don't have to, but I told Tommy we'd be there."

Then she understood. "It's business then?"

"No, just Tommy and his girlfriend, and a few other people. They really wanted to meet you, and I wanted you to meet them. You're the guest of honor, so to speak."

"But you know I'm usually in bed by then. Late-night parties aren't really my thing."

"There weren't any late-night parties in Seattle, I know. But it's not unusual here." He examined her face. "You don't like them."

"It's our first night together," she said, trying not to sound like she was complaining or criticizing his choice of entertainment, and wishing he would read her mind. She didn't want to go out.

"I thought you'd enjoy meeting some of my friends. I didn't mean to rush it. If it's too soon, just tell me."

"I'd be happy to meet them, but maybe another night might be better for throwing me in their face."

"I'm sorry. I couldn't wait. But I understand. I can still call it off."

He looked so disappointed that she couldn't bear it. "It's not really fair to back out on him at the last minute like this. We can stop by for a quick drink anyway," Reggie said.

"You are fantastic, Reggie, my love. I should have realized that you would want to relax your first night here, especially since you're not used to late nights."

"Yes, you should," she said sternly, but then she relented, adding, "Since you didn't, we'd better get going. How much time do I have to get ready for this shindig? I want to look nice and refreshed for your friends. Maybe I'll take a nap before we go."

"Oh we have hours and hours," he said. "I could nap with you."

"I wouldn't get much rest that way," she pointed out.

"Not if you're in my bed in that thing, you won't," he agreed, licking his lips.

"Uh uh. This much satin deserves a nice leisurely night to enjoy it. That's why I bought it," Reggie said.

"We have three or four hours," he commented.

"Is it three? Or is it four? I have to shower and dress and put on makeup, and you know how bad I am at that."

"I can shower with you," he suggested. "That will save some time."

"Sure it will," she said sarcastically. "No chance, Mo. I'm not going to be your excuse for being late," she said firmly.

He ignored her objection. "I can dress you, too. It would make a nice change of pace. Not that I don't love undressing you, but this would be new and novel. I bet I could even put on your makeup for you," he said. "I've watched lots of times while I was waiting for my turn in the makeup chair."

"If you wanted to shower and sleep with me tonight, you

shouldn't have made other plans," Reggie chided. "I didn't come all the way to California for a quickie."

He looked shocked, but he quickly recovered. "I can't believe you said that."

"I meant it, too. You're going to have to wait for a more propitious time to get your reward. It was going to be good, too," she taunted.

"You're full of surprises tonight, Reggie. I can't wait to see if you really live up to your promises," he challenged.

"You're just going to have to wait and see, aren't you?"

"You're killing me, sweetheart," he groaned.

"Good," she said.

"What's that supposed to mean?" he asked.

"I was looking forward to tonight, too," she said. "Anticipation is a wonderful aphrodisiac, don't you think? I was almost enjoying the wait, but I can't say it didn't leave me a little . . . tense, shall we say. I feel like I'm ready to explode."

He groaned again. "Oh God. Reggie, you're doing this on purpose, aren't you?" Langston accused.

"I refuse to suffer alone," she replied offhand.

"You're not," he confirmed.

"Good," she said again.

Twenty

Langston loved having Reggie in L.A. with him. For the first time since he'd known her, she wasn't working, so they got to spend almost all their time together. He wasn't signed up for a new project yet, so they had plenty of time to go to places like the Fine Arts Museum and the J.P. Getty Mansion. They had fun together. He reveled in the newfound confidence her presence here had given him. He had won her over after all. He felt like the luckiest man on earth.

He especially liked having her all to himself. His time wasn't completely his own, though. He had appearances to make, and since he had fulfilled his promotional obligations for *Under His Skin,* he could do the things he put off when his every move was ruled by the hectic schedule imposed by making the movie. Reggie did almost everything with him. He went to the Media House, an alternative educational program at a high school in one of the poorest areas of Los Angeles called the Fourteenth Street Corridor. He owed them an interview at their television station. He loved showing Reggie the place and the hope there. The program was designed to give teenagers who were at high risk for dropping out some direction and academic opportunities and job skills that would not otherwise be available to them. The kids, who were underprivileged minority students, were amazing individuals. After a few minutes with them, he felt like he'd never been away. And he adored the look of pride on Reggie's face when she saw him with the kids. He definitely scored points with that one.

On the other hand, she wasn't much interested in his real work, which consisted of being courted for films by agents, producers, studio folk, and other Hollywood personalities. Reggie didn't like the Hollywood "scene" at all, and declined to attend the power breakfasts, pre-power breakfasts, lunches, dinners, and drink dates during which various insincere individuals pitched him on what they could do for him. The meetings were nonsensical, he agreed, but they were necessary. She skipped most of them.

Langston hadn't signed up yet for his next film project. Most of the scripts he was sent were for buddy cop films, action and suspense, and independent black films about gangsters, prisons, money, or sex. He had a decent film about baseball from Spike Lee, and a nice star vehicle from Kopelson, part *Fugitive* and part *Negotiator,* that he could see himself doing. But Tommy and he were hoping that once people saw *Under His Skin,* they would offer him character roles.

He had actually attached himself to a small doomed project that was based on an unpublished book by an unknown romance writer, which his little sister had recommended he read. It was a period piece about race relations in the U.S. during the Second World War. The lead character was an eighteen-year-old black boy who fell in love with a young white girl before he went off to fight for his country. He came back expecting to be treated differently by the whites in his small southern hometown. After the much more equal treatment he received in the Army, and the heroic welcome he received when his platoon liberated white European cities, he thought he and the white girl might have a future together.

Reggie liked that project best, and she thought that he should concentrate on using his connections to get it made into a movie. "Tommy, can't you do something?" she asked his agent. They had gotten to know each other a little better, although they would probably never be the best of friends. She thought Tommy was a little too full of himself.

Tommy thought she was too smart for her own good. "Even if a big studio purchased the rights to the story, and even if they could set up a deal to film and distribute it, it could take ten years to write a script, get good producers and the kind of director the story deserves, the money to actually make it, and insurance to satisfy prospective investors." Tommy explained.

She turned to Langston. "It's worth a try, isn't it?"

"Not if it gets swallowed up in development hell," Tommy answered for him.

"Reggie, Tommy means the chances are so small that it's not worth it to invest the time on it."

"Tommy is a cynical soul and you sound exactly like him," she replied. "When *Under His Skin* opens, you can force one of those companies that want to work with him into getting that project going."

"It doesn't work that way," Langston said. Her face fell. "I appreciate your enthusiasm, Teach, but Tommy knows what he's doing."

"I'm sure he does," she agreed. "But he works for you, doesn't he? So if you want him to try something different, he should try. He can always tell his big-shot connections it was your idea."

Langston stopped her. "Whoa babe, I don't want to look stupid."

"You're not stupid. Neither is Tommy Ray, and neither am I. We just have different priorities."

"So," Tommy said, smiling. "You want to fire me, Reggie?"

"Of course not," she and Langston said at the same time. "Just light a fire under you," Reggie continued.

"Forget it," Langston ordered. "Tommy knows what's best for my career." He saw something in her eyes change, grow dimmer or darken, and he knew he had lowered himself in her estimation.

Tommy wasn't the only friend of his whom she took on. She never said anything about anyone specific, but she let him know what she thought. She was, as he might have expected, completely intolerant of drug use and alcohol abuse. "All these people obsessed with their image and their 'healthy lifestyles', shoveling white powder up their noses and spending hundreds of thousands of dollars on clothes for one evening and cars they leave in the driveway for their neighbors to admire is sick,"

Reggie said. She could neither condone nor suffer silently the eccentricities and excesses of his wealthy neighbors and business associates. In the end, they had to agree to differ and to avoid certain subjects altogether.

But she was here. And she was his. She savored the successes of, and suffered the setbacks to, *Under His Skin* like she was its biggest investor. Reggie even made him sneak into a theatre with her to watch it with an audience of "regular people," so he could see how it was perceived by the crowd. When they were on the same track, she made him feel good about his work, himself, and his future. It came so naturally to her, but his efforts to return the favor didn't seem to produce the same effect at all. He cooked for her, and she barely ate. She said that all the beautiful people out here made her feel self-conscious, and she was going on a strict diet. He told her he liked her just the way she was, but it didn't seem to make any difference. He bought her clothes, toys, decorative knickknacks, and she thanked him, but they didn't seem to cheer her up.

One day he brought home a painting by an artist whose work she had admired at a party at Dionne Warwick's house.

"You bought this for me?" she asked incredulous.

"For us," he said, wrapping his arms around her as she stood staring at it propped up on the couch. "Do you like it?"

"Of course. It's beautiful. I feel like it should be in a museum, not in our living room."

"This way we can see it whenever we want," he replied.

"But why should we be the only ones to enjoy it?" she questioned, and he realized right then that as much as she liked it, she would feel guilty every time she looked at it. She hung it on the living room wall and seemed to forget about it, until a couple of weeks later when he told her he had donated it to a museum.

"That's wonderful," Reggie exclaimed with all the joy he'd expected her to feel when he bought the painting for her. "Let's go see it."

He tried to talk about her with his best friend, but Tommy didn't seem to know what to make of Reggie. He liked her well enough, and was prepared to love her for Langston's sake, but he knew she didn't approve of him. He took it with a good grace. His agent was, above all else, a realist and he definitely didn't think her idealism would serve her well in Hollywood. His friend and manager Scott was a romantic. He loved her immediately.

"She is fantastic, Mo," he said after he met Reggie. "Hold on to that one."

Both men agreed on one thing, though, Reggie was like a fish out of water. He had his work cut out for him if he was going to try to make her a part of his life.

Reggie couldn't seem to get comfortable in her new life. It felt strange to wake up every morning in Langston's bed. It was nice, but it was also disconcerting. She didn't feel quite herself in this new setting. She told herself it was because she wasn't working. It was the first time in over ten years that she didn't have a job, so it was no wonder that it took some time to adjust to her changed circumstances. But within herself, she knew that wasn't the only problem.

It was completely appropriate for her to feel uprooted, displaced, and confused. After all, she had just completely rearranged her life. But sometimes Reggie wondered if she might have gone too far, too fast. She loved Langston, but his lifestyle was not for her. She admired the work he did with inner-city children, and she liked the way he shared himself with her. He loved her. She didn't doubt it. But she was beginning to wonder if that was going to be enough for her to make a permanent commitment to him. She spent her time trying to get to know him, really know him, and let him know her.

Within a month, she started to feel like a member of his family. Tricia called every few days, and she had long talks with the woman, about writing, about books, and about her son.

"If he gets a few more good roles, like the last two, he'll be set," she told Tricia during one of their early morning phone calls. "Then maybe he can take half a year or so off, and start working toward his degree." They both agreed it was a shame he didn't think he could achieve this one goal. "We could do it in Europe, where he isn't so recognizable," Reggie suggested.

"Sure, I'll just go to Oxford," Langston said. She had thought he was asleep. He sat up in the bed next to her. "Good morning." He kissed her. "Hi, Moms," he said to the telephone receiver.

"You could attend Oxford, if you wanted to," Reggie insisted doggedly.

"Right." he said sarcastically.

"You'll never convince him," Tricia said on the other end of the line. "He'll have to apply and when they let him in he'll see what he's capable of."

"You can be the brains of the family, Teach," Langston said cheerfully.

"And have people thinking you're the good-looking one? I don't think I can settle for that. Besides, who would believe it?" Reggie joked.

Tricia cleared her throat. "Should I call back later?" she asked.

"No, no. We'll argue it out later," Reggie said. Langston rolled over onto his back and put his hands behind his head in a pose that communicated perfectly that he was patiently awaiting her attention.

"Good. I called to find out when you're planning to come see us." Tricia asked.

"You're not planning anything special, are you?" Reggie said nervously. She was looking forward to a quiet weekend with his family. She'd had enough glamour and excitement in the last month.

"No, no. But everyone will want to meet you." Tricia responded.

"We're thinking of the weekend after next. Would that be okay?" She looked at Langston, who nodded his agreement.

His mother said, "Fine."

"Good." Reggie said relieved.

"I've got to get going," Tricia ended the conversation. "I'll talk with you later."

"Good-bye," Reggie said.

"Bye, Moms," Langston added as Reggie hung up. "Finally." He pulled Reggie over on top of him. "Alone at last."

"We should probably get up," she suggested, but she kissed his chin.

"Why?" he asked.

"It's morning. See?" she pointed toward the window.

"I don't have to be anywhere until after noon," he said. "And I need fortification before I can lunch with Scott. He's going to nag me about work, I can feel it."

"So get a job," she teased. "You deadbeat."

"I'm working on it," Langston retorted.

"I don't think this qualifies as job hunting," Reggie told him.

"Rehearsal for my next love scene," he replied. "Now shut up and let me work. I need to concentrate." he said, nuzzling her neck.

"I would hate to break your concentration but . . . I have a question. Why have you waited so long to go home? You wrapped up the film two months ago, and you traveled all over the country on that publicity tour. Why not make a stop off in Detroit? Or invite your family here to visit you?"

"I was busy trying to impress this woman I met," he said against her skin as he trailed kisses from her throat to her shoulder.

"Impress?" she questioned as she pulled his head up by his ears.

"Okay, I was trying to seduce her. She is very hard-headed and it took a while."

"That is no excuse for neglecting your mother," she chided gently.

"She likes you better than she likes me anyway." he said.

"You know she's just using me as an excuse to get you home," Reggie disagreed.

"Don't bet on it. She likes me fine, but it's you she's really interested in."

"I'm not going to argue with you about it, but—" Reggie began.

"Good," he cut her off. "Now that we've got that out of the way, let me tell you more about this woman I like."

"I guess that could be interesting" Reggie said feigning reluctance.

"Very interesting. She's beautiful, and strong, and intelligent, and funny, and she has a little beauty mark, right here." He kissed her collarbone. "It drives me wild with desire. Especially when it peaks out at me from behind the collar of one of her blouses, which isn't often." He lowered his voice. "She's a bit of a prude," he said conspiratorially.

"She sounds like a drag to me," Reggie commented.

"She's not a drag," he protested indignantly. "She's a classy, elegant lady."

"Sounds too good for you," Reggie retorted.

Twenty-one

Langston didn't know if he would ever understand this woman. He loved her more each day, but she seemed to slip further and further away from him. The only time they were in sync was during a few rare moments, once when they enjoyed a sunset together walking down the beach, and again when they finished reading the same book at the same time, closed it, looked over at each other, and said, "Well . . ." at the same moment. Then they laughed and talked and caressed each other, and he felt for a few seconds that he'd achieved what he'd always hoped he would—perfect union with another human being who loved and respected him just as he loved and respected her.

Reggie was, he was almost certain, the woman who should be the mother of his children someday. But he couldn't get a handle on her. He could never predict how she would react to some new experience they shared, and, more importantly, she definitely didn't seem to be adapting to his world.

It was a problem without a solution. He didn't even know what lay at the root of it all. One morning over breakfast he tried to talk to her about it. "Reggie, what do you want in the long run?" he inquired.

"Whew, that's not a simple question to answer," she said with a wide smile. "I guess I want to be happy."

"Are you happy here, with me?" he pressed further.

"I'm very happy with you," she said, but the light that had shone in her eyes a moment before had dimmed. "If I weren't, I wouldn't be here."

"So you think this is working out well?" he couldn't resist asking. "You're not sorry you came?"

"I'm definitely not sorry," she answered hesitantly. "And I think we could work things out. I'm not sure where we're going, though. Are you?"

"I think we're . . . we're getting closer and really getting to know each other," he replied.

"Me, too," she said. "Is there any special reason why you're asking me this now?"

"No special reason. No," he answered slowly.

"Good. I thought maybe you were worried about visiting your mother." They were going to Detroit that weekend for his mother's birthday so that Reggie could meet his sisters. "I'm the one who's supposed to be nervous, not you. They're your family. They can't decide to take an instant dislike to you."

"My mother met you already," he pointed out. "You were a hit."

"But that was before we began living in sin," she teased. She spoke to Tricia at length on the telephone when his mom called him for her weekly chats, so he knew Reggie had to be joking. But now that he thought about it, she had seemed a little tense about this visit.

"I'm sure she's got our wedding gift picked out already," Langston said soothingly. Reggie looked at him as if he were insane. "And my sisters will love you," he continued as if nothing had happened. But that surprised look stayed with him. It couldn't be a shock to her that his mother was anticipating their wedding. Her mother was, too. Just the night before, he heard her say to Jenny on the phone, "He hasn't asked me yet, Mother. You know what they say about counting chickens. It applies double to counting grandchildren." That hadn't been out of the ordinary. Everyone they knew seemed to take it for granted that eventually he would marry her. He did himself.

It gnawed at him. That look. It gave him the same nagging feeling he got when he'd forgotten something he was supposed to do. And the feeling persisted. They packed for the weekend. He bought an engagement ring and considered a number of ways to make a marriage proposal romantic and unique and unforgettable. They drove to the airport, parked the car, and boarded the plane. After they took off, sitting beside each other, Reggie read a book while he pretended to read the newspaper. He finally got up the nerve to ask her what she was thinking when she looked at him like that.

"When?" she asked, confused.

"The other morning, when I said my mother probably had our wedding gift picked out already, you looked as though I just confessed I was the man who killed Nicole Simpson."

"I don't remember that," she said.

"So what were you thinking?" he asked.

"Since I don't remember this happening, I don't remember what I was thinking," she said acerbically.

"Can you make a guess?" he pressed.

"I probably could if I absolutely had to," she said doubtfully.

He nodded. "I would appreciate it."

"I might have been thinking that we've never discussed marriage," she said offhand.

"What would you say if I did ask?" he couldn't help probing.

"Are you?" she asked, smiling. She thought he was kidding.

"I could," he said challengingly.

She laughed. "Langston, read your sports section."

He felt his face get warm, whether with frustration or embarrassment he wasn't sure. "Reggie, this is no joking matter."

"Isn't it? Mo, you're not seriously talking about marrying me. You're not ready for that."

"What makes you say that?" he asked, thinking of the ring in his pocket.

"Everything. You're like a little boy. You don't have the first idea of what it is to love as an adult, to forget yourself and really be there for them. For me. It's okay. That's worked for you with everyone in your life, including me. But it doesn't exactly make me want to marry you." She didn't sound angry or hurt or even disappointed in him.

"But . . . but," he stammered. "Why? What are you doing with me then?"

"You said you wanted me. I believed you. I loved you for it."

"And that's all?" he said, shocked.

"You make me feel beautiful. I love being with you. There are some advantages to being with a man who loves like a kid. You're fun and open and wild. It's wonderful to be around you."

"I do love you," he insisted.

"I know you care about me. I don't really fit into your life, and that's forced you to make compromises I never would have expected you to make. I know how hard it's been for you to give up going to parties because of me. If I met you in your natural habitat instead of on my home turf, I don't think we would have made it this far. You've even tried to change things as far as you could stretch them without completely rearranging your life. I'm satisfied with that, for now."

That wasn't what he wanted to hear. Even when she said, "Really. I love you, Langston," he wasn't mollified.

"I'm not a child. I'm a man," he erupted. "Reggie, you're talking to me like I'm fourteen years old. I can't believe you're saying this."

"I'm not trying to insult you. I don't have a crystal ball. I don't know what will happen between us. I like to think we'll have a lot of fun together, and maybe we'll learn something from each other along the way. You've already given me so much."

His anger dissipated somewhat, but he was disturbed by her attitude. "Regina, we have to talk."

"We are talking" she said.

"I mean really talk about this. I can't believe you'd just dismiss my proposal like that."

"What proposal? I didn't hear any proposal. You've got me exactly where you want me. There's no need to propose." He couldn't argue with that, because she was at least partially right. He bought the engagement ring in reaction to her look of surprise when he mentioned marriage. He was motivated as much by the desire to prove her wrong as he was by his desire for her. "Don't ask me to marry you just because your ego is at stake. I don't need that."

"What if it's my heart that's at stake?" he couldn't resist asking.

"Is it? Or is it your pride?" she asked in response.

The flight to Detroit was more than two hours long, but after her last remark, he couldn't bring himself to speak again except to ask the stewardess for a stiff drink when Reggie ordered a mimosa. Langston was disconcerted. He didn't know what to do. There was an element of truth to everything she said, but on the whole, he felt misunderstood. Betrayed.

Zora was waiting for them at the gate, and Reggie and his oldest sister took an instant liking to each other. Once he introduced them, he didn't have to speak again during the entire ride home. He didn't think they noticed his silence.

Zora gave Reggie a rundown on the family. "I'm the oldest. So you have me to thank for his best qualities." She waggled her head toward Langston. "I beat them into him. With a little help from my sisters, Joey and Lorraine. Joey's the middle girl. She was named after Sojourner Truth. Between her middle-child syndrome and the name, she has all kinds of problems, as you can imagine, but basically she's cool. Can't keep a man but she's got her kids and a great job, so she doesn't really need one." Reggie laughed, but the laugh subsided as Zora gave her an appraising look. "I'm serious. My husband Frank thinks he's indispensable, but if he wasn't such a good dancer, he'd be out the next time he got home late for dinner."

"And she calls Joey neurotic," Langston chimed in from the back seat. "Meanwhile, Zora married the first guy she dated who was taller than her with her heels on." Zora adored Frank. Everyone knew it. Though she pretended to be so tough and unemotional, deep down she was a big bowl of mush.

"She even tells people she just married the guy so she'd always have a dance partner." Langston's outspoken, funny older sister was his rock, but though she'd provided the mothering Tricia Downs hadn't been able to, the family as a whole always treated her as if they couldn't stand her bossiness or her chronic interference in their lives.

"It's no joke, Langston," she threw at him over her shoulder. "It's tough being five feet eleven inches and female."

"She was scarred for life when she hit five foot eight in the sixth grade," he told Reggie.

"Oh be quiet," Zora ordered. "My littlest sister, Lorraine, is at the house with the rest and she can't wait to meet you, Reggie.

You'll like her. She's the nicest member of the family, and her boyfriend Ziggy is a sweetheart, too."

"Who else is at the house?" Langston asked.

"The kids, and Rufus is coming, too."

He seemed surprised. He explained to Reggie, "He's our step-father."

While they were getting their bags from the trunk of the car, Reggie asked him, "Are you all right?"

"Fine," he answered curtly, and slammed the trunk closed.

"Fine," she repeated, but in a lighter tone that indicated to him she was just humoring his childish tantrum, waiting for it to blow over. She followed him into the house.

The whole family was waiting there, except for Langston's stepfather, Rufus, who was due later according to Tricia. They were a big crowd. Langston's visits home were rare enough by themselves to merit a family gathering. The fact that he brought a girl home with him made his mother's brunch an event not to be missed.

Tricia Downs greeted Reggie like an old friend, and the rest of the family was as eager to talk with her as Zora had been on the drive from the airport. Although his oldest sister had filled Reggie in on Joey's full name, Zora had neglected to mention that Lorraine was also—like her siblings—named after a famous black author, Lorraine Hansberry, which his youngest sister lost no time in telling her. "She told me she thought about naming me Gwendolyn for Gwendolyn Brooks, the poet. I wish she had, maybe then I'd be more literary or something. Anyway, then it would fit in better with Zora, Langston, and Sojourner."

"Don't complain," Joey admonished. "You were the lucky one."

"I've been calling myself Lori lately," she said to Reggie.

"I'll remember," Reggie promised.

"Lorraine is a lovely name," Tricia interjected. "All of my children have beautiful names that also happen to be tributes to some great people."

"Face it, Moms. You were hoping we'd be writers," Langston teased.

"I'll admit I hoped at least one of you would share my obsession with the written word," she confessed without embarrassment. "But I didn't stand over you with a whip and force you to write."

"You did when we were little," Zora reminded her.

"You'll be glad I made you keep those diaries some day," she told her eldest daughter. "Would you like to see them?" she asked Reggie.

"Oh no!" Langston protested, and his sisters clearly felt the same way. "Believe me. You don't want to waste your time."

"Maybe later," she consoled Tricia. The doorbell rang. "Saved by the bell," she said thankfully.

The arrival of Langston's stepfather put an end to the conversation, at least for the moment. The house was completely wheelchair accessible, but it always seemed to take a while for Rufus to settle in and get accustomed to moving around the old house again.

It took Langston time, too, to get comfortable with Rufus each time they saw each other. After that, he couldn't keep his attention fixed on Reggie anymore. He knew she'd be fine. She was completely at ease with the Downs clan, he noticed. She charmed his sisters, held the babies, and talked to the children at length. Watching her draw them out, he could imagine her at the front of a classroom, speaking about creative writing and the English language which he knew now, after all their time together, was a special passion of hers.

He knew a lot about her. Today he had learned even more. He knew exactly what she thought of their relationship. And he learned something about himself that he'd failed to recognize before. He was exactly the immature, selfish man she had accused him of being. He was hurt by the words she had spoken on the plane, but it was his pride that was hardest hit. He had to admit the truth.

It was ironic that, for all his wounded feelings, he was more concerned with changing her mind than with changing himself in order to become more acceptable to her. He wanted to propose now. To pull out the ring and prove her wrong. But he'd only be doing exactly what she had said he would. It was a reaction to her rejection, not because he wanted to change his life. He didn't. He liked his life. He wanted her to become a part of it, but only if she could support his choices. He was an idiot. He acknowledged it within himself. All he could think was that Reggie Primm was going to marry him, whether she knew it or not.

When he thought back over the last two months to when he met her, he realized he hadn't changed at all. He had pursued her, as she said, because she was different. And once he got her, he couldn't let her go because she was the best thing that ever happened to him. Langston Downs was in love with a woman who wanted more than the sexiest man in America. She wanted what he always said he wanted: a partner and a playmate, a lover and a friend. The difference between them was that she was willing to give all of herself, while he was afraid to give anything away. It was funny that he always thought of himself as an open, vulnerable lover, and Reggie as the rigid one.

She came to L.A. to try to make this thing between them work. He never even considered moving to Seattle, except to dismiss it immediately when she brought it up. He didn't even consider what it might cost her. Sure he knew he was asking a lot, but in his arrogance he thought he was giving her something equally valuable in return. Himself. He hadn't given her much of anything. He hadn't thought to make a single sacrifice in return. He had never thought to grant her simplest request, that he keep their relationship a secret from the press. It would not have been that hard to do. But even in the face of her pain, he only challenged her to rise above the humiliation she was subjected to daily. And she did it. For him. He was an idiot.

Twenty-two

Langston's mother, and most of his family, lived in a nice suburb of Detroit, but he took her to the house in which they'd grown up, which was a tenement not far from Detroit's famous Museum of Fine Arts, in an area that looked like it had been bombed some years ago and never rebuilt. The neighborhood consisted of block after block of red brick townhouses, many of them clearly abandoned, interspersed with the occasional over-grown lot and a few blocks of houses that were better cared for. The people on the street were all different ages, sizes, and shades of brown, and, if their attire was any indication, different income brackets. There were bums in layers of clothes that looked as if they might smell really terrible. There were also men and women in suits, on a Saturday, obviously on their way to and from work. There were children from five to fifteen in torn jeans, both the designer and the hand-me-down kind. It was a mix with only one common denominator—the color of the people's skin. If she saw two Asian and two white faces, it was two more of each than she expected after driving through the area for five minutes.

But after seeing the crumbling apartment building, in which Mrs. Downs and her four children lived in a three-bedroom apartment until the late eighties, they drove a few blocks to Detroit's Museum Of Fine Art. It was one of the nicest museums Reggie had ever visited. It was huge, with an amazing collection of both famous and lesser known paintings, including some of her absolute favorites.

"I never knew Detroit had such an amazing art museum."

"My mother brought us here all the time. And to the movie theater downtown, which has been renovated and proclaimed a national landmark since, and to the restaurants in Greektown, and to so many other incredible places in Detroit. Although we saw few white faces on our block or at school, ours were often enough the only black voices at the symphony or the ballet, so it all balanced out."

"When did you leave the neighborhood?"

"When I signed my first deal with the pros. But my mother didn't want me to do it. She spent our childhood working her butt off, but she never failed to take advantage of any opportunity to show us there were more important goals than making a paycheck," he said proudly. "She wanted me to go to college, get a degree before I started working. She didn't care about the money."

"She is an amazing woman," Reggie said. "Do you ever wish you listened to her? Waited, I mean?"

"Not really. You know I would like to have a degree, have a proper background in academics and all that. But I'm happy with the choices I made. I think I turned out okay."

"She's very proud of you," Reggie said.

"Not half as proud as I am of her," Langston responded. "You remind me of her."

Reggie was stunned. "That's the nicest thing you could say to me," she said finally. Sometimes the extravagant compliments he paid her made Reggie think he didn't see her at all, as when he told her how beautiful her legs were to him. But this single heartfelt statement made her feel like flying.

"I mean it. You have that strength and independence, and her brains."

"So do you, Langston." She wished she could convince him of that. She just couldn't get him to see that his inferiority complex was not based on anything real. No one who knew him could see him as stupid. No one but Langston himself. She planned to devote herself to changing that, if he would let her.

He shook his head. "I'm not like you. You can do anything."

"You educated yourself, and that's not easy to do. Especially since half your so-called friends treat you like a commodity—"

she stopped herself before she could start another argument with him about his chums at home. She hated what Hollywood did to him. She hoped that someday, maybe, she could get him away from the place—at least for a while. If they stayed together, she had every intention of getting him to take some time off from making films so she could take him to Europe or Australia or anywhere where he could spend a couple of years getting his bachelor's degree.

If they stayed together.

Reggie knew it was a big "if." He was convinced that his new career would prove to himself and to everyone else that he wasn't a dumb jock, all brawn and no brain. He thought acting would validate his existence. She couldn't persuade him that he didn't need to prove anything to anyone but himself. He was surrounded by people who lived by the adage, "You are only as good as your last picture." It was a strange, other-worldly town that valued its famous, talented inhabitants more for their fame than for their talent.

She didn't want to bring up that bone of contention when they were here, among his family and his real friends. He didn't think his friends in Los Angeles were wrong to treat him like a dumb jock, but here, where he was expected to behave like the sensible, capable man his mother raised, he lived up to those expectations without a second thought.

"I blew my chance," he said sheepishly. He pointed at the painting on the wall in front of them. "I could have learned all about this painting and the artist, but I couldn't resist the lure of the big money." He shrugged. "I was young. And I did what I thought I had to do."

"What did your stepfather have to say about that?" she asked.

"Rufus didn't think he was qualified to give me advice. He's disabled, paralyzed from the waist down because of a car accident. So he understood why I wanted to make that money for Mama and the girls. He would have made the same choice himself. He moved out when I was ten because he couldn't support us. He'd come back, then leave again when he couldn't take it anymore, watching Moms do it all."

"How come you never mentioned him?" Reggie asked gently.

She was so surprised when she met the man because no one told her about him, not Langston nor his mother.

"They're divorced. They are still friends, and I know he loves my mother and us, but he couldn't handle being in that chair. He thought it made him less of a man. It didn't. Not to any of us. But he gave up, just quit and sort of faded out of the family. We loved him, but it felt like we had one parent, my Moms. She took care of everything."

"She is a very forceful woman," Reggie said.

"When I was growing up, she was the one I wanted to be like, not him. I just knew a wheelchair wouldn't have stopped her. The women in my neighborhood were strong. They took care of all of us and made sure we did right, and they were tough, too. But they raised us with love." His eyes misted over as he thought about the past.

"And hope," she said softly.

But he heard her. "Faith," he said, his voice ringing out in the tall-ceilinged room. He looked around, embarrassed, but when he met the curious glances of the other museum visitors, he just smiled and lowered his voice and continued. "They were full of it. And they instilled it in us. No matter how unfair the world seemed, or how hard, my mother kept pushing and praying and persuadin' us that there was always something good waiting right around the corner, if you believed."

"My parents thought that, too, I think," she confided. "They mostly taught us just by being so involved and so fearless. They made a great team. I thought when my father died that my mother would go nuts alone in that big house by herself. But she didn't. She kept right on. You know she was a social worker until she was forced to take retirement. She was a good one. She told us about her work over dinner, and we all wanted to be social workers, too. Even John.

"How come we never talk like this at home?" he surprised her by asking.

"I don't know. I guess these things don't come up that much in L.A. and before that we had . . . other things on our minds. But I'm glad we're talking like this now," Reggie answered. "I like seeing this side of you. Now I'm sure I've made the right decision."

"What decision?" he asked.

"To go home, to Seattle."

His mouth dropped open. She closed it with a fingertip. "I didn't mean to mention this until we went back, but this just seemed like the perfect setting, the perfect moment. It's so peaceful here, and I feel good, being here with you."

"The perfect moment for what?" he asked.

"To tell you that I don't like L.A. I can't imagine making it my home."

"For someone who says she's enjoying herself, you certainly chose an odd place to drop a bomb like that."

"I'm hoping that there won't be an explosion, you see."

"But you know there will be. You know I'm not going to let you go."

"It's a decision I had to make for myself."

"I can't believe this," he said, astounded. "It hasn't even been a month. How can you give up on us after only three weeks?"

"I'm not giving up," she vowed. "I love you, Langston, and I want to keep seeing you. I don't want to leave you. But I have to go home because if I stay in Los Angeles, we'll end up hating each other."

"I could never hate you," he protested.

"You will. I can't stand the life you lead in Hollywood. It's awful, so fake. I can't stand to watch you getting sucked into those parasites' mind games." He cringed. "It hurts me. And I know that my criticism hurts you, but I can't keep my mouth shut about these people who want to know you, do you favors, etc."

"What do you want me to do, Reggie? Just tell me and I'll do it. Don't leave."

"I told you on the plane, I've seen how hard you've tried to include me in your life. It just won't work. I know now why so many movie stars have homes in places like New Mexico and Texas and Montana. I always thought it was an affectation, but now I understand the necessity. They need a break from the film industry, which permeates everything from trying to drive home safely on a freeway full of idiots talking on their cell phones, to trying to get the attention of a salesperson in the Gap who's more interested in serving a fourteen-year-old television star. They want to get as far away from limos and lunches and lime-light as they can."

"If you don't like L.A., we don't have to live there," he said reasonably.

"You do. At least, you seem to think that 'scene' is the key to your future. And you don't want a house on exclusive Bain-bridge Island any more than you want a ranch in Wyoming. Neither of them would be any more natural to you than Malibu. Real life for you is this place, the people who truly know you and love you. I thought you were too embarrassed about your life in Tinseltown to invite your family to live with you there, or at least to visit regularly. Now I understand. It's not embar-rassment that makes you keep this part of your life so separate. It's a sane, simple solution to an insane situation."

"I could commute to Seattle," he suggested, sounding des-perate.

"You would hate that. You need a home. You said it yourself. You spent all those years on the road, and I don't think you would be happy spending half your time traveling back and forth between your work in California and your home in Washington. Do you, Langston? Think about it. Meanwhile, I think it's time to go home."

"When?" he inquired, his voice hard.

"I mean home to your mother's place," she said soothingly. "We can talk about this later."

He turned with her, and they walked back out the way they came, but after a minute, Langston said. "I agree with some of what you said, but I think you're wrong about some of it. I couldn't be prouder of you, of how you handle yourself, and how you refuse to be sucked into the game playing. You never embarrass me. You have some problems of your own—your insecurity about your appearance, for example—and they make you blind to the fact that you really fit in very well to my lifestyle."

"I didn't think I did," Reggie said, feeling somewhat offended. He couldn't even look at her.

"Let me finish." She nodded. "Maybe I am trying a little too hard to fit in myself, but I've only been doing this for a year, and I have a lot to learn yet. I am busy starting a new career and trying to make a home for myself, and the changes might affect my choices, but one thing I'm absolutely sure about is that you do belong in my life. I feel it more each day. You haven't had enough time to adjust yet, but I think you can do it if you want to. I'm not sure why you're fighting so hard against making a few compromises—"

She couldn't help herself. She had to interrupt. "A few compromises?!" she exclaimed.

But he overrode her. "I know you're homesick for your friends and family. You're very close to your mother and your nephew and Bebe, and I can hear in your voice how much you miss them every time you speak to them on the phone, but it's not like you'll never see them again. We can move to Seattle, maybe not right away, but as soon as I get more established. I think we could live anywhere we want."

"*I* know we can," she said snidely, but he wasn't listening. They had reached the car, which he had borrowed from his mother for the day.

After he climbed into the driver's seat, he continued, "I thought a lot about what you said on the plane out here and a little part of me guessed that this might be coming. But what you see as an inability to compromise, I see as exactly the kind of sacrifice you think me incapable of making. True, that sacrifice was for my career, but don't you think that if I can make the necessary compromises for my work, I'll be that much more capable of making them for something that's infinitely more important to me, namely you?"

"Honestly, Langston, I don't know. Your dedication to your career is clear. You worked really hard and even risked life and limb your entire adult life. But you've never risked anything for a relationship. Or if you have, I don't see any evidence of it. You are in your mid-thirties and by your own admission, you've never even had a long-term relationship before."

"That's because I never knew you before," he said simply.

"That's sweet. But I'm not sure it's true," Reggie replied dryly.

"Could you try to open up a little. Don't be so hard," he said.

"I could, but I'm not one of these fat people who is always nice and jolly." Reggie knew she sounded churlish, but she was still smarting from his remark about her insecurity.

"Oh God. I'm sorry I said anything about that, Reggie. But I definitely didn't mean to imply that you were fat."

"Why not. I am. Anyway, let's not get into that again."

"Fine with me. I want to talk about this decision you've made about moving to Seattle."

"I don't want to argue with you anymore. Let's just have a pleasant weekend with your family, and we can discuss this when we get back to Los Angeles."

"So you are coming back with me?" he asked.

"Of course."

"That's good," he said. "Then let's talk about this later. We're almost home." For the rest of the drive, they discussed the itinerary for that evening and the next day, which included a visit to his friend Sammy's house. On Monday they were returning to the West Coast, and Reggie figured they could hammer all this out then. She didn't want to leave him or end their relationship, but she couldn't just go on the way they had been. She couldn't take living like they had for the past few weeks. She would be miserable. He was a different man at home than he had been in Seattle or than he was here in Detroit.

She hated Los Angeles, the hypocrisy and apathy. Langston was a caring, giving man, but in Hollywood that only meant that he would lend his name to any worthwhile charity, and they exploited it. Even Tommy, who she believed was a true friend, was a cynic when it came to that aspect of their lives. She tried talking some sense into both men just a week before, when they were invited to a charity dinner.

"Why go to a five-thousand-dollar-a-plate-dinner? Just send the five thousand to the American Cancer Society."

"The rich buy plates to rub elbows with the famous who attend," Tommy had said.

"Langston is rich and famous," she had commented.

"So he gets to choose," Tommy said. "He can buy the dinner or attend it so others will pay big money to sit at his table."

"Or both," Langston chipped in.

"Which is what he usually does," Tommy explained.

"And you don't find it ironic, and somewhat sad, that the men and women at the dinner will spend as much on the clothes they buy to wear to the dinner as they do on the dinner itself?"

"Ironic perhaps, but if that's what it takes . . . "Tommy shrugged. "Come on Langston, tell her."

"Tell me what?"

"To get people to give, you've got to give them something," Langston said.

"People don't want to think about cancer research or birth defects or babies with AIDS. So dinners like these make it easy for them not to think about the actual people they're helping. Instead, they pay a lot of money to dress up and hobnob with famous folks," Tommy continued.

"Tommy, how can you just accept that?"

"That's the way it is, babe," he answered. She knew his heart was in the right place, but Reggie couldn't believe that his friends and associates were equally well-intentioned.

In contrast to Tommy Ray, Reggie liked Samantha Moore from the moment she met the woman who was Langston's best friend from high school.

"It's been too long, Mo." Sam, as she introduced herself, gave him a hug as warm and friendly as any of his sisters' hugs.

Reggie liked the lady's house, too. It was unusual. It was completely open; the only room with walls was the bathroom. The big open space that remained was separated into areas by the furniture within each section. A big brass bed dominated one area, with dressers and racks for hanging clothes nearby. A dining area was demarcated by the large country table and benches alongside. The living room, where the three of them currently sat, contained a huge overstuffed sofa and matching chairs.

"Nice place, Sam," Langston said to their hostess as she served them drinks.

The walls were painted bright white, and the tall windows and large skylight let in so much light that there was no need, even though the sun had started to set, to turn on any electric lights. "Need I ask who designed it."

"You know I did," she said.

"I like it," Reggie interjected.

"Thank you," Sammy said. "She's nice, Mo."

"All my friends are nice," he said arrogantly.

Sam balled up a napkin, dipped it in her ice water, and threw the wet mass at him, barely missing his head. "Don't brag," she said. "I could contradict you. I met your friends when I was out in L.A. and I wasn't that impressed." Reggie shot Langston a triumphant look. He rolled his eyes. "This lady is different."

"Thank you," Reggie said, liking Sam better with each passing minute. "You're an artist?"

"I try," Sam said modestly.

"She is great," Langston said, waving an arm to indicate the artwork on the walls.

Reggie looked around at the paintings and photographs that hung on the walls. "You did these?" she asked, impressed.

"Let me show you around."

Sammy's work glowed. Reggie's favorite painting reminded her of Langston. She looked at the other woman for confirmation. Sammy was watching her, amused. "I thought you might recognize him," she said, pleased.

"It's wonderful," Reggie said.

"You should marry this girl," Sammy told Langston.

"I'm willing," Langston said. "Talk to her."

Sammy looked back and forth from Langston to Reggie, who was staring at him in annoyance.

"Sorry, I didn't mean to bring up a touchy subject," Sammy joked. But she looked puzzled.

"No problem," Reggie said. "Langston thinks he's being funny."

"Sure," Sammy said uncertainly.

"Ignore him and tell me more about your work."

"There's not a lot to say. I paint. A few people seem to like my work, and I'm hoping it will catch on. That's about it."

"I'm sure when people get to see it, they love it," Reggie said sincerely. "Have you had any shows?"

"Little exhibits at the library and the university. A local restaurant hung some of the larger pieces and agreed to sell them on consignment. But it's hard to get into the large galleries. You know how it is. It's more who you know than what you do, and I've never been good at playing those games."

"Have you thought of hiring a manager or a publicist?" Reggie asked.

"Not really. I don't know how much that would cost. And the only people I know from art school who have people working for them are already making it. They can afford to pay someone."

"It might be worth it to hire someone, even if you're not spending a lot at first. A lot of publicists, including myself, work with a budget. The client tells us how much they have to spend, then we figure out how best to use the money—and it includes a price for our work, usually. Anyway, that's how I work, and I know a lot of others do, too. It wouldn't cost you anything to find out."

"True," Sammy mused. "You're a Hollywood publicist?" she inquired, sounding surprised.

"No, I'm from Seattle. I have my own company there," Reggie explained. "I can't imagine doing business in L.A. There's too much hype involved in the film business. I only like to take on projects I really believe in, and from what I saw in Hollywood, I wouldn't last long with an attitude like that. But I don't want to become one of those people who takes on clients just because I think they're going to be successful. I hope all my clients are successful of course, but commercial viability isn't the main thing I look for in a project."

Langston listened intently to them talk. "That's why you don't want to work in Los Angeles?" he asked.

"For the most part," Reggie said. "And I miss Seattle. I had a base there. I had contacts and clients. I'd like to keep my company open if I can."

"That makes sense," Sammy said, nodding wisely. "How do I find a local publicist? And how do I find out if they're any good?"

"You can try the Yellow Pages, and your friends," Reggie

advised. "And as for whether you can trust them, that's something you have to decide for yourself. Ask questions about how they work and what ideas they may have for you. If you like the answers, then you can discuss their terms."

"It was fascinating listening to you and Sammy talk about P.R.," Langston said as he drove her back to his mother's house.

"It reminded me of why I like my work," she said with a satisfied sigh.

"What did you mean when you said you want to keep your company going?"

"I referred my current clients to other people, and I sent out a letter saying I was planning to take an extended vacation and I'd contact them with further information when I knew where I was going to be," Reggie explained. "I didn't know what I was going to do next . . . whether I'd close my company or whether I'd be able to keep it open."

Langston was clearly astonished. "You never expected this relationship to work, did you?" he asked. "You always planned to go back to Seattle."

"I didn't plan it. I just left my options open," Reggie said. "I wasn't sure what would happen between us. I was hoping it would work out differently." He looked at her in patent disbelief and she knew he wasn't convinced. It didn't matter. "This isn't the worst thing that could happen, Langston. I think this relationship can work, if we both commit to it. I can visit you. You can visit me. It could be very romantic."

"I thought you didn't believe in long-distance relationships?" he said.

"I never wanted one. They seemed too hard to maintain. But you changed my mind. I don't want to give you up."

"So don't," he said. "Stay with me."

"I don't want to live with you, either," she said wryly. "Besides, absence makes the heart grow fonder, didn't you hear?"

"My heart is fond enough," he said, dispirited.

"This is exactly what you wanted a month ago," Reggie reminded him. "Think about it."

"I like having you with me," he said.

"I like being with you. That's why we'll still see each other," she reasoned. "And who knows, one of these days we may figure out the perfect solution."

Twenty-three

Their return trip home was a quiet one. Langston didn't want to be the one to bring up the subject of her leaving, and Reggie didn't seem to be in any hurry to do so either. But it occupied his mind most of the time, leaving little room for anything else. They gained three hours when they flew in from Detroit, so it felt like they arrived an hour after they left, but the time dragged. The plane ride, the drive home, even the walk to the front door with the bags, seemed to take forever. The shadow that hung over him could not be ignored.

He made love to her that night like a man possessed. He concentrated on coaxing out of her every sigh and every moan in her body. He wanted Reggie to ache as he did, and this was the only way he knew to achieve that. He watched her for a little while when she slept, trying to think of how he could get her to stay, but he fell asleep without thinking of any kind of effective plan.

The next morning at breakfast, he couldn't restrain himself for a moment longer. "Why do you have to go?" he asked. He sounded like a whiny child when he wanted to sound forceful and adult.

"I miss my work. I miss my life," she answered instantly.

"You can share my life. You can work here."

"The projects I'm interested in publicizing won't sell in this town."

"You could teach again."

"I loved teaching, but I don't want to go back. Not right now, anyway. Besides, I told you, I only referred my current projects to other firms. I don't think it would be hard to pick up almost where I left off. And I like what I do. I'm good at it."

"I know. I was a client, remember?"

She ignored his sarcastic tone. "How could I forget? That's why you fell in love with me, isn't it?" she batted her eyelashes at him.

He smiled as she had intended, but he said, "This is not a joke, Reggie."

"Just trying to lighten the mood around here," she commented. "Somehow our roles seem to have been reversed. You're supposed to be the fun, light, breezy one who is always telling me not to take life so seriously."

"I seem to have done my job too well. Now you're the one who wants a casual affair, and I'm the one who can't see the point."

"Think back," she suggested. "You'll remember."

"Just how long do you think that arrangement is going to last, Miz Thang?" he said, feeling desperate and trying not to sound it.

She jumped on the chance to change the subject. "Did you just call me Miss 'Thang?' " Langston knew that tone of voice. She didn't like being called by that name. He didn't have to wait long for her reason. "I do not see the appeal of using street slang when there are so many more elegant choices available."

He considered bringing up the real issue at hand—her leaving. But it was easier to talk about words that didn't mean anything than to find the words that did. "At least I said *Ms.* Thang. No one can accuse me of being politically incorrect," he countered. Usually he enjoyed these little debates of theirs about words and their usage. It was a passion of hers that he had appreciated from the beginning. He liked listening to her talk about it, and he liked arguing with her. She was so cute when she got all flustered. Their banter made him feel clever and witty, and he rarely felt that way before he met her.

"I don't see what is so cool about speaking a language that has no real meaning for you. The kids who invented it have a whole frame of reference for its use."

"We hear it used. That gives us a frame of reference, too," he argued halfheartedly.

"That gives you a vague understanding of the meaning. You don't know where the words come from. Your friends certainly don't. They would need a translator to understand the kids in that high school where you volunteer," she pointed out.

"It's the language of today. Their own kids speak it, even in Beverly Hills. Why shouldn't they?"

"When their slang is co-opted by the mainstream, the kids who came up with it have to invent even more outlandish terms in order to rebel," she said. "What I'm trying to say here is that as soon as your friends start speaking the language, it's not cool anymore anyway. So why do they bother?"

"I don't know, Teach. You tell me. Maybe they are joining in the kids' rebellion. Or they could be trying to prevent it by joining in."

"Maybe it's a little bit of both," she answered. "Honestly, I don't know why these people do anything they do."

"Whoa, honey, I heard your own middle-aged brother use the phrase 'macking the hotties' the other day," he commented.

"This disease is not confined to L.A., I agree. My brother was trying to make a joke about his son looking for a hot date in front of his wife, so he used a phrase he didn't think she would understand. That serves a purpose. A sick, demented purpose, but one that is easy to understand. Here, they've made a hobby of it. These are grown men and women, well-educated, well-groomed, wealthy folks, and they're competing over who knows the most slang? It's ridiculous."

"I give up. You're right."

"Damn straight," she joked.

He smiled, but he wasn't getting the usual kick out of their debate. "As long as it doesn't hurt anyone, I don't see what the big deal is."

"That attitude is why I can't stay here." He felt his smile fade. He hadn't expected that. "You put up with anything these jerks do. Maybe it's not harmful, but it's childish and pointless, and they should be called on it. Asked at least why they do it. You aren't comfortable telling people that they're being foolish. I don't feel comfortable keeping my mouth shut when I see these white people acting like fools."

"So tell them. I don't care," he said, irritated.

"Yes, you do. You care what they think, and that includes wanting them to like me and accept me. I don't think that will ever happen here."

"Are you saying that my friends are racist?" he asked, shocked.

"No, no more than I am. Just . . . intolerant and cliquish. I thought when I left high school behind I was through with all that. But your so-called friends and colleagues are so concerned with hype and appearances and fame, I feel like I'm back at St. Mary's."

"Don't you think that may be your problem, not theirs?" Langston argued.

"Maybe, but whether I'm the one who's being childish or they are doesn't matter. Trying to fit in made me miserable as a kid. As an adult, I refuse to do it again."

"No one's asking you to," he protested.

"You roll your eyes when I talk. I've seen you. I'm not going to stop voicing my opinion, even if it runs counter to some big shot who might bankroll your next picture. Maybe you'll get used to that, and maybe you won't, but I need to find out before I make a permanent commitment."

"I can change."

"I don't want to change you. I love you. I just want . . . I don't know," she said, sighing. "I want to be sure we can live with each other, keep loving each other."

"You're the most stubborn, opinionated, infuriating woman I have ever met, and I don't want to change a thing about you," he said.

"That's the nicest thing you have ever said to me," Reggie answered.

"So if we like each other so much, why can't we make it work?"

"What if we get married or something and then you discover that I'm an anathema to your career. What would you do?"

"I'd figure something out. Some way to be with you and still work," he said, frustrated.

Her head snapped up and she looked him in the eye, her expression knowing. "That's all I'm trying to do, Langston," Reggie said simply.

"But I wouldn't leave," he said.

"That's exactly what you did," she responded. "You had to leave, to go home, to get back to work. So do I." No matter how many different ways she tried to explain, he didn't think he would ever understand. Although he had wanted originally just to have a long-distance relationship, he couldn't imagine it now. He liked having her at his dinner table every night and in his bed every morning when he woke up. It appeared, though, that he didn't have any choice. He wasn't going to change her mind.

Reggie was absolutely right when she said that he himself had planned to have exactly the relationship she was describing when they first met. But now that he had had more, he didn't want it. He wanted to go forward, not backward. He was ready for commitment, for marriage. She had decided he wasn't prepared to take that step, but he knew that together they could make it work. She was wrong.

She was wrong about moving back home, too. She was just running away because she was scared. She admitted that the thought of marriage terrified her, but she said it was because of him, because he wouldn't be able to adjust. It was she who wouldn't or couldn't adjust. And the compromise she was offering was not an acceptable alternative. He couldn't live like that.

"Just how long do you think it would last?" he asked, realizing that though he asked the question before, she never answered it. "You said yourself it was hard to do."

She hesitated, thinking a moment before she replied. "It would last for as long as we both wanted it to. Until one or both of us grew tired of it. Or one or the other found someone else," she added slowly.

He shook his head. "That isn't going to work for me," he said. "I need more of a commitment than that."

"I can't give you any guarantees," Reggie said. "There aren't any."

"I'm not asking for guarantees," he averred. "I just don't want to be kicked in the teeth. If I can't win out over Seattle, how can I hope to compete with other men . . . especially men who live in the damn place."

"Langston, this isn't a question of winning or losing. Nobody, and certainly no city, means more to me than you do. Don't you understand? I'm not choosing it over you. I am choosing Seattle over Los Angeles, but not over you. I want us to be together. We will be together. Geography doesn't matter—not unless we make it matter."

"But that's what you're doing," he accused.

"It's not. I'm just . . . not going to make it so easy for you to have me in your life anymore." She looked up into his face. "I'm sorry, Mo. I just can't do it."

She started packing that night. Not much, just a few things that she didn't need to use every day. He knew it was for his benefit. When he finally came to bed, she lifted the sheet so he could slide in next to her. He lay with his back to her, feeling like a little kid—sullen and hurt. But he didn't want to face her.

She spooned him, resting her head between his shoulder blades. "Langston, I love you," she said softly, snuggling up against his back.

He wished that made him feel better, but it didn't. She was determined to leave anyway.

"I love you," he finally admitted.

"I don't want to get a phone call telling me my mother will never be able to see me again," she said, as though that settled it.

He felt her slowly slipping away from him, and he couldn't do anything about it. Reggie had made up her mind, and she began to make arrangements to move back home as if it were the most natural thing in the world. She spoke to her mother and sisters about her house and the tenant who had been happy to move out by the end of the month once she offered him a rebate of two months rent—which was all the rent he paid. She avoided subjects like that with him, but she didn't try to keep any of her plans secret. He overheard her making plans to send a notice to her clients and contacts about her grand reopening.

She was sitting at the kitchen table, discussing it as she ate a tuna salad sandwich. "I don't want to make a web site, Bebe. Everything on the computer always sounds easier than it is." She listened to her friend as she ate a bite of her sandwich. "I just don't think it's necessary to go to all that trouble. Not until I see if business gets going again without it." She noticed him watching her, and she covered the mouthpiece with one hand and whispered, "I'll be off the phone in a minute, honey." She waved that same hand in the air to indicate Bebe was still talking.

Slowly she arranged everything, and her departure date crept closer. He tried in vain to accept the idea that Reggie was leaving. He tried also to stay out of her bed, but he couldn't. Their nights were his only solace. They were still heaven.

The days were hell. Each one started with the usual warm, sunny, Southern California morning, but he didn't welcome them. He wished time would stop moving forward. He called his mother and told her that they weren't going to be living together, thinking she might have some advice or comforting words. Tricia Downs didn't seem at all surprised by the news that Reggie was going back to Seattle, and only sounded curious about how their relationship was going to work now.

"I don't know, Mother. I'll visit her. She'll visit me. We'll take vacations together maybe."

"I'm sorry, Langston," she said soothingly.

"Me, too, Moms," he said, unconsoled.

For all her busy activity, he knew Reggie was sad about the direction they were going in, too. But it didn't help. He felt like she was abandoning him. Maybe she also felt betrayed. There didn't seem to be anything he could do about that since they never talked about her leaving anymore. Neither of them had anything new to say. His life was no longer under his control, and there was nothing he could do about that either.

She left on a Wednesday: an ordinary day of the week. He had lost, and he had never felt more hopeless.

Twenty-four

Reggie wouldn't have called hers a joyous homecoming, but there were some heartwarming moments, as when her little nephew Freddy first saw her and ran toward her with a smile so wide it made her heart fill. Her emotions were so close to the surface, she almost cried. She was so happy to see everyone, it felt like she had been away for years, rather than just a month and a half. But she already missed Langston. When she thought about it, Reggie realized she spent almost every minute of the last eight weeks with him, so it made perfect sense that she felt bereft without him.

It was good to be home, though. Her mother's eyesight had deteriorated a lot while she was away. She kept telling herself that being there would not have made a difference, but the disease seemed to slow down once she came home. She knew that it was only because the damage seemed more gradual when she saw her mother every day. Jenny was handling it, as she did everything else, with unflagging faith and optimism. But Reggie was glad she was there for her.

She missed Langston from the moment she stepped on the plane. It created an ache inside her. Her family filled the void with the warmth and love she'd missed while she was away. It seemed odd to be so sure, so quickly, that she made the right decision. Given her choices, and as much as she wished Langston were there with her, it was a great relief to be back home.

It was wonderful to see Bebe again as well. They had been inseparable for so many years. This wasn't the first time they

had been apart for more than six weeks—Bebe went to Europe
for a term abroad during college, and Reggie traveled abroad
after they graduated—but when she left her friend this time she
thought they would never *live* so near each other again. Visits
weren't the same. Now that she was back, she realized how much
that thought had upset her.

"How could I let myself drop everything for a man?" she
asked her friend on Friday night at the bar. "I never thought I
was the kind of woman who would do something like that."

"Let me tell you something, Reggie," Bebe drawled. "Every
woman's the kind of woman who will do something like that. I
am. You are. So is every man."

"Oh sure," Reggie said. "That's why you hear so many stories
of guys chucking their careers to move thousands of miles."

"You may not hear about it as often, but guys do it, too."

"Not Langston," Reggie said morosely. "He would not even
have had to give up anything to move to Seattle. He wanted to
stay in L.A. because he didn't want to give up a cute little house
on a beach." She held up her glass in a silent toast to the subject
of their conversation. "I'm not bitter, though," she added as an
afterthought.

"You're too big a person for that," Bebe said, then laughed at
her own joke. For the first time in a long time, Reggie laughed
at a fat joke made at her expense. The sting was gone.

She supposed she owed that to Langston. But she wasn't in
the mood to be grateful. "The signs were all there from the
beginning. That boy doesn't know the first thing about loving a
woman."

"I find that hard to believe," Bebe said.

"Emotionally," Reggie clarified. "He may be in his thirties,
but with the life he's led, he's got the emotional maturity of a
seventeen-year-old." She downed her tequila, hoping to catch
up with Bebe, who appeared to be very happy.

"They say that's when men peak sexually. Seventeen." The
lawyer was slurring her words pretty badly. Reggie figured it
was probably time to call Neal. She would do that as soon as
she finished telling her best friend about the sexual prowess of
a certain thirty-five-year-old ex-football player. She had to say

she doubted the accuracy of Bebe's sources. No seventeen-year-old could outperform Langston Downs.

"I miss him," she admitted reluctantly.

"You're not going to get all maudlin on me, are you?" Bebe asked.

"No way." she vowed. "I wouldn't do that to you, Bebe."

"Good. I didn't bring you here to watch you cry into your drink. We're supposed to have a good time tonight."

"And we will. We won't even think about him."

"You go, girl," Bebe urged.

"I am a powerful, independent, black woman who does not need some piece of beefcake to validate me."

"Right on, sister!"

"He was lucky to have me." she finished her drink. "And a fool to let me go."

"You know it," her friend agreed wholeheartedly.

"He knows it, too," Reggie said definitely.

"He'll be back!" Bebe shouted.

"I only have to crook my little finger, and he will come running." Reggie snapped her fingers, once, then again.

Bebe craned her head awkwardly to look toward the door of the bar. "He's not here yet." she reported.

"Good. I don't want him back." Reggie explained. "I was just demonstrating what I have to do to get him back."

"Good for you. Be strong," her best friend encouraged.

"I'm doing my best." Reggie said, a little plaintively. Then she downed another shot.

She tried not to think about him. She worked hard. She got her stuff out of storage and returned her little house to its proper state. She visited friends, and family members. She kept herself very busy so she wouldn't have to think.

Reggie was home a full week before she wound up at her mother's place for lunch without any of her siblings or their children.

"So," she said, sitting down at a table laden with her favorite foods, fried chicken, macaroni and cheese, and brussels sprouts. "I've been wondering when we were going to talk."

"We talk every day," her mother said innocently.

"I know," Reggie said, loading her plate with Jenny's mouth-watering cooking. "So what do you want to know?" she asked, taking a big bite of a golden chicken breast.

"What really happened?" her mother asked.

"It wasn't worth it," Reggie said simply.

"Relationships are hard work," Jenny said. "You knew that."

Reggie took a bite, chewed and swallowed it while she considered how to answer. "Langston didn't," she said finally.

"You knew that, too."

"I thought . . . I don't know what I thought," she admitted. "I didn't think I would be so lonely."

"I'm sorry," her mother said. They ate in silence for a few minutes. Reggie didn't think that was the end of it. She was right. "You still love him?" Jenny asked.

"Yes, I do." Reggie admitted. "We're going to keep seeing each other. I'm going to live here, and he's going to live there."

"That makes it hard," Mama said sympathetically.

"I doubt it will be harder than living there," Reggie answered. "Aren't you glad to have me home? I'm glad to be here. I missed seeing you. I missed everything." She changed the subject. "I can't believe Ginnie's walking so well," she said of her oldest sister's youngest child.

Her mother went along with the ploy, so Reggie supposed she'd answered her questions to her satisfaction. However, she was left feeling very unsatisfied. That night, ensconced in her old bed in her own little house, she thought about her mother's words. She did love Langston. And she wanted to live with him. But she didn't like the way he lived, his friends, his profession, or at least the luncheon part of it, the parties and events. Most of all, she didn't like him as much in Malibu. In the poverty-stricken neighborhood they visited, she saw him shine. He loved working with those kids. She thought he could be a very good teacher. But she didn't want him to give up acting if he didn't want to. She just wanted him to believe in the value of what he did.

He was able to help her get over her insecurities, but he wouldn't even acknowledge his. Not really. Not when it counted. Sure, he told her he wished he could get his degree, but whenever the subject of his education came up, he made jokes or changed the subject. She couldn't fight all their battles alone. She couldn't make the relationship work by herself, and she couldn't make him grow up. Langston had to realize what he wanted from his life. He wasn't going to find it trying to make a house into a home by cooking gourmet meals for himself and watching the sun set over the Pacific.

"I made the right decision," she said aloud. But she really missed sleeping next to his big warm body.

She had been home two weeks when Darrell called. "I read that you split up with the superhunk," he said sweetly.

"No, I'm still seeing Langston," she corrected him.

"Oh," he said. "Good." She had to give him credit, he sounded as if he almost meant it.

"It's nice to hear from you. How are things going?" she asked.

"Great," he said. "I mean, business is good. I was asked to a dinner, and I, uh, was wondering . . ." He let his voice trail off, but it was clear he hoped she'd accompany him to the affair.

"I don't know," Reggie said. This was an area she and Langston hadn't discussed yet. She definitely didn't want to bring it up this soon after making the move.

"You need permission from the old man, huh?" Darrell joked. He was still a nerd. But he was the nerd who took her to her prom.

"What's this thing for?" she asked, hoping it was just some frivolous party so she wouldn't feel guilty if he missed it.

"You know that dinner party I had—to raise money for the museum?" Darrell asked.

"Yeah, I remember," she said, her heart sinking. It was a very worthy cause. "Are you doing it again?" Guilt reared its ugly head.

"They're giving a little party to . . . honor my contribution."

"Really?" Reggie said. "Cool."

"You deserve it, too. You helped me a lot with that. So will you accompany me, milady?" It was a simple decision. She was going to go.

"To bask in your reflected glory?" she said, tongue in cheek. "Of course I will."

She told Langston about it that evening, emphasizing that this was a purely friendly outing and nothing more. He wasn't thrilled about it, but he didn't object, and Reggie breathed a big sigh of relief. "I can't wait to see you," she enthused.

"Next weekend," he said for the tenth time that week.

"I'll tell you all about the dinner then," she said.

They talked about a script he was somewhat interested in, and she told him about her newest client. They dragged the conversation out for as long as they could until finally Langston said, "I'd better go. It's getting late, and we've got to get up early tomorrow."

"We do?" Reggie asked, surprised.

"You have work, and I have a pre-power breakfast," he said.

She laughed. "Pre-power breakfast? What the heck is that?"

"Coffee and bagels with some development v.p.," he scoffed.

"Sounds fascinating," she said sarcastically. "Good luck."

"I'll talk to you tomorrow night. Sleep sweet."

"I miss you," Reggie said. They spoke on the telephone every day, but it was vaguely unsatisfying, like eating baked potato chips instead of fried ones.

"Me, too," he said, then broke the connection.

Reggie hung up the phone reluctantly and prepared for bed, glad that he wasn't upset about her "date" with Darrell. And a little surprised. He acted jealous of her friendship with the other man a few weeks before. Perhaps Langston had just needed to see her as an independent figure in order to get over his irrational feelings about Darrell. Or maybe he had already started to distance himself from her because she wouldn't live with him. Whatever the reason, she wouldn't worry about it, she decided. She would just accept it and enjoy her evening out. With Darrell, it was always an elegant, expensive affair.

Reggie wore one of the dresses she bought in California to the dinner. She spent a good deal of time on Sunday choosing the gown and then bathing and moisturizing her skin with sweet-smelling potions. She amused herself for two hours primping and preparing, enjoying the entire process as she had never done before. Reggie took great delight in arraying herself in the lovely lingerie she bought for Langston's pleasure. She couldn't remember ever staring at herself in the mirror so much, or ever feeling as satisfied with the results of her efforts.

This was a tangible reward of letting herself care for the sexiest man in America. She had learned to appreciate her own special brand of beauty, and while she didn't think she was in any danger of becoming vain, it was nice to feel good about her appearance. Shallow as many of the people who occupied his world were, she finally understood why they set such stock in their image. If they saw themselves as attractive, they felt attractive, and feeling attractive was a heck of a lot better than feeling fat and frumpy.

Darrell was his usual charming self, and she had a lovely time with him. They talked about high school and mutual friends and their businesses. And about Langston Downs. Darrell followed his football career and was an admirer of the man.

"This is so civilized," she commented as they drank their brandy after dinner. "Talking to the man who took me to the prom about my . . ."—she lowered her voice—" . . . lover."

"He seems like a good guy in interviews and stuff," Darrell said.

"He is a good guy," Reggie confirmed.

"I was so surprised when you told me you really were dating him, but you look happier than I've ever seen you." He raised his glass. "Salud."

She drank. "Why were you surprised?" she asked. Darrell was the one man she knew who always found her appealing. She appreciated that now. Before, she thought he was blind and prejudiced, but since she'd seen herself in the mirror that evening and realized how flattering the long, black, sequined evening gown was to her full figure, she thought he had rare powers of perception.

"He's taken a few hits . . . to the head," he explained. "Not that there is anything wrong with that, but I didn't think you would have anything in common with a football player."

"You were wrong," she said simply. "There's a lot more to him than that."

"I'm sure there is, if you're with him. I wish you every happiness in the world," Darrell said with genuine feeling. "I guess I'll have to find a girl of my own, now."

"Why did you never look for one before?" Reggie asked, curious.

"I always hoped you'd come around and see that you had the greatest guy in the world hanging around hoping for the slightest hint of encouragement," he answered.

"I knew you were the greatest," she claimed. "But there was no chemistry between us. You must have felt it—or the lack of it."

"I know. But I love you, sweetheart. I thought the rest might come with time."

"I can't believe you considered settling for that," Reggie chided him. "You deserve so much more. Some wonderful woman is waiting out there to fall for you and lust after you and love you."

"So speaks a woman in love," he said. "Now I'm really convinced I don't stand a chance."

"I'm sorry," she said soothingly. "I do love you, as a friend."

"I guess I'm going to have to learn to dance to that rap music."

"Why?" Reggie shouted. "You dance beautifully to swing and big band and Latin music. Try meeting some women who like that. I guarantee you that they will love having you for a dance partner. Who knows what may develop from there."

"Thanks, Reggie. I needed that," he said.

When he dropped her off at home, she gave him a tender kiss good-bye. "I guess I won't be seeing as much of you in the future," she said. "Especially once you find your Ms. Right."

"I will always have time to see you," he promised.

"And me you," she vowed in turn. She walked up the short walk to her front door and let herself in, then turned to wave good night. As she closed the door behind her, she saw his limousine leave the curb. Just then a large arm wrapped around her waist.

She let out a shriek before she heard Langston's voice. "Hi, Reggie," he said.

"You scared me to death," she told him.

"I wanted to surprise you." He kissed her hello and walked toward the kitchen.

She followed him. "You were checking up on me, weren't you?" she said as he walked over to the stove to check on the teakettle, which was rattling a little but not whistling yet.

"No I was not," he said, feigning indignation at the accusation.

"Look me in the eye and tell me you didn't fly in here to make sure I was home all night," she said, smiling.

He didn't turn around. "I did time the kiss."

"I knew it," she crowed. "You were jealous."

"All right, I was a little bit jealous and curious," Langston confessed. "It was worth it anyway to see you in that dress. You look beautiful."

"I do look nice, don't I?" Reggie said, preening. "You bought me this dress."

"Ah ha!" he said, pleased. "I suppose that means that I can take it back any time I want to."

He advanced on her, and she backed away, giggling. "No chance, Langston Downs," Reggie protested. "It's mine."

He was shaking his head. "Uh uh," he scooped her off her feet and carried her into the bedroom, where he deposited her on her feet in front of the bed.

The long slide of the zipper down her back released the tension inside her. Reggie turned and ran her hands down his arms, then rested them on his hips. "You really want this dress?" she asked. "I don't think it will fit you."

He watched as she slid her arms out of the sleeves and skimmed the top down her torso to her hips until it fell to her feet. She stepped out of it and he bent down and picked it up. He threw it on the bed behind her. "You keep it. I'll take what's left," he growled.

She smiled. "You will, will you? And what do I get?"

He unbuttoned his shirt as he kicked off his shoes. His bronzed chest rose and fell as if he'd been running a race. "More?" he asked.

Reggie nodded, sitting down on the bed to watch him undo his pants and take them off. She held out her arms and he walked to her until he stood in front of her at her bedside. He bent over and kissed her and reached around her to run his hands down her back. It had been so long since she felt this good.

"I miss you all the time," he murmured into her hair. "I need you."

"Me, too," she purred.

She splayed her hands across his chest, then leaned forward to trail butterfly kisses down his chest to his abdomen. He smelled of soap and shaving cream, and tasted like himself. She had missed that.

"Come back with me," he said.

"I can't. I'm sorry," she said, her lips still moving over his taut skin. "Now that I'm back here, I don't think I could leave again. My mother is handling everything on her own, but I want to be with her. And the rest of my family." She dipped her tongue into his belly button, and felt his stomach muscles contract. She wished they could make love and forget everything else.

She raised her head to look up into his face. He was looking down at her, his eyes sad. "This isn't going to work for me, Reggie. I can't think, concentrate on my work, or anything."

She closed her eyes so he wouldn't see his sorrow reflected there. This was not unexpected, though she had hoped he wouldn't give up so soon. She knew a long-distance romance was a chancy proposition for the most mature, steadfast man, and she should have known Langston couldn't handle it—not even for two weeks. It was no big shock that the sexiest black man in America would want a woman who could fit better into his life, his house, his dreams. She just couldn't be that woman.

Twenty-five

Someone kept hanging up on his answering machine. The phone rang until the answering machine picked up, then the caller hung up before the recording could come to an end. As soon as the machine disconnected, the phone would ring again. Langston ignored it for a while, then found himself listening to the irritating sounds: brrinng, brrinng, brrinng, click, brrinng, brrinng, brring, click. At first Langston thought it might be Reggie, though that didn't seem like her style. By the third call, he realized it couldn't be her. It might be a reporter. Or a fan.

By the sixth time, he couldn't take it anymore. He picked up the phone. "Hello?"

"Hello, Langston," his mother's voice boomed over the line.

"Was that you hanging up on the answering machine?"

"Yes. I wanted to speak to you, and I had a feeling that you were there."

"Why didn't you just leave a message? You know I would have called you back?"

"Not right away," she answered. "I know you're hiding out there after what you did to Reggie."

"Huh? I didn't do anything. She ended it, not me."

"Right," Tricia said, her voice dripping with sarcasm. "That sweet little girl who clearly loves you to death was the one who broke it off."

"She did. I mean, she decided not to live with me anymore, which is the same thing."

"How is that the same thing?" she asked. "I left your father twice *after* we were married, and I didn't consider it 'over,' any more than he did. He came after me."

"We're not married, Moms. She doesn't even want to live with me. I don't think she's looking for a proposal."

"Never mind what she's looking for. What do *you* want son?"

"I want to marry her and live together and have kids. I want it all."

"Did you tell her that?

He could tell by her tone of voice she expected him to say no. He was glad to be able to surprise her. "Yes! But she didn't like my lifestyle here, so she didn't even want to live with me, let alone make a commitment."

"She said no to you?" Tricia sounded shocked. "Jenny gave me the definite impression that you never asked."

"Well I did," Langston said. He felt like he had in childhood when he'd been unjustly accused of some offense committed by one of his sisters.

"I'm sorry, Langston, I thought . . ." Her voice trailed off. "I should have known better. I know no son of mine would be stupid enough to let the woman he loved get away without putting up a fight."

"Uh huh," he muttered, but he started to wonder as she blathered on, *Did I fight hard enough?* It was true that he did go after Reggie in Seattle. Well, he did visit her and ask her to come home. *She* was the one who said no. She was the one who gave up on them. Not him.

"You're no idiot," his mother was saying. "You've never given up on anything you wanted in your life—except college, and one of these days, I know you'll go back and get your degree. I thought Reggie might help you with that, but . . . anyway, I'm sorry. I should have trusted you. Wait until I get my hands on Jennifer Primm. How dare she suggest that she and I should get you two together if you can't handle this yourself?"

Langston thought of Reggie's mother and his ganging up on them, and shuddered. That was all he needed—his mother and her mother arranging his and Reggie's lives as if they didn't know what they wanted. Hadn't he told Reggie more than once that he thought they should marry? She always treated it as a joke. That was a large part of the reason that he never tried to give her the ring. He didn't want to scare her away by showing her how serious he really was.

"I'll speak with you later," Tricia was saying.

"Uh, Mom?" he said hesitantly, ending her tirade.

"Yes, son," she answered.

She waited patiently while he tried to figure out how to ask her to help him fix the mess he had made. "I . . . might not have phrased my proposal in the best of terms."

"Why?" she asked, suddenly suspicious. "How did you ask?"

Langston thought back over the various conversations he had had with Reggie. "I begged her to come back to Los Angeles with me. I told her I was ready for a serious commitment."

"And?" his mother asked.

"That's pretty much it. I mentioned that I thought we would be happy together, happy married, stuff like that. I'm an actor, not a writer," he said, trying to excuse himself.

"So Jenny was right. You never asked," she said, sounding disappointed.

"I think I told her once that she was wrong, and I was ready for marriage."

"Langston, what is the matter with you?" his mother scolded.

"I've never done this before," he defended himself. "Cut me some slack."

"No, I will not cut you any slack. You acted like a big, selfish, thoughtless child. You're too handsome and too sexy and too damned lucky with women."

"Lucky?" he cried in disbelief. "You consider this lucky?"

"I knew things came too easily to you, but I thought you finally started to grow up now that you were on your own, especially after I met Reggie. She's good for you. She won't let you stay a spoiled brat. She's not your mother."

"You think you spoiled me?"

"I know I did. In every way I could. But I think it was a mistake, because now you think everything should be that easy and, Langston, I'm telling you, just because you've never had to really work on a relationship before doesn't mean this one wasn't worth having."

"I know that. That's why I tried so hard," Langston insisted. "It wasn't enough for her. I don't know if anything I could have done would have been enough for her. What if I moved to Seattle and proposed, and we got married and then she decided it wasn't enough? Where would we be then?"

"So you're going to give up now?" she asked, incredulous. "Before you've really tried."

"I don't want to give up, but what do you want me to do?" Langston was stumped. "She won't come back to me."

"You are a grown man. You have to take responsibility for your actions."

"I do," he proclaimed, indignant.

"Did you ever think of going to her and asking her what she wanted?" Tricia asked simply. "Or consider telling her straight out how you felt?"

"Uh, no," Langston said after a moment. "I guess I never thought of that."

"You might want to try it," she suggested. "Communication is an extremely important part of any relationship."

"I think I heard that somewhere," Langston tried to joke.

She was not amused. "If you don't go after that woman, you are an idiot."

"Maybe I am," he answered. "I've always suspected it."

"I'm sorry, Langston. I shouldn't have said that. You are not an idiot. You just have to take a chance."

"Will you help me?"

"I shouldn't, but . . ."

Tricia and Jenny's plan was simple enough. They had planned to trick he and Reggie into showing up at the same place at the same time, and then lock them in. Now that they had his cooperation, it was even easier. He flew to Seattle and drove to Jenny's house and she called Reggie and asked her to come to lunch. He and Reggie's mother talked for the better part of an hour. He really liked her. They settled a lot between them. Twenty minutes before Reggie was due to show up, Jenny started to make lunch.

"You don't need to actually make lunch," he pointed out. "She's coming here to talk to me, right?"

"Yes, but it will be lunchtime. She'll be hungry." Jenny kept on working.

"We can go out and grab a bite," he said.

"I'm going to have a word with her, too," she said. "In fact, why don't you go sit out in the backyard, and I'll call you when it's time."

Langston tried not to let his consternation show. She blithely ushered him out the back door and returned, humming, to her chore. He sat at the picnic table and enjoyed the quiet of the early summer day. The flowers Jenny planted in her little garden were blooming, and the birds were singing. The grass under his feet was green and lush. Slowly, Langston relaxed. He felt good. Better than he had in weeks.

He didn't hear her enter the house, but he did hear Reggie greet her mother as she entered the kitchen. "Hi, Mom. Something smells good," she said.

"Sit down. Lunch will be ready in a minute," Jenny told her. "What would you like to drink?"

"Iced tea," Reggie said. "I'll get it." She appeared in the window so suddenly, Langston felt his heart jump. But she was looking at the pitcher of sun tea that was sitting on the windowsill and didn't see him. A moment later he heard her ask, "Shall I pour you a glass, too."

"Okay." He heard the tinkling of the ice cubes in the glasses, and settled back, wondering when Jenny planned to get the ball rolling. "Baby," the older woman said, and he sat up at attention. "I want to talk to you."

"I figured," Reggie replied. He could picture her wry smile. "What's up?"

"I've been thinking about you and Langston."

"Mom, we've been over this already," Reggie said. "The sex was great, but the man—"

Jenny stopped her. "This isn't about him. It's about you." Langston presumed she interrupted her daughter because the truth might hurt him. He could have told her that his own mother had taken care of that. She had reduced his ego to virtually nothing. But he was grateful for Jennifer Primm's discretion. He wanted to know what Reggie thought of him and of their relationship, but if she was too disparaging he didn't know if he could summon the nerve to confront her.

"You ran away," Jenny said.

"I hated his life. It was so phony, so pointless. He could do anything, be anything. It was a waste.

She believed in him. Even after he'd been such an unmitigated ass, she still thought he could be more than a big dumb jock. Luckily, he believed it, too. Now. *Thanks, love,* he said silently.

"You told me, but that's no reason to give up on the man. You hate his life, but you love him, so you work on it. Isn't that what you went to California for?"

"He doesn't want to work on it. He didn't there. And he won't here. There's nothing I can do about that," she said. Again, he thanked his luck. She didn't sound bitter, just resigned. He could change that. He hoped.

"Maybe you should try harder."

"Maybe I should have. I didn't expect it to be so hard. I was on my own, doing everything myself. He didn't help. He didn't even know there was anything wrong."

"Did you tell him?" Jenny asked gently.

"I tried," Reggie said sadly.

Langston couldn't wait any longer. He stood and started toward the door.

Jenny's next question stopped him. "Are you going to?"

"I don't think I'm going to get that chance," Reggie said. "I blew it, Mama."

"You can always tell him now."

"Call him, you mean? I thought about it. But what's changed? He hasn't. And I don't think I can."

"I think you can," Jenny said. "Would you be willing to try?"

"I don't know. I keep thinking about it," Reggie said.

Jenny appeared at the window. "You don't have to call him." She waved to Langston to come in. "He's here."

He was through the door in seconds. Reggie was sitting at the kitchen table, frozen by shock, her fork halfway to her mouth.

"You don't have to say anything," he said.

She put the fork down very deliberately, and stood. "Mama?"

"I'm going to leave you two alone," Jenny Primm said, then headed toward the front of the house.

"I don't want to give up either," he said, not moving. He was afraid if he tried to get closer, she'd run away again. "And this time, you won't have to do everything alone. I'm going to move here, to Seattle. Long-distance romance bites the big one."

She smiled, but she still watched him warily. "You said you couldn't work if you didn't live in Hollywood."

"I was wrong. Actually, I was scared. It was the first home of my own and I was afraid that if I moved, I would never settle down anywhere. I'm a little bit backwards for thirty-five, in case you hadn't noticed. I blame it on my misspent adult years, playing a game for a living."

"There's nothing wrong with playing football."

"There is when you use it as an excuse not to grow up. When you came to live with me my house became a home, not before. I've figured it out now. Wherever you are, that will always be my home."

Reggie sat down, suddenly. "That's . . . very nice," she said, but she didn't sound convinced.

He stepped forward, and she looked down at his feet, as if willing him not to come any closer. He halted where he stood. "I was lonely when you moved back here, but it didn't compare to how lonely I was when I realized I would probably never see you again, never get to hold you, or argue with you, or feed you, or make love to you."

"Me, too," she said breathlessly.

He took another step toward her. This time her eyes never left his face. "I love you, Reggie. I can't stop. I tried." He took another step, drawn to her by the need to hold the hands that lay so still in her lap, and kiss away the bewildered expression on her face. "I told you I was stupid."

She smiled again, and he closed the distance between them and sat down at the table in the chair next to hers, facing her. "I love your honesty. You thought I was embarrassed, but actually I was proud that you always said what you thought. I was ashamed because I hadn't said anything before."

"It didn't seem like it," she said.

"It's true. I was never ashamed of *you*. I was ashamed of myself because I didn't have the strength of my convictions, like you did. But I can change." She nodded. "I have changed. But you have to help me. I'm not smart enough to figure it all out by myself." She shook her head, but he didn't give her a chance to argue with him. "You can't give up on me. I need you."

"Langston, you—" she started.

He cut her off. "You don't have to decide right now. Just think about it, okay?" He stood up.

"Where are you going?" she asked.

"I'm back at the Westin Hotel. Until you tell me yes. Or no. But first, I have to tell you you were right about one other thing as well. I wasn't ready before. I didn't realize what a spoiled brat I was until you left. Even then, Mom had to tell me."

"Your mother did that?" she asked, shocked.

"She told me straight out that I was lucky to find you, and an idiot if I let you go," he confessed, looking down at his hands, which somehow had gotten hold of hers.

"I always liked Tricia," she said.

Langston looked up and couldn't believe what he saw. She was smiling tenderly at him. "There's a lesson to be learned here," Reggie said. "One should always listen to one's mother."

"I couldn't agree more," he said, suddenly feeling very hopeful.

"It wasn't just you, Langston. I was running scared, too. I was so sure for so long that no man could love this body that I hate . . . but thanks to you, I like it better now. My mother's been talking to me, too. She made me realize what I was giving up. And why. It wasn't you I didn't believe in. It was me."

She waited until he looked up at her face before she continued. "Partly because of that, I didn't think any life could be as satisfying as the one I made for myself. It was almost a relief when Lalaland proved so disappointing in comparison to home. I was actually happy when sharing your life seemed so unfulfilling compared to living on my own."

"But . . . " he prompted.

"I was getting to it," she said, her eyes twinkling mischievously. "You were the one who persuaded me that I wasn't the ugly duckling I thought I was. You convinced me that you were attracted to me. So it's possible you could make marriage to an idiot appealing, too."

"Thanks a lot," he said in mock indignation.

"Seriously, coming home wasn't nearly the relief I thought it would be. And life without you, even here, was not at all fulfilling anymore. So I guess I'm stuck with you."

"Yes," he said seriously. "You are. So why not just make it official and marry me."

She looked surprised and then pleased, and he finally pulled the ring box from his pocket. "Okay?" He'd been carrying it for the past month and a half, transferring it from one suit jacket pocket to the next, and from pair after pair of jeans, slacks, and shorts. "I've been dying to put this on you since the day you said you couldn't marry a big kid."

She covered his hand before he could open the box. "I'll wear it on one condition."

"What?" he asked nervously.

"Our mothers get to 'do' the wedding," she said firmly.

"Done," he said quickly. Then he took out the ring and put it on her finger. She admired it and held it out for him to see, and he kissed her hand.

"Let's go tell Mama. Okay?" she asked.

He stood and walked to the phone on the wall. He put one finger to his lips to indicate she should be quiet, then he picked up the phone. He listened for a moment, then brought it to her. On it, their mothers were busily chatting away about the success of their plan.

He gently cradled the phone. "They've got the thing practically planned already," he said smugly as he came toward her.

"You rat!" she accused. Langston wrapped his arms around her waist. "I'm just learning about this relationship stuff," he said happily. "I need all the help I can get," he admitted, before he lowered his lips to hers.

"You said it. It pays to listen to your mother."

Coming in July from
Arabesque Books

ISLAND MAGIC by Bette Ford
1-58314-113-8 $5.99US/$7.99CAN

When Cassandra Mosely needs a break from her work—and from her relationship with Gordan Kramer—she vacations in Martinique and finds herself in a new romance. But Gordan is determined to win her back and with a little island magic, the two just may rediscover their love . . .

IMAGES OF ECSTASY by Louré Bussey
1-58314-115-4 $5.99US/$7.99CAN

Shay Hilton is shocked when her ex-fiancé is murdered in her apartment, but when she comes face to face with her prosecutor, Braxton Steele, she is overcome with desire. When a storm traps the unlikely couple together, it's the beginning of a passion that will change both of their lives forever . . .

FAMILY TIES by Jacquelin Thomas
1-58314-114-6 $5.99US/$7.99CAN

When Dr. McKenzie Ashford discovers that her new boss, Marc Chandler, may be responsible for her mother's death, she is determined to obtain justice. She never imagines that her quest might uncover long-hidden family secrets . . . or that her heart might be overcome with love for Marc.

SNOWBOUND WITH LOVE by Alice Wootson
1-58314-148-0 $5.99US/$7.99CAN

After a car accident, Charlotte Thompson develops a case of amnesia and seeks comfort in the arms of her handsome rescuer, Tyler Fleming. But as they fall in love, Tyler realizes her true identity as the person he holds responsible for the tragedy that nearly destroyed his life. Will he be able to give his heart to this woman that he has hated for so long?

Please Use the Coupon on the Next Page to Order

Turn up the Heat With
Arabesque Books